# Loving Liam

## Book One in the Cloverleaf Series
## Tales from Birch Valley

*By Gloria Herrmann*

*Loving Liam*

Limitless Publishing, LLC
Kailua, HI 96734
www.limitlesspublishing.com

Formatting: Limitless Publishing

ISBN-13: 978-1-68058-305-2
ISBN-10: 1-68058-305-0

# *Dedication*

I dedicate this book to my family, for without them none of this would be possible. They have shown me the true meaning of support, love, and family. I can't express enough gratitude for all their advice, encouragement, and countless prayers. These amazing people who I'm so lucky to have in my corner are my inspiration, my guiding light, and my heart.

# *Chapter One*

## Liam

Liam O'Brien rubbed his temples, begging the stirrings of a headache to go away. While resting his eyes, the single fluorescent light in the empty classroom buzzed indistinctly. His headache had been brought on by the deafening chatter of his fourth grade students. Rambunctious and excited energy had filled the classroom all day with the anticipation of winter break. Liam needed the time off and was almost as anxious as the students were for it to start. Yawning, he stretched long arms that were covered in the sleeves of a thick red sweater above his head. Peering out the massive window, he noticed the sky had darkened and snow was beginning to fall gently. His stomach gurgled loudly, and images of the cold pizza and beer waiting for him in his fridge intruded on his thoughts.

\*\*\*

Liam turned onto the long, snow-covered driveway lined with various pines and tamarack trees and pulled up to his quaint cabin nestled right outside the town of Birch Valley. The home itself was simple, but the land surrounding it looked almost magical, especially in winter. The temperature had been bitter cold, and all the trees were frozen stark white. The small lake Liam fished at during the warmer months lay tight with ice. The air was filled with an array of fresh natural scents like that of damp pine needles and frozen earth, along with hints of smoke from neighbors heating their homes with fireplaces or wood stoves. Liam had bought the cabin a couple of years after teaching at the only elementary school in town. He'd instantly fallen in love with the property that was home to most of the local wildlife, mainly deer, Canadian geese, hawks, and wild turkeys.

Liam stopped the engine of his aging, red pickup truck, gathered his coat and backpack, and trudged through several inches of new snow that had buried the path to his front door. Once inside the cabin, he tossed his belongings onto a plaid couch that sat directly in front of an overly large fireplace inlaid with river rocks. The mantle was a giant, solid piece of honey-colored tamarack wood with bold knots. The fireplace itself was a work of art and the main focus of the otherwise simple cabin. Liam kept the decor in his home sparse and spent most of his time at his childhood home with the rest of the lively O'Brien family.

The blinking red light on his phone caught Liam's attention as he knocked the clinging snow from his boots. His mother had no doubt left him a message. She was notorious for calling him all the time, despite living only five miles away and seeing him several times during the week, including every Sunday for their family dinner.

Not that Liam was the only one she called, or rather checked in on regularly. He had an older brother, Patrick; a younger brother, Daniel; and a baby sister, Maggie, all of whom he was close to. Liam's brothers lived in town and had taken over their father's construction company. Maggie had moved to Seattle the second she could, deciding the town of Birch Valley, with its one traffic light, was just too small for her. She'd always craved adventure and was attracted to the bright lights and overwhelming activity of the big city. A set of rugged mountains and a five hour drive were now all that separated her from the family.

Liam moved toward the blinking light and pressed Play on the machine.

"Hello, my darling son, it's Mom."

Liam almost chuckled at how she always announced who she was. Her sweet voice seemed to fill the room, sounding the same as it always did.

Mary O'Brien went on with the usual description of how she and Liam's father had spent their day, including who she had run into at the only grocery store in town.

"Liam, dear, I need you to bring that extra cot over Sunday. Maggie and my sweet Melanie are coming over for a visit."

Liam's heart warmed at the thought of his younger sister and her six-year-old daughter. He hated that they lived over on the coast, even though they wasn't all that far away, and missed Maggie being able to partake in the craziness that was their rowdy Irish American family.

Maggie had gotten married at twenty-one. She had been a receptionist at the same law firm where her husband, Michael Trembley, was an attorney. They had met at an office Christmas party held at the Space Needle and instantly fell hard for each other. Their whirlwind marriage and Maggie's pregnancy soon after surprised the entire family, but everyone genuinely adored Michael and were happy to welcome him into their lives.

Liam didn't have a chance to erase the message before the phone let out a shrill ring. He knew who was calling without even glancing at the caller ID.

"Hi, Mom," he answered.

"Hi, sweetie, did you get my message?" Mary replied.

Running his fingers through his somewhat overgrown hair, Liam couldn't help but smile.

"Yeah, Mom. I just got in a couple minutes ago." He sank onto the plaid couch and swung his long legs up to prop his feet onto the large, rustic coffee table.

"Oh, how was the last day? I bet those kids were very excited. I know I'm thrilled that it's Christmas break."

Liam could hear the excitement in her voice. Mary was well known for going all-out on decorating her home during the Christmas season. It was her favorite holiday, to the point that the Christmas spirit itself seemed to possess her.

Without letting him respond, Mary continued, "I was hoping maybe you could swing by tomorrow morning and help your father and me finish hanging lights. I would love for everything to be done by the time Maggie and Melanie arrive."

"Of course I'd be happy to. So is Michael coming along too?" Liam asked eagerly.

"Hard to say. Maggie mentioned he was busy with a pretty big case. I'm sure he'll be able to come closer to Christmas. It's just so hard for him to get away. Such a shame. I enjoy seeing him. Also, I have enlisted the help of Patrick and Daniel, so we should be able to get everything perfect tomorrow."

"Good. I would hate to think they'd be left out of all the fun of hanging lights in twenty-five degree weather," Liam joked, slightly dreading having to help but knowing full well his mother would equip them with plenty of hot chocolate and the best sugar cookies in all of Birch Valley, if not the world.

"Well, I won't keep you, sweetie. Just wanted to ask for that cot for Melanie. I hear your father and Grandpa Paddy coming in now, so I'll let you go. Love you, dear." Mary hung up before Liam could get in a word.

Grinning as he hung up too, Liam made his way to the fridge for that pizza and beer he'd promised himself.

\*\*\*

The air was frigid and the wind snapped at Liam's face as he wrangled a large ladder through the door of his father's garage. On the porch, Daniel O'Brien was fussing with several large boxes filled to the brim with a tangled mess of lights.

"You know, I'm not sure why Mom doesn't just leave the lights up on the house all year round," Daniel complained. His already rosy cheeks were turning a deeper shade of red as the freezing air chapped his skin. He worked the knots of lights, growing more frustrated by the minute.

Hefting the ladder against the side of the house, Liam sighed. "With it being this cold, that's not a bad idea. But then, I doubt she would make us all those famous cookies of hers."

Liam turned as he heard the front door shut and saw Patrick making his way toward them.

"Glad you decided to come join us. What was keeping you, the nice warm house?" Daniel teased.

Patrick playfully glared at Daniel. "Don't worry, I didn't eat all the cookies, if that's what you're worried about," he replied while starting to untangle a gnarled ball of lights.

The three brothers looked so different that at first glance, they didn't seem to be related at all, except for their mesmerizing, deep emerald eyes. Liam stood as tall as Patrick but had sandy-brown hair, a lean but muscular body, and a shy, yet welcoming face. He was well known for his boyish charm that accompanied his constant grin. Patrick had what people typically referred to as black Irish features: wicked black hair and a strong, well-defined jawline that always sported five-o'clock shadow. His eyes were bright against his deeply handsome features and danced with a hidden light. The dark, mysterious air about him drew the attention of the women of Birch Valley.

Daniel was six inches shorter than Liam and Patrick and of a stockier build, and his hair had a reddish hue. His expressions were friendly and joyous, and a smile was constantly perched on his face as he was always laughing.

The three men always gave each other a hard time, as brothers do, but the love they shared was immeasurable.

After climbing back onto the ladder, Liam braced his body against the steel frame as he ran another string of lights along the edge of the roof of his parents' older Craftsman-style home. Below him, someone grabbed at the ladder and gave it a slight tug.

"Hey, don't fall, Liam." Daniel laughed.

"Knock it off, you knucklehead. Some people are actually trying to work here," Liam teased back as he continued to hang the lights.

"We need to hurry up, guys. I can barely feel my fingers, and I lost the feeling in my toes like an hour ago," Patrick said.

"You are such a complainer, Patrick. Come on, Liam, that should be the last strand of lights we need to put up. Then we can all head in and get poor little Patrick all warmed up before he catches a cold," Daniel joked.

After Liam climbed down the ladder, the three brothers stood admiring their handiwork as snow started to fall lightly, sparkling against the reflection of the twinkling lights.

"Not bad. I think it even looks better than last

year," Liam offered as he heard the front door close. He turned around and saw their mother's plump figure making her way out onto the porch.

"Oh my," she gasped. "It's just lovely. You boys did a terrific job. Now scoot inside for a bit of hot chocolate and some cookies that just came out of the oven."

Following her orders, the men all trudged through the door after their mother. Liam inhaled the warmth inside his childhood home as he peeled off his layers of coats and sweaters and hung them on the oak coat hanger.

"Mom, it smells great in here," Daniel exclaimed, taking off his heavy work coat and practically running toward the kitchen.

"Daniel O'Brien, you get those boots off. I don't want you tracking in all that snow," Mary scolded as she set a plate piled high with various homemade cookies onto the table.

Liam looked into the den across from the kitchen and noticed his father and grandfather sitting together skimming over the newspaper, each adding his own commentary about what he was reading. The two aging men were surrounded by a soft glow from the fire burning slowly in the brick fireplace.

His grandfather looked like an older version of Liam's father with dark hair and the deep-set green eyes all the children had inherited. Known to everyone in the family as Grandpa Paddy, he was an Irish immigrant who had settled in the small community of Birch Valley. After laboring for many years, he'd started a construction company and taught his only son Pat the trade. Pat then came to work with him and eventually took over the business. The construction company had gained a solid reputation thanks to Grandpa Paddy's hard work and honesty and his insistence on instilling those values in his son and grandchildren. The construction company, now run by Liam's brothers, still had that reputation.

"Hey, Dad and Grandpa Paddy. You two missed all the fun outside," Liam announced as he leaned in the doorway and smiled at his two male role models.

The men looked up from their papers and turned their heads toward him in unison. Grandpa Paddy had a pipe dangling from the corner of his mouth, and Pat looked over the tops of his glasses and gave his son a slight smirk.

"You know your mother. She always has to decorate this place like the North Pole. But you got it done, son, right?" Pat shifted his gaze from Liam back to his paper as he turned the page.

"Yeah, it looks really good, actually. It started snowing again, and Patrick complained he was cold, so we decided to see if Mom would treat us to some of her famous homemade sugar cookies." Liam yawned, and his stomach gurgled as he thought of the treats.

"Well, lad, you'd better hustle on into the kitchen before Daniel helps himself to your serving," Grandpa Paddy added before turning his attention back to his paper. "Be a good boy and bring your granddad a couple of those delicious goodies. Be quick about it too." His Irish brogue was still as thick as ever, despite him having been in the US for more than sixty years.

Liam softly jogged to the kitchen to retrieve some sweets for his grandfather. After opening the cupboard and choosing a small plate, Liam then grabbed several of the warm baked goods to bring back to the den. As he popped one in his mouth, his mother sighed.

"Dear, have a seat and eat at the table, won't you? I don't want you dropping crumbs about." She scurried over to him and brushed a couple of tiny crumbs off his midnight-blue, cable-knit sweater.

After planting a kiss on top of her head, he asked, "What would I do without you, Mom?"

Rolling her eyes and encircling him in her arms, she said, "Probably leave a trail a crumbs."

Liam laughed. "I do it in case I get lost," he said, exiting the kitchen.

After dropping off some cookies to his father and grandfather, Liam joined his brothers at the dining room table. It was the same one they had used when he was a kid, and he had so many memories of the family seated around it. That was the special thing about this home—his mother didn't change it around much. She also prioritized creating memories and traditions that could be passed on. Now that some of her children had provided her with grandchildren, she really tried to make every event or occasion into something special.

"So Liam, how was the last day of school yesterday?" Daniel asked while dunking a sugar cookie into his steaming mug.

Grabbing a cookie for himself, Liam replied, "Crazy as usual. The kids were so thrilled for

Christmas, it was difficult to keep their attention on anything else."

Patrick yawned as he announced, "I really should be heading home. I still need to pick up the boys."

"Probably just afraid Mom might find something else for us to decorate," Daniel added as he motioned toward Patrick before helping himself to another cookie.

"Yeah, I need to head out soon too," Liam said, turning his head toward his mother, who was washing dishes at the sink. "Hey, Mom, what time is Maggie arriving tomorrow?"

Mary shut the water off and turned toward him. "Well, depends on the snow, I suppose. I know she mentioned getting an early start, so probably no later than afternoon. I expect you all to be here in time for dinner. I'm making a pot roast, Melanie's favorite."

"My favorite too. I can't wait," Daniel said.

"What isn't your favorite, Daniel?" Patrick teased as he poked his brother's larger waist.

Daniel laughed and tried to grab Patrick to pull him into a headlock. Liam smiled as he watched his brothers, both grown men, acting like children at their mother's table. A little roughhousing and general teasing gave Liam the sensation they were stuck in time. Seeing his mother's face looking soft and lost in thought as she watched them, Liam could tell these moments were precious to her.

\*\*\*

When Liam arrived at his parents' house the

following day, he could hear children laughing and his family's voices as he walked up to the red-painted front door. Upon opening it, Liam saw Daniel on the floor in the living room with his niece and nephews piled on top of him. Liam watched the wrestling match, fully amused at seeing his younger brother pretend to be overtaken by two toddler boys and a six-year-old girl.

Daniel met Liam's eyes. "Help," he cried playfully as he allowed himself to be pinned on the floor by the toddlers, Finn and Connor.

The boys were Patrick's children, and the cutest three-year-old twins ever, according to the entire O'Brien family. Each boy had the mischievous emerald O'Brien eyes but had inherited their mother's wild blond curls.

Melanie held a special place in Liam's heart; she was the first to make him an uncle. She had a cherub face, bobbed hair the color of rust, and the O'Brien eyes, only hers had flecks of gold in the deep green.

As soon as the children noticed Liam, they quickly scurried off Daniel.

"Uncle Liam," they shouted in unison.

Crouching down low to give all three a hug, Liam said to Daniel, "I guess they love this uncle more."

"I see how it is." Daniel laughed as he got up. He then tickled the children, causing them to scurry toward the kitchen, where their grandmother was preparing Sunday dinner.

"Where's Maggie at?" Liam asked as the two men went to go sit down in the living room.

"She's in the kitchen with Mom. She was acting kind of funny, though," Daniel said. He was still trying to catch his breath from wrestling with his niece and nephews.

"Funny how?" Liam questioned.

"I don't know really. I'm not good at figuring women out, but she wasn't acting normal, you know what I mean?"

"Well, not quite. Guess I will have to see for myself in a minute," Liam said.

"Don't say I said anything. I don't need to be getting into any trouble with her or Mom," Daniel teased.

"Where's Patrick at? I see his little munchkins are here," Liam said, smiling at the thought of his two nephews.

"I think he is going over some business stuff with Dad and Grandpa Paddy," Daniel replied as he stretched out on the soft leather couch, adjusting the pillows and settling into a comfortable position.

"How's work been?" Liam sat across from Daniel in a matching dark brown leather recliner. Patrick was much like their father, serious and always concerned about the business, particularly after his wife Beth had died in a car crash three years ago. She had been pregnant with their twin boys when the accident happened, leaving Patrick a devastated widow and a new father. Through the thickness of his grief, Patrick was raising his sons with the help of his family and Beth's parents, who also lived in Birch Valley.

Daniel interrupted his thoughts. "Work has been sort of slow, especially with the holidays coming up. But I sort of don't mind because we'll be busy as heck in the spring and summer."

"How's Patrick been?" Liam asked.

"Eh, Patrick's been Patrick. So nothing new there." Daniel shrugged.

Liam heard footsteps making their way down the hall just before Maggie appeared at the entryway of the living room.

"Liam, Melanie said you were here. I didn't hear you come in." She leaned her slender figure against the wall with her arms crossed casually over her chest. Her soft, chestnut hair framed her heart-shaped face and fell just past her shoulders.

"Glad you made it in with all this snow we've been getting. How was the drive over from Seattle?" Liam asked, trying to read his sister to see if she was acting strange as Daniel had suggested.

Maggie yawned, covering her mouth and said, "It was okay. We got an early start this morning. The highway was pretty clear for the most part, and they weren't requiring chains over the mountain pass."

"Well, that's good. So Mom is making something good for dinner?" Liam asked, still not getting the feeling that anything was wrong with his sister.

"She has a pot roast going. Actually, dinner's almost ready. I just got done having the kids help set the table."

"Great, I'm starving," Daniel chirped.

Both men stood, stretching and eyeing each other.

"I'll let Mom know you guys are ready to eat,"

Maggie said as she turned away.

As soon as she was out of earshot, Liam looked at Daniel and said, "I didn't think she acted funny or like anything was wrong."

"I don't know, Liam, but earlier she did act like something was wrong. Maybe she's fine now. You know how women can be, all moody and stuff," Daniel said as he led the way to the dining room, from which wonderful smells of pot roast and vegetables were wafting.

Liam took his place at the large table, where his family was gathered. Meals at this house were always loud and filled with the sounds of dishes clinking and several conversations happening all at once.

Grandpa Paddy was seated at one end of the table and Liam's father at the other. They were having a lively debate regarding something they read earlier in the newspaper. Maggie was bringing different dishes to the table as Mary brought a pitcher of water out and began filling everyone's glasses. Connor flicked a spoonful of peas across the table at his twin, making Finn cry loudly.

"Connor, don't throw peas at your brother," Patrick scolded, wiping the loose peas off the table.

Melanie giggled and forked in a mouthful of creamy potatoes. Daniel sneakily flicked a lone pea at Connor and quickly looked at his plate and started eating.

"Mary, come and sit down. You are working too hard, lass," Grandpa Paddy commanded in his deep brogue.

Maggie took her seat next to their father, who

eyed her and asked, "Where's Michael? What has he been up to these days?"

Shifting uncomfortably, Maggie replied, "He had a lot going on this week, Dad. He needed to get some loose ends all tied up before the holidays."

"Well, he's missing out on a terrific pot roast tonight, I'll tell you that," Pat commented before he put another piece of the succulent meat in his mouth and sent a sweet look toward Mary.

"Yes, my compliments to the chef," Grandpa Paddy added when Mary took her place next to him.

"Yeah, Mom, everything is great," Liam said before taking a sip of his water.

"Grams, you are such a good cook." Melanie motioned to her mother for another helping of potatoes.

"Well, thank you, everyone. I'm just so glad we are all here together. Too bad Michael isn't here," Mary said as she helped herself to some peas while giving her grandson a warning look as he aimed another spoonful of peas at his brother.

Daniel seized the opportunity to flick another pea, this time at Liam.

Liam just rolled his eyes. This was his family, and he adored every one of them.

# Chapter Two

## Rachel

The sun was high in the cloudless sky, and Rachel was sweltering as she jogged up the concrete stairs. She was panting hard but remained in rhythm with her friend Chelsea as they neared the top platform that gave them a magnificent view of the Pacific Ocean.

"I can't believe you're serious about this, Rachel!" Chelsea said with annoyance before she sipped from her hot-pink sports bottle that matched her workout attire.

"I think I just need a change of scenery, and it's a great opportunity for me." Rachel looked beyond the vast, blue waters, trying to imagine what moving to a new place would be like. She could feel the warm rays of sunlight on her shoulders and trails of sweat running down her back.

Rachel Montgomery had always lived in Newport Beach, California. She assumed she would spend her entire life here, as she had no reason to venture out of this well-sought-after area. To most, living in the wealthy beach community would be a dream come true, but it was all she had ever known, so perhaps she was a bit jaded. Her father, a well-respected plastic surgeon, had a successful practice that kept the richest members of society looking youthful. Her mother, who had divorced her father when Rachel was still quite young, spent most of her days shopping and living off her hefty alimony checks. Rachel had an older brother, Ethan, who was busy carving his own path in the world of medicine. She, however, had gone in a completely different direction, deciding to work in education administration. She was currently the vice principal at a prestigious elementary school.

"I think it's insane that you would even consider leaving all this," Chelsea exclaimed as she gestured around them with her arms.

Chelsea had a longstanding history with Rachel. They both had attended the same prep school, both had fathers who were plastic surgeons, and had somehow managed to maintain a real and deep friendship—quite a feat in the shallow community they'd both grown up in.

"I know, I know." Rachel looked at her longtime friend, who seemed to be growing more annoyed by the minute. She dabbed the sweat off her face and neck with a small sports towel and added, "Chelsea, it's hard to explain, but I guess I just want to see what else is out there. I don't feel whole here, if that makes sense."

Rachel fussed with her pixie cut nervously, sweeping sun-kissed bangs away from her eyes. She wasn't completely confident she was making the right decision. This was giant leap of faith, and she was usually pretty cautious. She always weighed out every option and calculated all the risks. So when she announced her plans to accept the position of principal at a little elementary school in Birch Valley, Washington, her family figured she must have lost her mind. They didn't realize she felt as though something was missing in her life. She didn't know if she was experiencing an early midlife crisis, but Rachel felt as though this opportunity just might help her resolve these unsettling feelings.

"Oh Rachel, I don't get it. I mean, what could a tiny, middle-of-nowhere town offer you?" Chelsea questioned as she stretched her toned frame before bending down to touch the tips of her running shoes. "You're my best friend, and I can't imagine you being two states away."

With nothing else to add, Chelsea spun around and started back down the concrete stairs, her bleach-blonde ponytail swishing back and forth. Rachel followed, knowing full well how disappointed Chelsea was by her choice. Her parents hadn't taken her decision to accept the position well, either. Only Ethan had championed her desire to venture out.

After leaving their favorite workout spot, Rachel and Chelsea each got into their matching silver BMW convertible sedans. Waving good-bye, Rachel sped off toward her home. She had a great deal of packing and finalizing some last-minute details to do if she was going to be all set for the move by the end of the year. As she drove, Rachel started to succumb to thinking this idea was ridiculous. After all, she was relocating during the holidays to a state she'd never even seen. She silently prayed this wasn't a colossal mistake.

\*\*\*

Rachel looked down at her pretty manicured toes and her tan legs, which stood out against the pale carpet of her small bedroom. She then turned her gaze to the boxes stacked evenly against one wall. She was deep in thought and going over a mental checklist of things she needed to do when her cell phone chirped with a text message from her mother, asking if she was available for lunch tomorrow. Rachel typed back a reply, wondering why her mother hadn't just called instead. This was what their relationship had been reduced to: a text here and there, an occasional call to go shopping or dining out at some exclusive restaurant Rachel would much rather avoid.

Her relationship with her father wasn't much different. He stayed in contact more than her mother but mainly with a call, an email, or an occasional dinner. This had always been the norm for her family. They were each busy with their individual lives, and that probably would never change.

When Rachel was a child, nannies and housekeepers tended to treat her more how she imagined a traditional family would. They'd bandage a skinned knee when she fell off her bike and later listened and offered advice during those difficult teen years. These important people had provided Rachel with the care and love that should have come solely from her parents. On the other hand, her parents had provided everything else she could have asked for. Her mother and father did love her; they just had a monetary way of showing their affection.

Ethan had taken advantage of the lack of parental supervision and concern and enjoyed the perks of their privileged life. He tended to get into trouble quite often.

She worked on organizing her belongings for a couple more hours before settling in front of her computer to look up more information on the place she would soon call home. Sipping on a mug of herbal tea, she typed "Birch Valley" into the search engine, and a beautiful picture instantly popped up. Surrounded by small mountains and various trees, mostly pine and tamarack, the town looked like something out of a postcard for a quaint vacation retreat. Aspen and birch trees speckled along the river that ran through the town. Large mountains encircled fields that looked like patchwork on a homemade quilt and that could be seen for miles. This faraway place was very different from her vibrant ocean home.

Rachel had contacted a local real estate agent in Birch Valley to see about renting something. The problem, according to the agent, was that there were few rental properties, especially in the middle of winter. Still, she was fortunate enough to secure a small home. The agent had promised it was the best one available at the moment, and Rachel had agreed to a short lease, just in case things didn't quite work out.

One of the more difficult tasks was scheduling movers to haul her furniture and boxes. She arranged for them to pick up her belongings a couple days after Christmas, then planned to drive to Washington shortly after. Her goal was to get moved in and settled before she started her new position the day after New Year's.

Rachel shut down her laptop and felt an array of emotions as she readied for bed. Lying in the dark room, she contemplated once again the life she would be leaving for the life that could be.

***

Rachel nervously stood outside of a posh eatery, waiting for her mother, Evelyn, to arrive. An overly decorated gift bag containing her mother's Christmas gift was slung over her arm. She hoped the Chanel bag inside, in the latest color and style, would meet with Evelyn's approval. The weather was on the edge of hot, and as Rachel absorbed the sun's rays, she was thankful she'd worn her lavender sundress. Staring through her strappy sandals at her painted toenails, she grew impatient as she continued to wait.

When Rachel next looked up, her mother was rounding the corner of the building and walking toward her. For an older woman, Evelyn was in amazing shape. Her figure was lean and toned, and she wore her champagne-blonde hair in a youthful, layered cut. The brilliant sunlight bounced off her sparkling diamond earrings.

"Oh hello, darling." Her mother kissed her on each cheek in a very chic European fashion.

"Hi, Mom." Rachel started to feel underdressed as she took in her mother's crisp, white two-piece suit. Evelyn motioned for the hostess to seat them. Once seated, each woman was served water with a perfect slice of lemon. Sipping on hers, Rachel offered her mother a smile.

"So I was wondering if you've changed your mind about accepting that job," her mother said, curling her slender fingers around the elegant glass before sipping her beverage slowly. Her tone was dismissive, and she appeared to be more focused on their fellow diners, almost as though she was scanning the room to see if she could recognize any friends or perhaps even a celebrity.

Rachel was prepared for the questioning. She held the large gift bag up to her mother's eye level, seeing if she could distract her with her Christmas gift.

"I wasn't sure if I would see you again before the holidays, so I wanted to make sure you got this." Rachel held the bag out to her.

"Why, Rachel, that is very thoughtful of you, darling. I'm set to take a cruise down to Mexico in a couple days, so that is very smart of you to think ahead." Evelyn grabbed the gift and placed it on the ground next to her chair.

Rachel mentally rolled her eyes but was slightly surprised her mother hadn't opened the bag or even peeked inside it.

"I've also brought something for you." Evelyn

slid a card over to Rachel's side of the table.

"Thank you, Mom," Rachel said as she started to unseal the envelope. The card contained a check. Rachel didn't want to know how much was written on it, so she tucked it away in her purse without glancing at it.

"Well, now we've exchanged Christmas gifts, tell me once again why you're leaving? I just can't seem to wrap my mind around the idea." Her mother reached her well-manicured hands across the table for Rachel's.

"I know it seems crazy. I just thought the opportunity was too good to pass up." Rachel shrugged as her mother gripped her hand a little tighter.

"Have you spoken to your father about this absurd move?"

"I have, and we're meeting tomorrow for dinner. He isn't thrilled, either."

Evelyn eased her grip. "I can't quite understand why you would want to leave the school you are already working at. What about meeting someone and getting married? I'm sure you realize you aren't getting any younger."

"I like where I work now. The school is fantastic. I see this as a great opportunity for advancement. Right now, I'm really wanting to focus on my career, so I'm not looking to get involved with anyone." Rachel lowered her eyes. The very thought of getting into another relationship caused her to feel a pang of distress. She'd been there, done that, and had the broken heart to prove it. She'd also failed to mention that she felt as though something was missing in her life. There was no point in trying to get into some emotionally deep conversation with her mother.

Evelyn rolled her mocha-colored eyes, which were shrouded with false eyelashes and designer makeup. "Fine, I won't say another thing about it. If this is what you want, then so be it. Even if it is a huge mistake. But keep in mind there is no place like home, especially if you live here." She smiled as she looked all around them.

With that topic over and done with, the two women proceeded to dine on light Cobb salads, and the rest of the conversation focused on her mother. Soon, Rachel was anxious to leave the overly crowded restaurant and made eye contact with their server to get the check.

"Well, thank you again, Mom, for the card and lunch. I hope you enjoy your cruise and have a wonderful time," Rachel said as the two women exited the restaurant.

"Good luck with the packing." With a wave, her mother headed for her parking spot, her heels clicking against the concrete quickly.

Standing outside in the warm weather, Rachel absorbed the loud sounds of traffic. She wondered what her new home would sound like. Thinking about this huge move both excited and scared her.

\*\*\*

Rachel was taping up another box when her cell phone started to ring. She glanced down to see who was calling and noticed her brother's number on the screen. "Hey, Ethan," she answered quickly.

"Hi, Rachel. Wanted to see what your plans were for Christmas." Ethan's voice sounded distant and echoed. He was probably stuck in traffic on his Bluetooth. Rachel pictured him sitting in his Jaguar, irritated at the lines of cars that were probably surrounding him.

"No plans, just packing. I had lunch with Mom today."

"Oh, I bet that was fun." He laughed. "I was thinking maybe we could have dinner or something so I could see you off before you leave. When exactly are you heading out again?"

"I was thinking about leaving a day or so after the movers come to take all the stuff. I'm kind of anxious to get up there, and besides, I start the day after New Year's, so the sooner, the better," Rachel answered as she placed the box she had taped against the wall with the others.

"Wow, not too much longer before you're gone. Are you excited?" Ethan asked casually.

"I'm excited and nervous and wondering if this is a huge mistake," she confided. "Do you think it is?"

"I think it's great, so just go with it! It's about time you do something crazy."

Rachel appreciated her brother's support. After a little more chatter, they decided on a plan to have one last dinner before she left. She would miss Ethan but knew he was always a phone call away.

Not even a minute after she hung up, her cell phone started ringing again.

"Hello?" she answered.

"Hey, Rachel, just wanted to see how the packing was going," Chelsea said.

"Eh, it's about done. Why? Are you offering to come over to help?" Rachel teased.

"I'm actually on my way over and wanted to make sure you were home first."

"Okay, great. Just buzz when you get here." Rachel ended the call and scanned her living room.

The only things in it now were a line of boxes along the wall, a small couch and loveseat, empty bookshelves, and her entertainment center in the corner. Everything looked so sterile now that her personality was tucked away into those brown cardboard boxes.

Rachel had left the essentials to be packed last; her coffeepot and favorite mug were her most precious treasures. Though she figured Chelsea could help her pack some odds and ends, she was mainly looking forward to the unexpected visit with her best friend.

When Rachel heard the door buzz, she hurried to it. When she opened it, she found Chelsea smiling her perfect smile and embracing an expensive bottle of wine. Rachel let her in and took the bottle.

"You are awesome," she exclaimed, looking it over. "I might have already packed away my wineglasses," she added, doing a mental inventory of the contents left in her cupboards.

"We don't need glasses. This is a 'drink out of the bottle' kind of occasion," Chelsea said, smiling as she rummaged through Rachel's utensil drawer. "You didn't pack this away yet, and that's all that matters," she said, holding up a wine opener.

"I think I might have another mug I haven't packed yet," Rachel offered as she scanned the near-empty cupboards.

"Nah, I'm good," Chelsea replied and took the first swig out of the bottle.

Rachel joined Chelsea, who was now sitting on a barstool at the breakfast counter. She grabbed the bottle, took in the pleasant aroma of the rich liquid, then took a hearty drink.

"So I see the packing is really coming along," Chelsea observed as Rachel handed the bottle back to her.

"Yeah, I'm glad it's almost done. I still can't believe I'm leaving in just a couple days." Rachel surveyed the room.

Chelsea added, "I can't believe it's almost Christmas too. I'm so bummed you won't be here for New Year's. What about our tradition of watching the New Year's Eve special on TV and drinking way too much champagne together?"

A twinge of sadness crept into Rachel's chest. She'd been so busy packing and making plans, she hadn't really thought about the holidays too much. Or what she would be leaving behind.

"Once I get settled, I want you to come and visit. I hear the summers are amazing up there." Rachel reached out to her.

"I'm just really going to miss you, Rachel. We have so much fun together. You are always giving me the best advice about everything. I'm so sad you're moving away." Chelsea sobbed, ruining her perfectly applied makeup.

"I'm only a phone call away. Trust me, I'm

going to make sure we keep in touch. I'll miss you too, but now you have a new place to come and visit. Who knows? You might meet someone and even move up there. I will keep an eye out for some hot bachelors for you," Rachel teased and Chelsea smiled.

After tearfully discussing the move a little more, Chelsea headed home, leaving Rachel in the quiet space. The condo didn't feel like home anymore. All the walls were stripped of the colorful art she had collected over the years at trendy galleries. It lacked the smell of home too, scented now with various disinfectants and cleaners instead of the floral and vanilla candles she burned regularly.

Rachel now grasped the reality that this would no longer be her home in a couple of days, and a little jolt of panic intertwined with the eagerness which went through her.

\*\*\*

After waking up with a mild headache from a little too much wine the night before, Rachel padded to the kitchen in her bare feet to retrieve a much-needed cup of coffee. Her phone let out a loud chirp, echoing off the walls of the empty condo. Seeing her father's number appear on the screen, Rachel picked up the call.

"Hello?" she answered, still a bit groggy before sipping on her steaming-hot liquid lifeline.

"Hello, sweetheart. I wanted to confirm our dinner date for tonight," he said.

"Hi, Dad. Yeah, we're still on." Rachel

grimaced.

Wrapped up in all the last-minute details of her relocation, she had forgotten about her dinner plans with her father, Robert Montgomery. Good thing he had called. She never would have heard the end of it otherwise.

"Perfect. How about we meet up at that sushi place you like off the pier? Sound good?"

Rachel's stomach growled at the idea of food. She hadn't eaten dinner last night, instead choosing wine as her main course.

"Sounds great, Dad."

After setting up a time to meet and saying good-bye to him, Rachel added more coffee to her mug and settled in front of her laptop. She mapped out the route she was going to travel to Birch Valley and reserved a night's stay at a hotel at the halfway point of her two-day journey. Satisfied that things were now in order, she nibbled on a high-fiber breakfast biscuit. Everything was set. The movers would be here in two days to load her boxes and furniture, and she'd leave the following morning. Rachel planned to stay her at Chelsea's apartment for her final night in California, and she still intended to meet up with Ethan on Christmas to say her good-byes. Feeling perky from all the coffee, Rachel decided it was time to tackle the day.

\*\*\*

The sun was dangling low in the sky, and the early evening was warm with a light ocean breeze. Rachel arrived at the pier earlier than her father so she could watch the tide. Inhaling the salty air mingled with the pungent, raw smell of the sea, she made her way across the busy street.

Christmas lights were festively strung around store windows and the weathered railing of the pier. Rachel appreciated the holiday touches the shops had added to their displays. Christmastime felt odd to her this year, though, probably because she hadn't decorated her condo and wasn't going to attend any of the holiday parties she was usually invited to. Perhaps next year she'd come back to celebrate the holiday season with her friends, she thought as she continued to window-shop her way down the long pier.

Once she reached the end, Rachel gazed at a couple of sailboats drifting on the horizon against a backdrop of purple and orange clouds as she took in in the sounds of the rhythmic waves pounding at the edge of the shore. Rachel was tempted to go down to the water and stick her feet in as she remembered all the times she had anchored herself in the wet sand, taunting the sea to drag her in. She was already missing the ocean.

Sensing some time had passed, Rachel set off toward the only sushi place on the pier, a vibrant little restaurant with fresh seafood and an excellent atmosphere. Local bands would sometimes play there on the weekend. Tonight the restaurant was quiet because it was the middle of the week and tomorrow was Christmas Eve. As she made her way inside, her nose was ambushed with glorious smells. She looked around the room and quickly found her father, who was seated by himself at pub-style table

31

and looking concerned. His flawless, tanned skin set off his equally flawless white teeth. His salt-and-pepper hair was precisely combed back and impeccable as usual. He was dressed in a light brown blazer and casual khaki pants.

"Rachel, I was starting to get a little worried." He stood and glanced at his expensive watch, then hugged her before they both climbed onto the stools.

"Sorry, Dad, I lost track of time," Rachel apologized as she grabbed the menu and started browsing.

Looking over his menu, her father sighed and took a sip of his beer that had been served in an elegant and tall, frosted glass. "I'd like to know a little more about this so-called job offer."

Rachel leisurely sipped the water her father had taken the liberty of ordering her. *So it begins*, she thought. *He sure didn't waste any time. A "how are you?" would have been nice.*

"Well, where would you like me to start?" she asked.

"You can start by telling me about why you even applied for this position. I'm sure you can imagine how incredibly surprised I am," Robert said in a cool tone that matched his exterior.

Rachel swallowed back the tightness forming in the back of her throat. "It's an excellent move as far as my career goes. Besides, I think I'm up for the adventure."

Her father rolled his eyes. "Seriously, Rachel, you are hardly the adventurous type. That's why this is all a bit concerning to us and frankly, quite ludicrous, really."

She took another drink of water in hopes of calming herself. Her parents had every right to think she had lost her mind. What they didn't realize was how she felt and who she was. She wasn't content with her life as it was, plain and simple. She was having a difficult enough time grasping the concept that she was moving two states away from everything she had ever known. Somehow knowing this move was the greatest risk she had ever taken felt good and right.

Rachel let out a deep breath. "I'm sorry, Dad. To be honest, I didn't think you or Mom would really care if I decided to take this job."

Her father closed his eyes and inhaled deeply. A waiter came up to their table, smiling wide with his pen and tablet open. Robert studied the young man, who started to shift nervously on his feet, then reached into the inside pocket of his blazer and pulled out his business card.

"I can absolutely take care of that for you," he said, handing it to him.

A surprised and insulted look washed over the waiter's face. Rachel felt confused and embarrassed as she tried and failed to see what her father was scrutinizing. The young man's face looked fine.

The waiter took their order quietly, avoiding eye contact with both of them, then scurried off without a word.

"Dad, what was that about?" Rachel asked.

Her father grabbed his beer and nonchalantly replied, "His nose." After swallowing a gulp, he added, "Don't tell me you didn't notice it. How could one not notice?" A deep, arrogant laugh escaped him.

Rachel felt terrible for their waiter as she recalled the times she'd been put under Robert Montgomery's magnifying glass. Her early teenage years were by far the most difficult. She hadn't quite reached puberty before her father suggested several procedures that would make her stunning. But unlike her mother and a lot of the people she knew, Rachel didn't desire physical perfection. Of course she had certain features she would like more of or less of, but she didn't want to do anything drastic, such as going under the knife to correct them. So she had taken an uncommon approach for Newport Beach by trying to exercise, eat right, and accept that she wasn't perfect. Meanwhile, most of her friends, including Chelsea, weren't opposed to going out for a Botox lunch date with their friends.

"So getting back to our original conversation, tell me a little bit more about this place you are moving to. Is it near Seattle?" her father questioned.

"Well, no, it's on the other side of the state. According to the map I looked up online, it looks to be about an hour or so north of a city called Spokane," Rachel said, trying to picture exactly where Birch Valley was.

"I see. How did you hear about the job? What about interviewing for this position?"

Rachel felt interrogated. "I heard about the position on an online job board for teachers and administrators. So I applied just to see if I could qualify for a principal position, after seeing that I met their requirements, and I was interviewed," she stammered.

"What about flying up to see the place? And how did they do your interview, over the phone?"

"At first I was contacted on the phone, then I did a webcam interview."

Her father snorted as he laughed, then sarcastically added, "Webcam? So they have Internet in those parts? I figured since they were so far from the only city that really even matters in Washington, they wouldn't be so hi-tech. I could understand if you were going to Seattle, but Birch Valley? Never even heard of it, and just seems a bit ridiculous."

Rachel swallowed against the lump forming again at the rear of her throat. Pushing her irritation aside, she answered, "Dad, I realize Birch Valley isn't Newport or Seattle or some other giant, fancy city, but this place has offered me an excellent opportunity I may not have received here or in a larger city."

"Perhaps if you have to go to some small town in the middle of nowhere to be a principal, then you're in the wrong line of work, Rachel," her father retorted.

Feeling the sting from her father's words, Rachel was about to steer their conversation in another direction when their food arrived, brought by a different waiter. The server placed various dishes around their table and paused nervously, looking at Rachel's father. "Excuse me, sir, my coworker informed me that you gave him your business card. I'm actually interested in having a couple things done. Would you mind if I got your card?"

Robert Montgomery flashed his perfectly straight teeth as he fished another card out of his jacket pocket. "Absolutely."

Rachel rolled her eyes. This was one of the reasons she wanted to get out of Newport Beach. She hoped the speck that was Birch Valley on the map wasn't nearly as shallow.

*** 

The condo was still dark when Rachel woke up the day following Christmas. The movers were scheduled to arrive today, and stress was starting to set in. She hurried to make coffee and cut up an overripe pear and banana for her breakfast. The morning sun was starting to streak the sky and light up her home. She ate quickly and downed her coffee before showering. Mentally going over everything as she dressed for the day, Rachel felt less tense and more confident, as though all her loose ends were being tied up.

As she waited for the movers to arrive, Rachel found herself with nothing to do, so she fiddled with her cell phone and checked her email on her laptop. As she came across a message from Ethan wishing her good luck with her move today, she couldn't help but smile. She and Ethan had spent a nontraditional holiday together over dinner and some drinks. Saying goodbye to him really hurt.

Checking the time, Rachel realized the movers would be arriving fairly soon. She made sure the stack of boxes was secure, then kept peeking out her living room window to see if a large transport truck was in the parking area. Like a child waiting for Christmas morning to arrive, she felt anxious and excited. Rachel had gone to double-check all her rooms when she heard a loud knock at her door. She practically ran to see who it was and was pleased to find a gentleman in denim overalls standing on the other side, holding a clipboard.

The movers wrapped the large furniture in heavy wool blankets to keep it from getting scratched or damaged, then made quick and easy work of carrying all her belongings to the truck, where they were stacked in neat rows and strapped down with bright orange and yellow nylon ties. One of the movers then latched the lock and got inside. Rachel watched as the truck left her standing alone in a parking lot filled with luxury sedans and high-priced SUVs.

Wiping tears from her eyes, Rachel headed back inside her former home. It was so empty and large now. Realizing there was no point in staying any longer, she loaded her suitcases in her silver BMW convertible. After she buckled herself into the plush leather seat, she took another long look at the condo before pulling out of the complex.

\*\*\*

After getting gas and grabbing some food to go, Rachel raced to Chelsea's apartment, where she planned to spend the remainder of the day and night before driving to Birch Valley. She pulled into an unoccupied spot on the palm-tree-lined street and set the car alarm. Balancing her purse, overnight bag, and a warm bag filled with the best burritos in town, she rang the doorbell.

"Yay! You brought lunch," Chelsea practically shouted when she opened the door.

Chelsea's apartment was very modern. Sleek lines and contemporary colors graced all the rooms. The living room contained a long, strikingly white sofa with solid-colored pillows in bright colors. The sofa and two attractive but uncomfortable matching chairs sat on a teal rug. A flat-screen TV was mounted between two large wall sconces, and an abstract piece of metal art sat in the corner. The entire room looked as though it had been staged for a photo shoot in an upscale magazine.

The kitchen, where Chelsea was leading Rachel, was equally modern. The stainless-steel appliances sparkled, and the polished granite countertops lay bare. Expensive dishes were stacked in uniform rows behind glass cupboards. Not one thing in it was out of place.

"Where did you want me to put my bag?" Rachel asked, sweeping her blonde bangs away from her eyes.

"How about the guest room?" Chelsea offered as she pulled two plates from the cupboard.

"Okay, that works," Rachel said, picking up her overnight bag and purse and making her way down the short hallway past the small dining area.

"Damn, these burritos smell and look amazing," Chelsea shouted after her.

Rachel smiled, glad she had brought lunch. She would miss their little visits like this. She hoped she would make friends in Birch Valley, but she had so much history with Chelsea and doubted she could find anyone quite like her.

After Rachel put away her things, she sat across from Chelsea at the chic designer table. Her friend scooted a silver vase that held a couple of bright roses to the side.

Nodding toward it, Rachel asked, "So who are those from?"

"No one. Well, actually, I thought he was going to be someone interesting, but he turned out to be really boring," Chelsea answered before sinking her teeth into the large burrito.

"That's a bummer," Rachel said before taking a bite of her own.

"Not a big deal, I promise you. He so wasn't my type, either. I wonder if you will meet anyone up there." Chelsea's brown eyes widened with the question.

"You know I'm not looking for anyone right now," Rachel replied, toying with a piece of her flour tortilla.

"You're never looking. I wish you'd be more open to meeting people and dating. It's been a long time, Rachel," Chelsea complained before licking a rogue bean from her finger.

Rachel rolled her eyes. Chelsea was always trying to set her up on dates or encourage her to go out. Rachel had been out of her previous relationship for about two years but had no desire to jump back into the dating pool just yet.

"I want to get moved and start my new job. Kind of see where life takes me for a while. Then I promise I will think about getting out there a little more," she said.

Chelsea shrugged her thin, bare shoulders, her tan dark against the pale blue tank top.

They finished lunch and decided to go for a walk around Chelsea's neighborhood to burn off the calorie-rich meal.

\*\*\*

Evening quickly transitioned into night, and Chelsea and Rachel said good night after gorging on some ice cream and a romantic comedy. Rachel lay in the guest room bed, relishing the crisp feel of the new sheets under her skin. She closed her eyes only to find her body buzzing with anticipation for the next day. She tossed and turned over and over, doing a mental checklist of what she would unpack first when she arrived. At some point, her tired brain calmed her feelings of anxiety and she fell into a deep sleep.

\*\*\*

The next morning Rachel hugged Chelsea tightly as they both tried not to cry.

"I'm going to miss you so much," Rachel sobbed as she dabbed her eyes.

Chelsea pouted. "My bestie is going to be so far away."

"You better come and visit me, and soon," Rachel demanded playfully.

"Maybe I'll come up for spring break."

Rachel gave her one more hug before she got into her car and pulled away, giving her friend a wave as she made her way onto the busy street. She got into the turn lane to get on the freeway, her belly full of nervous enthusiasm as she began her new adventure.

# *Chapter Three*

### Liam

While working on his second cup of coffee that morning, Liam paused briefly in reading the mystery novel in front of him to stare out his kitchen window. The thick, gray and white storm clouds threatened to burst open, and already white flakes were falling gently on branches heavy with snow that had fallen overnight. The cabin had a warm fire crackling as Liam returned his attention to the book he was reading. He treasured quiet moments such as these, free from distraction. Lost in the gripping tale, Liam heard the rumble of Daniel's truck as it pulled up in the driveway. The oversized piece of machinery was loud, a bit obnoxious, and a perfectly suited vehicle for his brother. Liam grudgingly tore himself away from the book, marking his place with a piece of scrap paper.

Christmas was closing in, and Mary O'Brien was

calling on her sons to cut down a tree today. Liam owned several well-treed acres, and his brothers planned on coming over today to see which one might meet their mother's approval.

Liam pulled his long arms through the heavy coat and went to meet his brothers outside. With the snow sticking to him as he tugged on a wool cap, Liam quickly approached Daniel's lifted truck.

"Hey guys, how's it going?" he announced with a wave.

Patrick exited the truck and nodded as he trudged toward Liam, and Daniel hopped out after him. His cheeks turned rosy as the cool, wet air touched them.

"Looks like a great day to cut a tree down," Daniel joked as his bright green eyes lit up.

Liam laughed, and Patrick grunted as he pulled his black, thick coat tighter around himself.

"Better than a blizzard." He grabbed Daniel's shoulder and gave it a good squeeze. "You guys want to come in for some coffee before we try and find Mom's perfect tree?"

"Sounds great to me," Patrick replied, already heading toward the cabin.

The three brothers entered the warmth of Liam's small living room. A short tree stood in the corner covered in soft, twinkling, white lights and a red and green garland. Liam had also cut some greenery from a few of his pines and firs and placed it on the beautiful tamarack mantle along with the more sparkling garland.

"Looks like you decorated for Christmas," Daniel said, pointing to the tree.

Liam nodded. "Yeah, I had some leftover garland from the classroom and figured I might as well use it."

"Better than my place," Patrick added. "I don't have anything up at all. I figure the boys and I are at Mom and Dad's place enough. Less hassle, I suppose."

"One of the perks of living at Mom's too, I get to eat well and the place always looks great," Daniel added, taking the chair closest to the fireplace. Patrick and Liam shared the large couch directly in front of the slow-burning fire.

"So what are the ladies of the house up to today?" Liam asked Daniel.

"I think Mom and Maggie are doing some last-minute Christmas shopping. Mom wants to decorate the tree tonight." Daniel stared off into the fire.

Remembering Sunday dinner and Daniel's concern about their sister, Liam asked, "How's Maggie doing? She still acting strange like you mentioned?" He stretched his long legs out and put his feet on the aged wood of the coffee table.

"You know, I don't know, really. She's acting weird still, but not as bad as when she first arrived on Sunday. Maybe she's just hormonal or something, who knows?" Daniel answered.

Patrick looked at Daniel while running his fingers through his wavy, black hair. "She acted a little stressed at dinner. I do know that she didn't seem like she wanted to talk about Michael. Especially when I asked her how he was doing. She was real short about it and then changed the subject."

Liam rubbed his chin, massaging the prickly, unshaven skin. "Well, maybe he's working too much. I know every time I call or text her, he seems to be gone. I think she gets lonely over there in Seattle."

"You might be right, but she has Mel, and I know she's always helping out in the classroom and stuff," Daniel said. "I bet if something really was wrong, she would tell us."

Liam wasn't so sure about that. Maggie had always been independent and rarely asked for advice. Liam was probably the closest to her, and she would open up about some aspects of her life to him. Perhaps that was why he didn't suspect anything was wrong with his sister. Liam was also shocked Daniel had noticed she was acting odd. Daniel was usually more of a joyful and playful kind of guy. He preferred staying away from any type of drama that might cause him the slightest discomfort.

Clearing his throat as if to change the course of the conversation, Daniel said, "So Liam, how's the dating going?"

Liam rolled his eyes. "Why do you care if I'm dating? I don't hear about you going out too often."

"I do. I just like to look around and see what's out there," Daniel playfully defended himself.

Patrick sat quietly, staring straight ahead, not looking at either brother. Liam noticed Patrick's demeanor turn slightly icy and decided to change the subject before Patrick's mood soured for the remainder of the day. "Well, looks like the snow has stopped, so we should probably get out there," he suggested as he extended his neck to peer out the only window in the living room.

Patrick was quick to reply as he got up from the couch. "Sounds great."

Liam frowned at Daniel in warning, and his brother looked back, surprised and confused. Liam simply shook his head as they went to get their coats on.

After tromping around the property for a while, they located a tree that would make Mary O'Brien quite happy. They loaded it into the bed of Daniel's truck, and Liam said he would meet up with them later that evening at the O'Brien home. With a wave, he sent them on their way and headed back inside to read a little more and warm up.

Hours flew by, and before he knew it, Liam was driving into Birch Valley, cheered by festive holiday lights hanging on buildings and wreaths on the doors of every storefront. The snow piled in the center of Main Street glistened beneath the soft lights strung overhead. The small trees lining the street were also decorated with lights as well as giant metallic ornaments. Antique lampposts wrapped in natural garland lit up sidewalks that had been cleared of snow. Liam passed the small courthouse and town hall, where the giant tree that stood proudly year round was now adorned with red bows and large, colorful bulbs and lights. The church where he grew up attending mass had lights that looked like candles in every window and a well-lit manger scene by the large front doors.

After driving past rows of beautifully decorated houses, Liam arrived at the home he grew up in. He opened the front door and was instantly hit with the lovely smells of dinner and apple pie. The tree from his property had been placed in the front bay window, where it stood barren and longed to be given that Mary O'Brien touch. The rest of the home oozed Christmas cheer as holiday music played in the background on an old radio. Patrick's twins were playing with toy cars on the rug in the center of the room, and Melanie came running toward him at full speed. She plowed into Liam hard, almost knocking his six-foot-two frame over.

Mary emerged from the kitchen, wiping her hands with a dish towel as she smiled at Liam. "Oh, sweetheart, thank you again for the beautiful tree," she said, warmly hugging her son.

"No problem, Mom."

"Dinner is about ready. I have Daniel in the basement gathering decorations for the tree," Mary said as she sashayed back toward her favorite room in the house, where she created all her delicious meals and treats.

Liam headed toward the basement. As he passed the den where his father and grandfather were seated in their regular spots, he peeked in for a quick hello.

"Oh, there he is," Grandpa Paddy said. His old pipe was dangling from his lips as usual while his famous O'Brien eyes glittered with mischief.

Pat raised those same eyes up to see his son. "Your mother is positively delighted with that tree from your place." He smiled at Liam.

"Oh, it was no problem at all. Glad she's happy. We took our time to find one she would approve of." Liam laughed as he joined the two men.

"Well, you lads did a fine job," Grandpa Paddy added in his thick Irish accent.

Liam decided to sit for a moment to catch up with his father and grandfather. He took a seat on an old plaid couch that had seen better days and which was situated directly across from the two reclining, wingback chairs. The room was furnished with a variety of Grandpa Paddy's belongings from his old house. Unlike the rest of the O'Brien home, which was well-loved but spotless and feminine, this room lacked a woman's touch, and everything was frayed and tattered. The sweet smell of tobacco hung like a light fog in the air, mingling with smoke from the slow-burning log in the fireplace. Several bookshelves stood almost to the ceiling, packed tight with a large collection of classics. Liam's father and grandfather were constantly reading, whether a novel from decades ago or the daily newspaper. Liam had inherited their love of reading, and it was his favorite subject to teach his students.

He loved the den. The low light from the lamps on the several side tables was bright enough to read by. The small, crystal bowl that always seemed to be filled to the brim with aging caramels and a rainbow selection of hard candies never moved from its spot on the end table next to Grandpa Paddy.

When Liam was in high school, his grandmother had passed away, and after a couple months of his mother insisting, Grandpa Paddy had come to live with them. Grandpa Paddy and Pat had worked together for as long as Liam could remember, and even today they spent most of their free time with each other.

Grandpa Paddy was unlike any other grandfather Liam had ever encountered. He was unique, not just because of his brogue, but in so many ways. He was playful almost to a fault, and mischief spun wildly in his eyes. Many times, his mother had held back laughter tightly behind her lips when she was annoyed with her father-in-law. There wasn't a mean bone in his aging body, yet he could get riled up over the tiniest thing. There was never a dull moment with Grandpa Paddy around.

After visiting and catching up, Liam remembered he was supposed to help Daniel. He marched off in the direction of the basement and almost collided with his brother.

"Hey, Liam. There's a couple more boxes near the door, if you want to grab them," Daniel said, barely managing to peer over the stack of cardboard boxes he was carrying.

Liam moved carefully out of the way and nodded. He went down to the basement, picked up the remaining boxes, and hurried to the living room to meet up with Daniel.

"Damn, you're quick. I always forget how my legs have to take two steps to your one." Daniel stood several noticeable inches shorter than Liam.

Liam laughed. As he started to open one of the boxes, Maggie joined them.

"Mom said you were here. The tree is just lovely, Liam." She shot a look toward the large, fragrant tree, avoiding direct eye contact with either brother.

As she stared longingly at the tree, Daniel and Liam swapped looks. Something was definitely going on with their sister. The slight quiver in her voice sounded unnatural and so unlike Maggie. Her demeanor was more aloof and distant than he could ever recall.

"So is Mel excited for Christmas? It's only two days away," Liam asked, hoping to gain more of a read on his sister.

Maggie turned slightly in his direction. "She's pretty excited. Melanie is very happy to be here with everyone. She is loving this snow too. We don't have any over in Seattle."

"Well, at least someone is enjoying the snow," Daniel added.

"So will Michael be coming over for the holidays?" Liam asked cautiously to see if this would get any sort of emotional reaction from Maggie.

"He's flying in tomorrow evening. Then leaving Christmas afternoon to get back to the office. He's trying very hard to make partner right now, so unfortunately he's putting in a lot of time." Her voice was flat.

Liam and Daniel again eyed each other. Liam now knew Maggie was having some sort of marital issue. He had no idea of the depth of the problem, nor did he really want to delve in and find out. Maybe he would chat with his mother about it. She always kept tabs on everyone in the family, so if there was anything going on, she was the person to ask.

Right then, their mother rounded the corner. "Oh

good, I see you brought all the stuff up from the basement. Well, I have the kids eating, so whenever you guys are ready, the food is warm." She spun around and was gone as quickly as she had entered the room.

"Sounds good to me," Daniel said, rubbing his stomach.

The three made their way into the dining room quietly. Liam took a seat next to Melanie, who was eating with vigor while Connor and Finn played with their food.

"Who is ready for Santa in two days?" Liam announced, placing a warm roll on his plate.

Instant grins and near shouts of what they wanted followed immediately. Liam enjoyed the enthusiasm children possessed, and it was one of the main reasons he'd decided to become a teacher.

"What do you want Santa to bring you, Uncle Liam?" Melanie asked, her smile extending across her entire freckled face.

"Maybe some new snowshoes or perhaps a reindeer? Yes, I definitely want a reindeer," Liam answered playfully with an exaggeratedly contemplative look on his face.

With an animated shout, the twins declared in unison that Santa would not be giving Uncle Liam a reindeer of any kind.

"Okay, how about Santa's sleigh? Think about how fun that could be. We'd all love that," Liam suggested.

Melanie frowned and sighed. "I'm afraid that isn't going happen, Uncle Liam. How else is Santa going to get his job done?"

"I suppose you're right. Well, maybe he will bring me a new fishing rod."

Melanie's eyes grew large, as though she was about to let the cat out of the bag. She placed her chubby hand over her mouth, and Liam was pretty sure he knew what he'd get for Christmas.

Everyone finally joined Liam and the children at the table. Dishes clinked as conversations flowed easily and loudly, just as it always had in the O'Brien home. They devoured the meal quickly, and the plates were cleared before family members migrated to the living room to begin decorating their lush tree. Mary had put on more Christmas tunes, this time Bing Crosby's *White Christmas* album.

Grandpa Paddy and Pat sat in front of the tree, giving orders to Daniel on the placement of the lights, and Melanie and the twins eagerly assisted their uncle Daniel with the colorful strands. Maggie and Mary sat on one of the leather couches, carefully going through each fragile ornament, recalling when it was made or purchased.

"The boys sure are excited about Christmas this year," Liam commented as he maneuvered another heavy box away from the tree.

Patrick's eyes glazed over with a sad wetness. "Yeah. Beth would have enjoyed seeing them get all worked up about Santa."

Liam knew it had to be difficult for his brother to experience holidays and other milestones now his wife was deceased. They had all loved Beth, and Patrick was right—she would have loved seeing her boys get thrilled about reindeer and elves and, of course, Santa bringing presents.

"I know, Patrick." Liam gave his brother a soft hug. There weren't too many words one could say at times like these.

Patrick nodded with his head turned toward his two sons, who were tugging on a tangle of silver and gold garland.

The tree was just about perfect when Mary brought in a tray of cookies and eggnog to celebrate the family's decorating efforts. Once they'd all emptied their cups and only crumbs were left, the twins and Melanie piled onto one of the couches in a slumber only children can have—the deep and uninterrupted kind of sleep, with soft breaths escaping from their milky mouths as the adults looked on lovingly.

"I better get them home," Patrick announced as he yawned and dusted some straggling cookie crumbs from his gray fleece sweater.

"I'll help you," Daniel said.

Mary began picking up the empty mugs as Maggie tried waking Melanie gently to take her to the room they were staying in. Liam offered to carry his niece, and Maggie gave him a grateful smile.

As Liam skillfully slipped his large arms around the six-year-old, she stirred for a moment and quickly returned to sleep. He carefully stepped into the room, placed the child in the bed, and pulled the floral quilt up near her neck. He then smoothed strands of auburn hair from her forehead before leaving a gentle kiss there.

Feeling Maggie's gaze on him, Liam whispered, "You coming back out?"

"No, I'm going to go to bed. Thanks for carrying her," she whispered back.

"All right, good night, sis," Liam replied, and he planted a soft kiss on top of her chestnut hair.

Liam joined his mother in the kitchen, where she was busy filling the dishwasher.

"Can I help?" he offered, grabbing some dishes from the wooden kitchen island.

"I have never been one to turn down help, let alone from one of my handsome sons." Mary smiled sweetly at him.

Liam chuckled. "You sure know how to butter us up to help, huh?

"Well, you can't blame me. With a family as large as ours, a woman needs all the help she can get."

Liam smiled at her and sighed heavily. "I felt bad for Patrick tonight."

"I know. It has to be hard, considering now that the boys are getting a little older. But I try to remind him that Beth is here, and she sees them growing up and what a fine job he's doing with them," Mary offered while rinsing a dish.

Handing his mother another dirty mug, Liam thought more about Maggie. It was time to see what information his mother had.

"You know, Mom, we have noticed Maggie seems a bit out of sorts. Any idea what's going on with her?"

Mary sighed. She was definitely aware of something. "You see, dear, Maggie's really having a hard time of it right now. Michael's working very hard to get partner at the firm. She misses him, and so does Melanie."

"It just seems a little bit deeper than just missing her husband," Liam said as he handed her another dish.

Mary took it from him and continued filling the dishwasher as she added, "I don't think you understand how it is for a mother at times, Liam. You see, you and your brothers all have done something with your life. Maggie did too, but she doesn't see just being a mom and wife as fulfilling."

"So why doesn't she go back to work?" Liam suggested, leaning against the counter to face her.

"It's more than just work. Maggie has her plate full, trust me. She has Melanie involved in so many activities, and she takes care of everything at the house. I just don't believe she sees her value, and she feels she is losing her identity. To everyone over in Seattle, she is either just Michael's wife or Melanie's mother. She doesn't have too many friends over there, or anyone who just knows her as Maggie."

Liam frowned but understood what his mother was telling him. Still, he had a hard time believing his confident sister could ever have any doubt as to who she was.

Mary continued, "Besides, as if that wasn't enough, Michael has mentioned wanting more children." She lowered her voice. "You better not go on and tell her I told you this. She shared a lot of this stuff while we were shopping this afternoon."

"I won't say anything, Mom, but when Patrick and Daniel came to my house earlier, we discussed Maggie. We all could tell something was going on."

"I know, sweetie, and I'm sure it'll work itself out. Michael is flying in tomorrow, and so I'm sure it will be lovely with him here," Mary said as she wiped her hands on a bright dish towel that had a tiny snowman pattern. After untying and hanging up her apron, which had a jolly-looking Santa on it, Mary turned to Liam and wrapped her thick arms around his slender waist. "You are a good son and an even better brother," she whispered, pressing her cheek against his chest.

Liam drove home that night with a heaviness in his heart and mind. As he pulled into his driveway, he said a silent prayer. The clear night sky was filled with diamond-like stars, and without a shroud of cloud coverage, the air was bone-chilling. The freezing temperature made the snow hard, and it crunched under Liam's boots as he hurried inside.

*** 

Christmas Eve arrived as Liam sat in his kitchen, enjoying his coffee and large bowl of oatmeal. As he nibbled on some wheat toast and turned the page of the novel he'd been reading, his phone rang.

"Hello?" he answered.

"Good morning, dear," Mary sang joyfully on the other end of the line.

"Morning, Mom," Liam replied as he tried tearing his eyes away from the book.

"I wanted to remind you to bring the gifts you got for the children and perhaps a couple extra pillows and blankets if you could," she said softly.

"No problem."

"Okay, sweetie, we'll see you when you get here. Perhaps you can let me know when you are leaving, in case I need anything from the store?"

"Sure, sounds like a plan," Liam said distractedly.

After they exchanged good-byes, Liam hung up and swallowed the last remaining bite of oatmeal. He closed the book and started humming "Jingle Bells" as he cleared his dishes.

Later that day, he would head to his parents' home to spend the night. After cookies were left out for Santa, stockings were hung, and the children were put to bed, the adults would usually sit together and enjoy a classic holiday movie. Liam had memorized most word for word, and he enjoyed every minute of it. Once they knew for sure that the children were sound asleep, they would lay out all the gifts. Liam hoped that someday he would have children and could experience that magic with them, but for now he relished this special time with his nephews and niece.

\*\*\*

Christmas morning was a flurry of activity in the O'Brien house with shiny wrapping paper strewn about and ribbons and bows scattered everywhere. Mary attempted to stay on top of the cleanup by picking up the wrappings after each gift was open, and Maggie tried wrangling all the gifts into a semi neat pile. Michael sat with the rest of the men, taking toys out of their packaging and installing batteries.

"Michael, so glad you made it, man," Daniel said as he worked feverishly on opening a small toy for Finn.

Michael smiled as he inserted several batteries into a rocket ship for Connor. "I was happy to sneak away for sure. Been so damn busy lately. It actually feels weird just sitting."

"This is hard work, getting all these darn packages open." Daniel groaned, surveying the countless items that had yet to be opened.

Liam was carefully cutting away a thick plastic string around a new doll for Melanie as he said, "But did you see the look on their faces?"

"Makes it totally worth it," Michael replied as Melanie ran up to give him a quick hug before scurrying back to her loot.

Patrick was opening another container of batteries when he said, "Every year it seems like they get more and more stuff. At least more stuff that requires batteries."

"So when does your flight leave, Michael?" Liam asked carefully, making sure Maggie was not in earshot.

A sudden look of disappointment washed over Michael's face. "Unfortunately, this evening. You know I only want to give them the best life. Making partner at my firm will give us that. But sometimes I wonder why I'm sacrificing all this time. It's such a drag not being able to be with Maggie and Melanie more, especially during the holidays."

"When will you know if you made partner?" Liam asked.

Michael sighed. "Well, I'm hoping to know

more by the end of winter or around spring. Keep your fingers crossed for me."

Maggie entered the living room again after having disappeared for quite some time and smiled sweetly at her brothers and husband. Liam could tell she was happy Michael was here.

"Just wanted to tell you guys that Mom has French toast ready," she announced, eliciting a loud cheer from the children.

After a delightful family breakfast, the kids resumed playing, and Liam said his good-byes to Michael and the rest of the family. Michael mentioned he would return for New Year's Eve, which was a lively evening for the O'Briens. Mary usually decorated their basement and set up game tables, and they would drink champagne and whiskey way past the midnight toasting hour. They would dance and laugh until dawn, and Liam was happy to hear Michael would be back for that.

# Chapter Four

## Rachel

Rachel had made it through California the previous day, and now her silver BMW was eating away at the highway. She'd never realized how long the Golden State was. The central agricultural area seemed to go on forever, with countless fields and groves as far the eye could see. Along the way, when boredom got the best of her, she would call Chelsea at various gas stations she stopped at, but Rachel did enjoy the solitude of the open road and the change of scenery. She had been excited to soar past Sacramento and was thoroughly exhausted by the time she made her way to northern California.

After waking up the next morning and being properly fueled with coffee and fully energized for the trek ahead, Rachel was thrilled when she sped past the Welcome to Oregon sign. Oregon was a pleasure to drive through. Thick trees covered the mountains, the peaks of which were covered with snow, and dotted the sides of the highway. The roads were wet, and a dense fog had slowed her journey slightly.

She was halfway through Oregon when she needed gas. Rachel parked, hopped out, and was preparing to swipe her credit card when a gas station attendant raced toward her. She looked at him in confusion as he quickly instructed not to fill her own tank. She felt like a fish out of water, not knowing what the proper etiquette was. Did she tip the attendant? If so, how much?

Rachel felt wary as she headed over the border into Washington. A mixture of uncertainty and excitement created nauseous waves in her belly. Trying to calm her tender nerves, she told herself this move was the right call and there was no turning back now. New Year's Eve was in four days, and she hoped she could go into it feeling hopeful.

As she pulled into a station for more gas, she hesitated, watching to see if other drivers were filling their own tanks. Happy to witness an elderly man pumping gas into his car, Rachel felt a sense of relief as she unscrewed her fuel cap.

When she was back on the desolate highway, with her stereo blasting a tune from the eighties, her cellphone erupted loudly.

"Hello?" she asked, turning down the music.

"Hey, wanted to see how your adventure was going," Chelsea chirped from two states away.

"I crossed into Washington a little bit ago. It's so different here. The area I'm in now looks sort of plain. Not a whole lot of trees like the pictures I saw," Rachel said, scanning the vast, desert-like landscape along the Columbia Gorge.

Chelsea laughed but then sounded concerned as she asked, "Are you sure you're going the right way?"

Rachel rolled her eyes. Chelsea was one to talk. The girl relied on her GPS even when taking a walk around her apartment complex. "Hey, you know me! I mapped everything out online, and yes, I'm going the right way," Rachel defended playfully. "I decided to take the shorter route, which doesn't take me through the western side of the state, you know, like by Seattle and stuff. I figure I can always go over there and visit one weekend."

"Oh, I want to go too! Maybe I'll have to fly up for a girls' weekend after you get settled, and we can go over there together and see that Space thingy," Chelsea said with enthusiasm.

"Space Needle," Rachel corrected.

"Yeah, that thing. So how is the trip going so far? Do you miss home yet? You ready to come back?"

"I haven't even been gone two whole days yet." Rachel laughed, picking up her speed on the open road.

Chelsea grew quiet for a moment. "Well, I miss you."

"I know, and I miss you too. I can't believe I start on Monday," Rachel exclaimed, reclining her leather seat back a tad.

"Pretty wild. So have you heard from anyone else yet?"

That was a loaded question as far as Rachel was concerned. She hadn't heard from her mother except for a short text message wishing her a safe journey, which was actually quite unexpected and appreciated. She'd also received a short email from her father that confirmed he was still disappointed with her decision to relocate. Her brother had called once to ask if this was really what she wanted to do. They had both made a promise to keep in touch, and he'd said he would try to fly up soon.

"I got a call from Ethan early yesterday and a text from my mother and an email from my father," Rachel answered dramatically.

She could picture Chelsea on the other end of the phone, her bottom lip sticking out sympathetically as she attempted to move her perfectly sculpted brows, which resisted from all the Botox in them.

Chelsea was a great friend, and she understood how Rachel's family operated. Her own family wasn't that different. Chelsea's father, also a successful plastic surgeon, was far too busy working to really know what was going on in Chelsea's life. He figured if he provided everything for his only little girl, he had done his job as a father. Chelsea's mother, though still married to him, was more focused on shopping and lunching with her elite group of friends, though she did take more of a personal interest in Chelsea than Rachel's mother ever had in her own daughter. Chelsea reaped the benefits of being wealthy without having to really work for anything. She enjoyed lunching and shopping, whereas Rachel didn't get any kind of thrill from either. Rachel, however, did accept some of the perks of having a successful and wealthy father, one being the luxurious ride she was driving.

"Well, that's good they contacted you at least. How is your devilishly good-looking and single brother doing these days?" Chelsea asked sweetly.

*Oh boy*, Rachel thought. *That is one relationship that had been attempted more than once and failed each time. Why can't Chelsea see they're never going to be a match?* "Ethan is still Ethan. I don't know what you like about him so much, Chelsea."

"I think it's pretty much just how damn sexy he is. Yup, that's it." Chelsea was laughing hard.

"Good grief, woman, have you no shame? You seem to forget he's also my brother, so I can't say I can put him in the sexy category," Rachel teased.

"Well, on that note, next time you talk to that sexy doctor, tell him I say hello." Chelsea's voice turned thick with feigned lust.

"Yeah, I'll be sure to do that." Rachel's sarcasm was equally as thick.

"Call me when you arrive at the hotel tonight. Where are you staying at again?"

"I'll stop in Spokane for the night. I figured the Realty office will be closed by the time I get in tonight, so I might as well see what Spokane looks like. That way, I will be super well rested when I see my new place tomorrow," she responded excitedly.

"God, what if it's a total dump, or, like, not what you thought it was going to be?" Chelsea's voice was laced with sudden panic.

"I'm sure it's fine. The woman I spoke with said it was the nicest one they had available. She seemed professional and not like some backwoods hillbilly, okay?" Rachel said as the image of a redneck real estate agent showing her a home in a swamp appeared in her tired brain.

"How did you know I was just thinking, 'What if that were the case?'" Chelsea squealed.

"Because I know you, and how worried you are, and how you are secretly hoping this doesn't work out, and that I will have to come back."

"Okay, okay, you totally know me. And yes, maybe I'm kind of hoping you go up there and hate it. But I do want you to know I want you to be happy, and I'm glad you are going on this adventure. Just really would have been fun to have gone with you," Chelsea said sadly.

"I know, but this is something I sort of need to do on my own. But I love you, and I promise to call you when I get in. I just hope it's sometime soon, because the scenery here is getting a little boring, to be honest," Rachel said as she passed more sagebrush and bald, rolling mountains.

"Well, drive safe." Chelsea disconnected the line.

"I thought they called this the Evergreen State. Where are all the trees?" Rachel wondered out loud.

As she ventured farther into the state and neared the large city of Spokane, she could see some trees, but they weren't quite like the ones she had seen on the Internet. She did, however, like Spokane. Bright lights and tall buildings surrounded her on a fast-moving freeway, but unlike any rush hour traffic she had ever experienced, the cars were actually moving at the speed limit and the drivers weren't weaving in and out, only to stop suddenly in front of other cars. Rachel got off at the exit that would lead her to the familiar hotel chain where she had a reservation.

After checking into a comfortable room, showering quickly, and texting Chelsea, she crawled into bed. Her eyes closed before her head hit the pillow, and Rachel fell into a coma-like sleep as exhaustion fully took over her road-worn body.

# *Chapter Five*

## Liam

Liam stretched leisurely in his bed, his naked chest warm under his thick comforter. He had overslept, but it felt great. Eyeing the digital alarm clock on the oak dresser across from his bed, he saw he hadn't missed the chance to have breakfast with his brothers at their favorite morning haunt, Herrick's Diner.

The little restaurant was one of the best places to eat in Birch Valley, and Patrick and Daniel went there almost every morning for coffee and breakfast. They also stopped in for lunch sometimes. Not that Liam could blame them; the coffee was terrific, the bacon was perfectly cooked, and they made some of the best pancakes in the county. When Liam had time off, he enjoyed catching up with his brothers at Herrick's. The O'Brien siblings had grown up eating there as kids, and the owners were kind people and an important fixture in town. They had kept everything about their diner the same for generations, from the menu to the slightly uncomfortable booths. Above the door, an ancient bell hanging on a weathered string would chime as you entered, the smell of diner food would slam into your nose, causing your belly to tighten with hunger, your mouth would salivate, and neighbors would wave or nod as you walked past them to slide into one of the orange, vinyl booths. Liam hadn't ever been to another restaurant that could cause so many bodily reactions to food or generate such a sense of community and belonging.

\*\*\*

### Rachel

The next morning, Rachel sat in the small dining section of the hotel. Aside from one other guest skimming the morning paper, it was empty and quiet. Large windows let in the cold morning sun, and the sky was filled with thick, gray clouds. Rachel stirred her coffee as she looked through the glass, taking in the foreign landscape. She could now see mountains covered with snow, which had been shrouded by darkness the evening before.

She pulled herself out of the trance the stunning view seem to have put her in and began to review her directions to Birch Valley. She was anxious to get on the road and see her new home. Rachel downed her coffee and went to turn in her room key.

Pulling the dirty silver BMW out onto the busy street that would ultimately turn into the highway leading out of this lovely city, Rachel put on her internal game face as she drove away from Spokane.

A thick line of trees greeted her as she crested a small hill. The sun shimmered on their frosted tips, and the splendid view enchanted Rachel as she continued her drive. The vastness of the landscape seemed to encompass her, and as her car went down the hill, she was submerged in an evergreen wonder. Tall pine trees lined the highway, and the road seemed to tremor and crunch slightly under her car. Slowing down a bit, Rachel tightened her grip on the leather-bound steering wheel and refocused her attention on the road. She had never driven on snow, and the sudden awareness of her lack of experience frightened her.

Rachel mentally kicked herself for not having considered what driving conditions might be like here. As tiny white flecks splattered against her windshield, she said a silent prayer, worrying she may have made a terrible mistake.

After passing several small towns, Rachel found herself coasting downhill and applied the brake a little too hard. Fear flooded her veins as the BMW fishtailed, but she was able to regain control of it. A large wooden sign at the side of the road announced her arrival in Birch Valley.

The town was surrounded by small mountains frosted with snow, and large barns and farmhouses blanketed in white lined either side of the road as she continued driving on the single-lane highway. As she entered town, Rachel reduced her speed and tried to take in everything. She noticed only one traffic light, which remained green as she passed it. Storefronts lined the main street, and the shopkeepers who were outside shoveling snow waved as she drove by. The buildings were old but looked to be well preserved. Beautiful Christmas lights were strung overhead, and wreaths decorated every store door. Antique lampposts had swirls of garland wrapped around them. Everything was so Norman Rockwell, she felt as though she had driven onto a movie lot.

Rachel snapped herself out of her daze and remembered she needed to locate the Realty office to get her keys. A smile crept across her lips as she noticed an antique-looking sign that said 'Birch Valley Realty' hanging off a building. She had made it. Excitement bubbled inside her as she quickly parked outside the office.

Surprised by the professional atmosphere upon entering, Rachel nervously approached the front counter that seem to be unoccupied.

"Hello?" she announced.

"Be right there," a woman's voice answered quickly as its owner emerged from a nearby hallway. "How can I help you?" she asked politely.

"Yes, hello, I'm Rachel Montgomery. I'm here to pick up some keys for a rental."

"That's right. I think Cheryl thought you would be in a little later." The older woman started looking through a drawer in a nearby desk for what Rachel guessed were the keys.

"I stayed the night in Spokane and wanted to get out here early. I know my movers should have stopped by to drop off everything." Rachel was starting to ramble. She began to feel uneasy as the woman continued to search for the keys.

"Well, my dear, I can't seem to find those keys. As for those movers, I know they called Cheryl and let her know they should be here soon. Looks like you beat them," she said cheerfully.

Rachel was confused. "Excuse me, they were supposed to be here almost two days ago," she started to complain.

A concerned look washed over the woman's face, and her laugh lines seemed to deepen as she frowned. "Let me call Cheryl and see what she knows."

"Okay, thank you. I'd appreciate it," Rachel replied, trying desperately to sound polite but feeling her aggravation rising.

The woman dialed the phone on the desk, smiled softly at Rachel, and turned away as the person on the other end answered. She lowered her voice as they began to speak, and Rachel strained to hear the details of their conversation.

After hanging up, the woman looked squarely at her. "Well, sweetie, looks like we're in a bit of a pickle."

"Oh?" Rachel knew whatever this woman was about to tell her was not going to be good news.

The woman took a step closer and inhaled deeply. "It would seem the movers got stuck on the pass."

"Excuse me? I'm not sure I understand. I made it through just fine. The roads were a little scary, but I made it in my car." Rachel motioned toward her BMW parked outside.

"You took the 90 highway here?" the woman questioned.

"No, I didn't." Rachel was quick to reply with a hint of snottiness in her voice.

"Okay, well, unfortunately the movers did, and they got trapped in that darn snowstorm we had right after Christmas." The woman looked worried. "Cheryl says she is going to be coming in. She's plowing her driveway right now. She suggested you stop over at Herrick's for a cup of coffee and meet her back here."

Rachel let out a huff. "I guess I don't have much of choice, do I?"

The woman frowned at her. "Afraid not, dear. Cheryl says she will figure out what's going on. Herrick's serves a lovely breakfast if you are hungry. Here's how to get there," she offered as she began to write the directions to the diner on a sheet of paper.

Rachel grimaced and accepted the directions with a nod before leaving. This was not how she saw her first day in Birch Valley going. The crisp air stung her face and ears as she jumped back into her car. She cranked the heater and tried to get her bearings.

The diner was right off Main Street and located on the corner. As Rachel pulled into the already-full parking lot, she spied a car slowly backing out and waited to swoop in for the spot.

\*\*\*

## Liam

After Liam showered and dressed, he was looking forward to sharing a nice breakfast with his brothers. He mentally perused the diner's menu, having a difficult time deciding between the waffles or pancakes. Still undecided, he grabbed his keys and coat, then made his way to Herrick's with a smile on his face and a growling stomach.

The parking lot was full when Liam noticed his brothers' work truck parked near the front entrance. When he saw a car backing out, he put his signal on to let the driver in the silver sports car who had just pulled up know it was going to be his spot. The parked car made its way fully out of the space, and before Liam could hit the gas, the silver BMW swiped it. Irritated and surprised, Liam honked the horn. He then sat there motionless as a woman with blonde hair cropped short in some fairy-like cut emerged from the car and pulled her sweater tight around her trim body. With her nose upturned, she didn't even glance to see where the sound of the horn came from as she went inside Herrick's Diner.

The small pinch of anger passed after a moment, but Liam was still staring at the car that had stolen his spot. Realizing the driver wasn't a local, he then eyed the California plates.

*Well, that explains that, I suppose.* After locating another parking space, Liam saw the petite woman exiting the diner with a large to-go cup. Seemingly unaware that he was watching her, she got into her fancy car and left.

Liam got out of his truck and made his way into

the diner, where he scanned the booths for his brothers. They were perched in their regular place at the far end of the counter.

Daniel gave him a wave and his usual bright smile. "Hey, buddy. You look a little pissed. Everything okay?"

Liam simply shook his head. "The nerve of some people. I was pulling in a little bit ago and was waiting on a space when this lady just stole it."

"Well, ladies first." Daniel laughed as he grabbed a piece of bacon from his plate.

"Yeah, I get that, but it was kind of rude, don't you think? I had my signal on. I was there first, and she didn't even look in my direction at all," Liam steamed as he flagged down the waitress to order some breakfast.

Patrick grinned. "Let me guess, was she that cute little blonde that was just in here?"

Liam ordered some pancakes and waffles. After having been riled up, he figured he deserved both. The waitress smiled as she poured him some coffee and walked away with his order.

"She caused a couple of stares, that's for sure." Daniel waved his bacon in the air as he talked.

"Pretty much only Daniel was staring," Patrick added playfully before he sipped his coffee.

"You know what else? Guess where she's from?" Liam asked. "California. Surprise, surprise, huh?"

"Hey, relax, man, she only stole your parking spot. I think you'll live," Daniel said gently, giving Liam's shoulder a squeeze.

Both men laughed as they turned back to their

meals while Liam grabbed the mug in front of him and tried to swallow down the irritation settling back in.

***

### Rachel

Rachel pulled away from the diner and quickly returned to the Realty office. She was surprised by the extreme friendliness of the people in the restaurant. Several waved or nodded in her direction as she waited for a cup of coffee to go. The diner itself had her feeling as if she had been transported to another time. The vinyl booths, the stools at the counter, even the waitress's uniform looked as though they were from decades ago. But she could admit the place smelled fantastic, and the coffee was some of the best she had ever tasted. Rachel actually looked forward to eating there eventually.

Her mood lighter, she opened the door to the Realty office.

"Oh good, you're back. This here is Cheryl." The older woman motioned at the finely dressed woman standing next to her.

"Good morning. You must be Rachel? So very happy to meet you. I must first apologize for some of the inconvenience that has occurred." Cheryl flashed a perfect smile that could rival the many Rachel had seen in Newport. She extended her hand to Rachel, who was thrown off by her intense professionalism.

"This unfortunate mishap will soon be resolved,"

Cheryl continued, locking eyes with her. "The moving truck company has assured me the drivers are en route and should be arriving no later than this afternoon. However, I do have those keys to the rental we discussed." Cheryl turned to the small desk to fetch them.

Rachel simply nodded. There wasn't a whole lot else she could do, and at least they would be arriving today. She suspected Cheryl was probably in her late forties or early fifties. She had a trim figure, but her skin wasn't as tight. Her skirt was formfitting and stopped several inches above her knee, her silk blouse brought out the flecks of gold in her hazel eyes, and her highlighted hair was layered in a short bob. She was very put together, but at the same time her appearance looked to be a bit on the side of desperate. She just oozed cougar.

Rachel noticed Cheryl's heels as they clicked against the hardwood floor. After seeing several business owners clearing snow off the sidewalks, she wondered how this woman was able to get around in those shoes without slipping on the snow and breaking her ankle.

Unconsciously, Rachel smoothed her sweater over her leggings, suddenly feeling underdressed.

Cheryl soon returned with the keys, jangling them at Rachel. "Let's go see that rental."

***

Rachel followed Cheryl's newer, sleek, black SUV down several streets, trying to find landmarks to remember the way to her new home. She found doing that to be difficult as her gaze kept wandering to her new surroundings. Freshly built snowmen stood lopsidedly in the yards of adorable homes that were still decorated for the holidays. So far Rachel had counted one market. It was a national chain type store, so that was a huge relief. This tiny place was unlike what she had pictured—tree-lined streets and small houses in neat little rows of postcard perfection.

Cheryl's SUV pulled into a small, recently plowed driveway not far from what Rachel assumed was the center of town. In the park directly across the street from the home, children waddled around, dressed in heavy snow pants and coats. Rachel smiled, thinking how perfect the park would be for her evening runs.

The home itself was a pale yellow with fading white trim and a metal roof dusted with snow. A large window gave an excellent view of the park, and the front door had been painted a deep forest-green and showcased a stained-glass window depicting hummingbirds and flowers. Not exactly Rachel's taste, but the stained glass was charming and pleasing enough to the eye. When Cheryl opened the door, the scent of new paint and the stale smell of a home not lived in welcomed Rachel, as did the gorgeous honey-colored wood floors and pale, natural light seeping through the various windows.

Letting out a breath of relief, Rachel was actually pleased with the home. It wasn't extremely modern, but the lovely details and craftsmanship could be seen throughout. Built-in bookcases and shelving, and carved archways leading into different rooms were eye-catching surprises as Rachel cruised through each room slowly, envisioning where she would put her numerous belongings.

"So what do you think?" Cheryl's voice echoed in the empty space.

Rachel smiled. "It's great."

\*\*\*

## Liam

Liam's mood greatly improved after stuffing himself with a heavy breakfast. He said goodbye to his brothers and decided to run to the grocery store for a couple of staples. The sun was shining now, pulling away from the storm clouds that had filled the sky earlier. Liam inhaled the sharp air. The sun was misleading; it was still damn cold.

At the checkout counter, Liam visited with a couple of neighbors, then chatted for a bit with the cashier as he paid for his items. Feeling happy as he exited the building, he realized he shouldn't have been so upset about the parking spot. He was normally an easy-going guy who wasn't really troubled by such small things, but for some reason her actions had rubbed him the wrong way. Seeing her license plate only made matters worse. Californians always came up to Birch Valley during the holidays for the excellent skiing, or during the summer for hiking, kayaking, and other outdoor activities, and they brought a rude and obnoxious me-first mentality with them that just didn't sit well with the community. Of course, not all Californians were terrible. However, a large number who seemed to flock to this tucked-away little treasure of a town had money and figured they could afford to treat the area and its people however they wanted.

Liam sighed and decided to enjoy the rest of his day. Maybe he would lounge around and finish that novel he'd been reading. He considered fixing up some soup for dinner and maybe taking in a movie. Either way, he decided a lazy day sounded great as he hurried home.

\*\*\*

## Rachel

After Cheryl left, Rachel kept checking through the large front window for the movers. She had already taken her luggage inside and had even run to the grocery store she had seen earlier and purchased some cleaning supplies, and the house now smelled of bleach and disinfectant. She'd checked in with Chelsea and given her the lowdown and was more than eager for the movers to arrive so she could start unpacking and get settled in.

Rachel had mapped out exactly where she was going to place some of her furniture. The home had two bedrooms, one bathroom, a living room, a fair-sized kitchen that contained a small dining area, and a small room that sheltered a washer and dryer. Rachel was particularly thrilled with this one because she'd had to use a shared laundry room at her condo in Newport. The appliances in the home weren't top-of-the-line or the newest, but they all seemed to be in good working condition, and Rachel figured she could always see about updating them later.

The living room had a beautiful brick fireplace and was the largest space in the house. The home had electric heat too, which came as a relief to Rachel, because she had no idea how to get the fireplace started. She was already creating a list of things she had to learn and things she would probably need to buy in order to properly be able to live here. She entered the dining room and discovered a deck outside of it, which was part of a generous but manageably sized yard. Several large trees stood at the end of the yard, as did a singularly large pine in the front yard. A line of snow-covered shrubs ran outside the large front window in the living room. Rachel considered purchasing some flowers when winter was over to dress up the place and added that to the now-growing list on the counter.

Soon, Rachel heard a loud rumble and looked out the large bay window. To her delight, she saw the moving truck pulling into her driveway. She threw open the door in excitement and instantly was hit with the harshness of the cold temperature. Relief flooded through her, and she grinned from ear to ear as one of the drivers exited the truck with a clipboard.

The movers were very apologetic as they quickly filled up her small home with her boxes and heavy furniture, and one of them explained how the storm had made the pass impossible to drive across. As they brought the last items in, the skies started to turn into a swirl of dark gray and white, the sun disappeared, and the temperature dropped considerably.

Rachel locked the front door after waving goodbye to the men. Then with her hands on her hips, she looked at the task before her and felt a little overwhelmed. Her new home was now littered with boxes and furniture. She let out a deep breath and prepared to get settled in.

***

The next day, Rachel's entire body was sore as she added freshly ground coffee beans to her coffeemaker. Yawning, she poured the water in and pressed the On button as she surveyed her handiwork from the late night she'd pulled. The living room was almost completed. She had set up her entertainment center and rearranged her couch and loveseat several times before finding their permanent placement. She'd emptied box after box, folded the empty containers, and stacked them in her spare bedroom. She had then set up her bedroom and snuggled in the fresh linens and a warm comforter before passing out sometime after one in the morning.

Today, she planned on putting all her kitchen items away and organizing the extra bedroom, which she hoped to turn into an office and guestroom of sorts. As cold light filtered into the chilly home, Rachel turned the heat up and pulled her thick sweater tighter around her frame. She wondered exactly how long winter lasted here and if it was always this frigid. She was already anxious for spring and missed the warm temperatures back home.

***

### Liam

Liam turned over in his large bed and stretched and yawned as he pulled the heavy comforter over his head. Tomorrow was New Year's Eve. He would only be privileged with a couple more wonderful days of sleeping in and lounging around before he was back to work on Monday. But Liam enjoyed his early mornings where he got to view Mother Nature as she woke up in all her splendid colors. He also relished the silence and his dose of caffeine before he entered a loud classroom filled with young faces and eager brains.

Liam's phone rattled next to him as it emitted a loud, shrill ring.

"Hello?" he answered, sleep still coating his throat.

"Good morning, dear. I didn't wake you, did I?"

"I was just getting up. How are you this morning, Mom?" he said as he sat up, his chest emerging from the warmth of his blanket.

"Doing quite well, thank you. I heard you had quite the run-in yesterday?" A hint of teasing laced her voice.

Nothing got past his mother. "Oh, did Daniel tell you?"

"Actually, Patrick mentioned it this morning when he was dropping the twins off to play with Melanie."

"I'm surprised. I figured Daniel would've told you. He really got a kick out of seeing me a little ticked off."

"Well, he failed to mention it, but I only saw him for a bit yesterday and this morning. Either way, I heard from my friend Janice—you know her; she works at the new real estate place Cheryl opened up—well, she told me a lady just moved up from California. She said Cheryl rented her Bob Flannery's old home. You used to mow his lawn, remember? That cute little place across from the park."

Mary sounded animated, and that worried Liam. "Yes, I remember that house. So someone new is in Birch Valley? Wonder why she moved here," Liam said, hoping the rude woman who'd cut him off yesterday wasn't the one who had just moved in, but he had a sneaking suspicion she was.

"Could the lady renting Bob Flannery's place be the same one you had the run-in with? Janice said the woman was younger and very attractive. Was that the person you saw? I wonder if she's single."

"Mom, I have no idea. And honestly, it wasn't that big of a deal. I hadn't had anything to eat or my coffee yet, so I overreacted a bit, you know? I didn't notice if she was good-looking or not," Liam tried to convince himself as irritation gnawed at him.

"Well, maybe the poor dear was in a hurry," his mother said sweetly. "Janice said her movers didn't show up until quite late. So I'm sure she probably didn't even see you, sweetie."

"I had my signal on." Liam was beginning to feel a tad defensive.

"I'm sure you did, dear. But never mind. Folks make mistakes, son, and one as minor as that is no reason for you to get all upset," she scolded.

Liam mentally rolled his eyes. "That's fine, Mom. She's forgiven, all right? Might not even be the same woman I saw."

"Well, Janice says she sent the poor dear over to Herrick's for a bite while she got ahold of Cheryl. So I'm thinking she just might be."

"Wow, Mom, she really gave you the play-by-play, huh?" Liam chuckled. Birch Valley didn't need a neighborhood watch of any kind as long as his mother and her friends were around. News spread quicker than wildfire in a dry field here.

"Sweetheart, you seem a little testy this morning. I think you need to get up and get a little coffee and food into you. I'll check back in with you a little later. Since tomorrow is New Year's Eve, I was hoping you could be a dear and pick up Michael from the airport. I need Maggie's help making all the snacks and decorating. We have a decent amount of people coming over for the party."

"Not a problem, Mom." Liam swung his nude legs to the side of the bed and slid his feet into his slippers. Cradling the phone in the crook of his neck, he wrapped himself in his robe.

"Remember, son, sometimes people have a bad day. I'm not excusing poor behavior, but sometimes we can be absentminded in our decisions, no matter how small they might be. Besides, it's not like we get a lot of new residents here, especially young, single ones." Her voice was smooth and loving as she continued, "I love you, son. Now go and get on with your day before it's gone."

"Love you too, Mom," Liam said. He hung up and padded to his open kitchen with plans to start a large pot of coffee.

Good grief. Now his mother had it in her head that this Californian, who obviously couldn't drive worth a damn, was single and cute. Granted, Liam had to admit she didn't look half bad.

\*\*\*

## Rachel

Rachel sighed as she dropped the flattened cardboard box down onto the growing pile. She was making progress in getting everything in its place. Swatting away at her blonde bangs, she peeked out the curtain to see what the weather was doing.

She had planned on running to the grocery store later in the day to purchase some much-needed essentials. The list she had been compiling since yesterday was becoming quite long, but she was nervous about venturing out now that snow had covered the street and the icy flakes kept pouring from the sky. Rachel had seen neighbors shoveling their walkways and a large snow plow truck scrape the street in front of her home.

Tomorrow was New Year's Eve, and a little pang of loneliness hit her as she realized she would be spending it alone. She added a bottle of champagne to her list as she thought more about her fond memories of sharing the holiday with Chelsea. Thinking of her best friend, Rachel wondered what she would make of all this snow and how Birch Valley looked. Chelsea would probably think Rachel had lost her mind moving somewhere so completely different. But even though Birch Valley was cold and unfamiliar, Rachel felt the newfound sense of freedom she'd hoped to find as she layered her clothing to go shopping

*\*\*\**

After Rachel had piled on as many sweaters as possible, frigid air blasted her in the face as she carefully walked to her car. The silver BMW was frosted with several inches of snow, and tiny icicles hung from the chrome grill. As Rachel used the arm of her coat to sweep off the snow, she felt someone watching her. She turned around slowly and saw one of her neighbors walking toward her. She was clad in a scarf and heavy winter coat.

"Howdy," she said.

Rachel smiled nervously. "Hello."

The older woman pulled away the thick wool scarf from her mouth. "I'm so sorry I haven't stopped by to welcome you. I'm Sue-Ellen." She extended a gloved hand.

Shaking it, Rachel replied, "Nice to meet you Sue-Ellen. I'm Rachel."

"How are you liking this weather? Where did you move here from?" Sue-Ellen asked, her cheeks rosy from the icy-cold weather.

"This is my first time really being around snow," Rachel said as she continued to attempt to sweep the snow off the hood of her car.

"Well, looks like you need a snow brush for your rig there. I'll see if I have an extra one in my garage. Do you have a snow shovel yet? Not sure if Cheryl left one here for ya."

"I was actually headed to the store now to get some supplies. I guess I wasn't sure exactly what I would need when I came up. It was still in the eighties when I left California a couple of days ago." Rachel laughed at the thought of how ridiculous she must look with the snow clinging to her coat.

"Wow, California? You sure are a long way from home, hun. What brought you up here?" Sue-Ellen asked as the snow started to fall a little faster.

"No kidding. It's different here but quite lovely, even with the snow," Rachel said. "I actually just got hired on as the principal for the elementary school here."

"Well, that's certainly a surprise. I had no idea Mr. Anderson was leaving. Granted, he's been working there since my children attended classes there." The woman shivered. "Well, before we both catch a cold, I will let you go. Wonderful meeting you. I'll come by sometime so we can visit some more."

Rachel started to feel the cold settling deeper into her core. "It was a pleasure, Sue-Ellen. I look forward to it."

\*\*\*

The car heater seemed to take forever to warm up enough to actually blow hot air. As Rachel drove down the quiet road, snow crunching under her tires, she admired the stillness. No one was outside, the trees were posed like frozen statues, and the only movement was plumes of wood smoke escaping from the chimneys of the small houses.

The wind chill was brutal as Rachel parked and scurried into the grocery store. Grabbing a shopping cart, she examined her list. Trying to find everything she needed without knowing the layout of the store was a bit of a challenge. She felt a pang of homesickness as she remembered her favorite grocery store back in Newport and the farmers markets she'd frequent with Chelsea on the weekends. As she cruised slowly down each aisle, taking stock of the inventory, Rachel was able to get most of the staples on her list.

When she was finished, she wheeled her cart up to a checkout counter that had only one other customer in front of her, who was chatting with the cashier as Rachel unloaded her items. When she finished, she waited patiently for the cashier to ring her up, but the woman was so engrossed in the conversation with the person in front of her, she didn't seem to notice Rachel. When Rachel failed to make eye contact with the clerk, she began to get antsy. As a last resort to get the cashier's attention, she coughed, and when both cashier and customer looked up at her in annoyance, she gave them a tight-lipped smile. The two then exchanged good-byes, and the cashier began to ring up her items.

"Hello, did you find everything okay?" she asked

before calling for another clerk to help bag the groceries.

"I did, thank you," Rachel said curtly, avoiding eye contact as she fished out her credit card.

An awkward silence fell until the cashier announced Rachel's total. She then thanked Rachel for her business as Rachel pushed the cart out of the lane. Once outside, she had to really work to maneuver it through the thick layer of slush on the slippery asphalt. She reached her car, and a sense of relief washed over her after she loaded all the bags into her trunk. Rachel then looked at her watch and was surprised to see it was only midafternoon. The sky was already getting dark. Back at home, the sun would still be shining on the endless blue ocean.

Now all she had to do was make it home and unload these groceries without slipping on the ice, she thought as she climbed into the BMW and turned her wiper blades on to remove the snow that had already accumulated on her windshield.

# Chapter Six

## Liam

As more snow fell on the mountains that sheltered Birch Valley, the swollen skies opened up, releasing sleet and rain in messy sheets.

It was New Year's Eve, a time to celebrate a year gone, the birth of new hope, and resolutions that would be broken within a couple months, if not weeks. Everyone was out and about, gearing up to ring in the New Year with family and friends.

The O'Brien women were busy with last-minute preparations for the evening ahead, and Liam was heading out to pick up Michael from the airport, which was over an hour away.

Liam pulled up to the busy terminal at Spokane International Airport just as Michael emerged from the large glass doors.

"Good to see you, Liam. I don't know if I'll ever get used to how cold it gets over here," Michael said as he quickly hopped into Liam's pickup and shoved his small suitcase by his feet.

"We've been having a bit of a cold snap lately. Glad you were able to make it out. We're going to have an awesome time tonight." Liam was in a fantastic mood. He planned on partying hard tonight because he only had one day to recover before going back to work on Monday.

After stopping at a fast food place, the two men got back on the road and made their way home to Birch Valley. The hour drive passed quickly because Liam enjoyed Michael's company and they had a great deal in common. Michael enjoyed fishing and was an avid reader like Liam but never found the time to do either anymore. He was also a die-hard fan of the Seattle Mariners and Seattle Seahawks and felt the countless stings from all their losses keenly.

One difference that separated the two was Michael's drive for success. Not that Liam didn't want to be a great teacher; he strived to change the young lives in his classroom. But elementary schools didn't have a corporate ladder to climb, and he was thankful for that. Michael's work ethic was similarly strong, but he wanted the recognition and glory that went along with the hard work and dedication. Because Michael had grown up in Seattle, a busy, fast-paced life was all he knew until he met Maggie, who had dragged him out to Birch Valley to visit her family. Soon after, he'd fallen hopelessly in love with them, the town, and Maggie herself.

"So what's the game plan at the house for tonight?" Michael asked as he shifted in his seat, trying to find a comfortable position. He was obviously used to driving a sleek, luxury sedan.

"Mom and Maggie have been cooking all day, and they have Patrick and Daniel helping set up the basement for tonight," Liam answered, scanning the road ahead for deer. As daylight faded, deer and elk often wandered into the middle of the highway. Liam had hit his fair share at this time of day, so he took extra precautions when traveling the dangerous highway.

"Did your mom invite a lot of people?" Michael questioned.

"Eh, the usual group of friends she has over. Her church friends and some of the ladies from her book club."

"Patrick or Daniel seeing anyone yet? How about you? Getting tired of being single?" Michael asked playfully.

Liam tried to stifle a chuckle. "Daniel's always looking. Patrick, well, you know, it's still pretty hard for him. He's getting better, I suppose, but he's not quite sure he's ready yet."

"And you?" Michael prodded.

"You know, I haven't really looked. There aren't a whole lot of available women in Birch Valley. Besides, I kind of like just being able to do my own thing without having to answer to anyone." Liam shrugged.

"Yeah, but there is something to be said for marriage, my friend. I love having Maggie and Melanie at home when I get back from work. I remember not wanting to settle down too, and then I met your sister, and that kind of just changed that," Michael said with a faraway look on his face as he peered out the window.

"I'm not opposed to meeting someone, especially if I met the right girl," Liam said. "It's funny you should bring this up, man. I had this little run-in with this lady. Well, she stole my parking spot. And the next day, Mom calls me and tells me all about this new girl that moved here. She went on and on about the possibility of this woman being single."

Michael turned to face him. "Wait, a new girl moved to town?"

"Don't sound all excited like Mom," Liam warned playfully.

"Hey, I'm serious. That's awesome. You just said there are no girls here. Well, hell, Liam, now one has moved to Birch Valley. She cute?" Michael pestered.

"I don't know. I didn't really get a good look at her," Liam said as he thought about the blonde with the pixie cut and upturned nose. "If anyone actually saw her, it was Daniel and Patrick. They were in the diner at the time. But anyway, I'm not even sure it's the woman that moved here." Still, Liam had a difficult time convincing himself of that.

"Did Daniel say if she was cute?"

Liam sighed as he rubbed his jaw, feeling the stubble that had grown there after his shave this morning. "Yeah, he thought she was good-looking, but that's kind of beside the point. I wasn't really looking to see if she was hot or not. She had just pissed me off."

"Oh, give me a break, of course you checked her out. I don't care how pissed off you were, you can't tell me you didn't notice how she looked."

Liam breathed a sigh of relief as they began making their way downhill and he saw the lights of Birch Valley.

"We're almost home. I can't wait to see my girls," Michael said as a happy grin crossed his lips.

\*\*\*

Liam turned off his truck after parking on the street in front of his parents' home. He could only imagine the flurry of activity going on inside. A whirlwind of orders coming from his mother welcomed them as he and Michael crossed the threshold. Maggie was carrying a large tray toward the basement when she saw Michael, and she raced over to give him a quick kiss.

After greeting her son with a peck on the cheek, Mary handed him a large serving bowl to take to the party area, and Liam followed his sister to the basement. When he entered, he was blinded by glitter and sparkles from every direction. Tables had been set up around the room, each covered with party hats and silver and gold confetti. The streamers hanging from the ceiling and the silver and gold garlands framing the windows made the room look even more festive. Meanwhile, twinkling white lights were wrapped around several pillars and draped loosely along the table that held the large punch bowl and a neat line of several trays and dishes. His mother and sister had outdone themselves this year with the decorating, so he could only imagine how great the food would be.

Several hours later, as guests began to arrive, Liam sat at a table with his brothers and Michael, working on his third glass of whiskey. Filling themselves with scrumptious appetizers and drinks, the men sat around laughing and telling stories as the time edged closer to midnight. Music played in the background, as laughter and happy chatter filled the basement, echoing loudly off the concrete walls. The children, meanwhile, ran past, filled with happy energy, Melanie in a puffy blue dress with matching ribbons in her hair, and the twins in matching little suits complete with a clip-on tie they kept losing. Soon, couples took to the small dance floor in one corner of the basement, and Liam watched as his father twirled his mother to the oldies music while they gazed at each other with love in their eyes. Michael then took Maggie to the dance floor, and they held each other close as they swayed to a slow song. Whatever had been bothering his sister over Christmas seemed to have fixed itself, because Maggie had looked content all evening, and she and Michael seemed to be in constant contact, looping their arms around each other's waists or giving each other a peck on the cheek or lips.

"So, Liam, anymore run-ins with the cute little Californian?" Daniel asked, interrupting Liam's thoughts.

"Yeah, thanks again, guys, for telling Mom," Liam said as he shot both of his brothers a small glare. "She's been pestering me about this girl ever since. She even had her friend Janice over there tell me her opinion about this woman." Liam motioned in the direction of Mary and Janice, who were helping themselves to some punch.

"Don't let it get to you. You know how Mom is," Daniel said lightly before finishing the last of his beverage.

"Yeah, I wouldn't make too big of deal about it. Mom just likes to meddle," Patrick added as he swirled the contents in his glass.

Liam took a full sip of the warm liquid, which burned his throat slightly. "I know. She means well, but it would be nice to not have her ask me about this woman every time we talk."

"I wish I would have a run-in with her," Daniel said with a wide smile as he got up to refill his drink.

"I bet you do," Patrick and Liam responded in unison.

Daniel excused himself and offered to grab another drink for his brothers before he wandered to the buffet table. Liam leaned back in his chair, stretching his long legs out.

Patrick yawned and looked at his watch. "Not too much longer," he said as he rubbed his face.

"It's been a fun night. Mom and Maggie sure did a nice job," Liam said, watching his grandfather taking Mary out to the dance floor. "Looks like Grandpa Paddy is getting down."

Liam and Patrick both laughed as they watched the elderly man bend and shake to the beat of the song.

\*\*\*

## Rachel

Rachel curled up on her couch, buried under a soft, wheat-colored throw. A half-empty bottle of champagne sat next to her while she flipped the pages of the romance novel she had been reading most of the evening. She took off her reading glasses and rubbed her eyes as she grabbed her cell phone from the end table to check the time. It wasn't quite midnight yet. She planned on calling Chelsea when the New Year officially hit.

Rachel was glad the holidays were basically over. She was looking forward to starting her new position on Monday. She still had no idea what the school even looked like and planned on driving by it tomorrow, as well as doing a little exploring around town if the weather permitted. With her home nearly unpacked and set up, she felt as though she was ready for her new routine to begin.

Taking a swig from the bottle, Rachel returned to her novel. Soon, her eyes felt heavy and started to close.

A loud ring woke her with a jolt, and in a slight state of confusion she searched for her phone. It had slipped between the couch cushions, and Rachel fished it out to see Chelsea's number on the screen.

"Happy New Year," Chelsea shouted as soon as Rachel hit the Talk button.

"Hey, Chelsea, Happy New Year," Rachel said, her throat scratchy and dry from her nap.

"Did I wake you up?" Chelsea asked loudly. Music was blaring in the background, and Rachel assumed her friend was at a party.

"I must have dozed off. Where are you?"

"I went to a New Year's Eve bash I got invited to. I just wanted to wish my bestie a happy New Year and good luck on Monday." Chelsea's words were slurred from obviously having a little too much to drink, and Rachel strained to hear them through the noise in the background.

"Thanks, you too. Hope you're having a good time. Be careful out there."

"I'm having a blast! Wish you were here. Well, I gotta go. Love ya, Rachel." Chelsea hung up before she could answer.

Rachel was a little bummed that she wasn't out dancing, laughing, and enjoying the light buzz from champagne alongside her friends. No point in throwing herself a pity party, she decided. After all, she was the one who'd chosen to relocate. Maybe next year she would be visiting Chelsea for New Year's and they could go out and celebrate.

Rachel closed her book, got up from the couch, and took the bottle into the kitchen, where she poured the remainder of the champagne down the sink. *What a way to start the New Year*, she thought as she watched the foaming liquid pool down the drain. She then went to her bedroom and crawled beneath the covers. The room was slightly chilly, so she burrowed farther into her comforter and drifted off to sleep.

\*\*\*

## Liam

When the clock struck midnight, everyone shouted and cheered as they entered the New Year. Toasting glasses clinked as couples kissed each other, and Liam and Daniel received their fair share of smooches from Mary's friends.

The O'Briens and their guests continued to celebrate for a couple more hours. Once the last of their friends had said their good-byes, Liam made his way into the living room and settled on the couch. With his head heavy from the night of drinking, he closed his eyes and passed out.

When he woke several hours later, Liam babied a mild hangover and ventured home after assisting with some cleanup from the previous night's festivities. Back at his cabin, he crawled into his own bed and slept until midafternoon. That evening, feeling fully recovered and renewed with a bowl of chili in his stomach, he prepared for class the next day and set his alarm for five in the morning.

*No more sleeping in*, he thought. *Back to the grind.*

\*\*\*

## Rachel

Rachel spent most of the day trying to decide which outfit to wear for the first day of her new job. She had narrowed her choices down to two suits, one pants and the other a skirt ensemble. She wanted to make a good first impression while indicating that she meant business and wanted to be taken seriously. Only in her early thirties, she was fairly young to be a principal.

A little later in the day, Rachel decided to take a drive to get acquainted with the neighborhood and locate the school. When she arrived there in only minutes, she was surprised at how close it was to her new home. As soon as the weather was warmer, she planned on walking to work sometimes, something she'd never had the opportunity to do back home. Her condo was fifteen miles away from the last school she'd worked at, and she would spend nearly an hour each way on the congested freeway. Being stuck in traffic was a way of life for anyone who commuted in southern California.

After readying herself for bed and setting her alarm, Rachel lay in the darkness. Fear of the unknown, interacting with people who didn't know her, and just the newness of all the responsibility she was about to be handed kept her from falling asleep. She tossed and turned, eyeing the alarm clock, then her cell phone as she struggled desperately to sleep. Finally, her brain had mercy on her and allowed her to fall into a restless slumber.

# *Chapter Seven*

## Liam

Liam grabbed his coffee and headed out the door. It was cold and the sky was still dark as he started his truck. He let it run awhile before making his five mile drive to work. As he drank his coffee and jammed out to a tune on the classic rock station, Liam was in a great mood, especially for a Monday. After pulling into the lot at the elementary school, he found his usual parking spot. Grabbing his backpack and coat, he then got out and headed to the large front doors of the school.

As he walked into the mail room next to the teachers' lounge, the school secretary Karen, a lovely older woman who had worked there since Liam had attended as a child, gave him a giant smile.

"Good morning, Liam," she said as she proceeded to place a memo in each of the teachers mailboxes.

Curious, Liam grabbed the papers from his box.

"Morning, Karen. How was your winter break?" he asked as he casually shuffled through the small pile, not really reading any of it.

Karen stopped filing and turned toward him. "Pretty nice. All the grandkids came to visit us."

"Oh, that's great. I bet you enjoyed seeing them. Maggie and Melanie spent the entire time at Mom's." Liam smiled but quickly scowled in confusion as he looked down at the paper on top of his stack. "Hey, Karen, what's this about?" He held up the memo she had just put in each box.

"Mr. Anderson says he wants to see everyone this morning during first recess." Her face scrunched with annoyance as she added, "He didn't tell me anything, which is a little odd."

"I guess we'll all find out together." Liam waved at a teacher who was headed in their direction. "Well, I'm headed to class," he said as he exited the room.

***

## Rachel

Rachel's eyes shot open. *Oh dear God! What time is it?* Noticing her alarm clock blinking 12:00, she sprang out of bed and grabbed her cellphone to see what hour it really was. *Oh no, it's after seven. I'm late!*

She hopped into the shower, lathered her body, dried off, and dressed with a speed she didn't know she possessed. She threw on her coat, grabbed her empty travel coffee mug and briefcase, and ran out the door. She prayed they had good coffee at the school because she was going to need it.

Rachel was thankful for how close the school was to her new home as she pulled into a spot next to the front doors. *Here we go*, she thought as the first bell of the day rang. She scurried through the enormous glass doors and made her way to a counter that was across from the entryway. Children of various sizes were hurrying to class, and their loud chatter bounced off the walls. Rachel smiled as a little girl waved and said good morning.

As she walked up to the counter, she noticed an older woman in the room beyond was filing paper into various mailboxes. "Good morning, I'm Rachel Montgomery. Mr. Anderson is expecting me," she announced politely.

The woman turned her attention to Rachel and gave her a warm smile. "Hello. Sorry, didn't hear you with all the kiddos coming in."

"Oh that's no problem." Rachel nervously clutched her briefcase as she rocked slightly on her chunky heels. She was glad she'd opted for the pants suit when a cold draft swept against her legs as the last stragglers hurried through the door.

"Let me go get Mr. Anderson for you. Rachel, was it?" the secretary asked sweetly as she scooted past the counter and down a hallway.

"Yes, Rachel Montgomery. Thank you again." Rachel scanned the interior of the school. It was an older brick building, and a large mural of Lewis and Clark's expedition was painted on the wall beside the entrance. Wide, exposed wooden beams held up the ceiling, the floor was polished concrete, and tall windows allowed plenty of sunlight to seep through.

Moments later, a tall man with a full head of white hair came toward her.

"Good morning, Rachel. Such a pleasure to meet you in person. Welcome to Birch Valley Elementary." His voice was deep and thunderous, and his presence demanded attention. Even though he was well into his seventies, he was intimidating. Her palms started to sweat as she gripped her briefcase tighter.

Rachel recalled her interview with this man. He'd seemed smaller when she'd spoke with him over their webcams. In person, he stood almost a foot taller than Rachel, even with her two-inch heels. He wore a light blue dress shirt and a tie that had a brilliant pattern of colors. His gray slacks were a shade lighter than her own dress pants.

"This is Karen Miller, our wonderful school secretary. There are not enough kind words for me to say about her. We have worked together for so many years, and she has been running the show that whole time." He laughed, patting Karen's shoulder warmly. "Karen, as you already know, this is Rachel Montgomery. Why don't we go to my office and I can start going over everything with you." He turned on his heel and led Rachel down the same hallway he had emerged from. "Karen, please join us."

Looking confused, Karen glanced curiously at Rachel, who managed a tight-lipped smile.

Once they were inside the principal's office, he sat behind a wide mahogany desk and clasped his large hands together. "Well, I'm so thrilled you finally made it up here."

Rachel had sat down in one of the two leather chairs in front of the desk, and Karen sat down slowly next to her.

"Yes, I had a great time coming up. Birch Valley is incredibly beautiful, though the snow was a little unexpected." Rachel swallowed the nervous lump in her throat, and her stomach twisted into queasy knots as she tried to calm her nerves.

Karen remained stiff, quiet, and observant, the exact opposite of how she'd behaved when Rachel first met her.

Mr. Anderson leaned forward. "Well, spring will be here before you know it. Now, on to business. Karen, I've hired Rachel to replace me as principal." His tone was even and firm.

Karen's face twisted in confusion and shock. "I'm sorry, I wasn't aware you were leaving the school, sir."

"Well, I went to the district right after Thanksgiving. I've been considering retirement for a long while, actually."

"Wow, I'm surprised. This is the first I've heard of it." Karen's tone was sharp, almost defensive.

Mr. Anderson sighed, as if he'd known she would react this way. "We've worked together for a long time, Karen, and I knew you wouldn't be thrilled about someone replacing me." He nodded toward Rachel, who felt even more uncomfortable as she watched tears fill Karen's eyes.

"No, I completely understand. I'm just a little taken aback that you didn't tell me, or anyone else here." Karen wiped a tear from her cheek.

"Now, now." He extended his reach across the desk and enveloped Karen's hand in his own.

"Perhaps I should give you two a moment," Rachel suggested.

Karen shook her head. "That won't be necessary, dear. I'm just a sentimental old lady."

"Now, Rachel has gone through the interview process with the district, and we felt she would be a great match for our school," Mr. Anderson continued. "She is from a charter school in California, where she was the vice principal, correct?" he asked, turning to her.

Rachel cleared her tight throat. "Yes, that's correct. I'm very excited about this opportunity and feel I can bring a lot to the staff and students here."

"Well, we're delighted to have you, Rachel. I hope you will forgive my little emotional outburst a moment ago." Karen's tone had softened as she squeezed Rachel's arm.

"That's okay. Honestly, I'm excited to be here and to get to know all of you," Rachel replied, feeling the sick nervousness lift.

"Well, excellent. I had Karen send out an announcement to all the staff today, instructing them we'll be meeting up during first recess. I'll introduce you to them at that time. In the meantime, I figure I'll show you basically what kind of ship I run here, and then I plan on handing over the reins to you within a couple of days. I want you to get adjusted and get your feet wet here."

"Perfect." Rachel responded, anxious to fully take the post.

\*\*\*

## Liam

Liam stood in front of his chalkboard reading out the roll call. Students answered if they were present, and Liam smiled at each one as he recorded their attendance. Excited energy filled the room as the students were clearly eager to share their experiences over the holidays. Time passed quickly, and soon the loud first recess bell rang. Students suited up in heavy coats and snow pants, then lined up in a neat row, patiently waiting to be dismissed. Once Liam saw that they were all well equipped to go out to the chilly playground, he let them go and headed to the cafeteria for the meeting.

Several teachers were already seated at the lunch tables, looking worried. Others were busy chatting away about their break. Liam looked for an empty place near the front and saw Megan Patterson, another fourth grade teacher who had a classroom right next to his. She smiled as she patted the space next to her, and he reluctantly sat down.

"Hey Liam, any idea what this is about?" She flashed him a bright smile. Megan had joined the teaching staff at the start of the school year. Her soft, brown hair was cut into long layers that framed her heart-shaped face. Liam guessed she was near his age and knew she was single because she had mentioned it to him several times, as had her mother.

"I have no clue. I asked Karen earlier, and she didn't know, either." Liam tried to look forward, facing away from Megan and her tight, low-cut, lilac-colored sweater that left little to the imagination. From the corner of his eyes, he saw Megan adjust the silk scarf hanging loosely over her cleavage, attempting to bring his attention to it.

Mr. Anderson walked into the cafeteria, and the room went silent as he waved and nodded at several staff members. Karen followed him, her skirt swishing against her leggings-clad legs. Another woman trailed after them, a petite blonde in a dark gray pants suit. Her red blouse drew attention to the otherwise nondescript outfit that was nonetheless well fitted to her small frame. Her light makeup caused her striking blue eyes to stand out, and Liam stared when he noticed her slender, upturned nose. The Californian who had stolen his spot at Herrick's was standing approximately ten feet away. His mind starting turning a mile a minute. *What is she doing here?*

The principal welcomed the staff back to work and then joked about how much he'd enjoyed himself over the break—so much that he had found a replacement and was going to retire.

The staff let out a collective gasp. Liam had to admit he hadn't seen that one coming, even though he expected the man to announce his retirement eventually. Granted, Mr. Anderson had been the principal when Liam and his siblings had gone to school there, but his leaving was the end of an era.

Mr. Anderson explained that he hadn't told anyone about his plans because he didn't want people to make a fuss. He also wanted to make sure he found the perfect replacement, and that was when he introduced the blonde woman.

"Hello, everyone, I'm Rachel Montgomery," she announced in a strong voice and with a wide smile that showcased her perfect teeth.

"Well, isn't she adorable?" Megan whispered to Liam. "A little young to be a principal, though, don't you think?"

Liam ignored Megan. His attention was now completely focused on the Californian, who now had a name. Rachel Montgomery. Now that Liam looked at her, she did appear to be a bit young to be running the school. She was also cute, as Daniel had said. She stood before them gracefully as she explained where she had come from, what her qualifications were, and how she planned to work closely with the staff to maintain the longstanding reputation of the school.

As she addressed the group, Liam couldn't stop looking at her. Rachel's mesmerizing eyes twinkled in the bright lights of the cafeteria, and he couldn't tear his gaze away from her smile.

*Oh no*, he thought. Not only was this Californian his new boss, but he was totally checking her out.

\*\*\*

### Rachel

Rachel inhaled deeply as she started her impromptu speech. The staff's astonished and blank stares fueled her nerves. They sat silently, questioning her ability, but realizing they had no choice but to work with her. Rachel was quite surprised by the ratio of staff to students.

Karen must have realized she felt a little unsteady because she patted Rachel's shoulder gently when Rachel had finished speaking, reassuring her that the speech was well delivered.

Another bell rang, and the teachers looked to Mr. Anderson, who excused them and thanked everyone for their time. The staff exited the cafeteria, talking in whispers of concern and surprise. Rachel overheard some of their hurtful comments and tried to sympathize with how they all must be feeling, but it was hard not to take their words personally.

"Well, the cat's out of the bag now," Mr. Anderson bellowed when the room was empty, a huge grin on his meaty face.

Karen looked at Rachel sympathetically and suggested, "How about I show you to the teachers' lounge where we keep the coffee?"

Only a couple hours had passed since Mr. Anderson had unveiled his plan to Karen, but despite the shock of the initial announcement, she had clearly taken a liking to Rachel. Rachel felt the protective and motherly concern from this woman and knew was going to love working with Karen.

# Chapter Eight

## Liam

Liam rubbed his temples as he sat in the empty classroom, thankful school had finally ended. He had somehow survived the day, which had started out quite promising, especially for a Monday. He was still trying to absorb the fact his beloved boss and childhood principal was now leaving the school. The fact he was being replaced by a smooth Californian, someone who didn't even know how Birch Valley operated, bothered Liam.

He shuddered as he remembered the visit Rachel had paid his classroom right after lunch. The students had been pretty receptive to her, and the respect they'd shown her made Liam proud. She was also kind to the students as she announced that she was happy to be their new principal and answered their questions, but her demeanor changed when she spoke with Liam. Tension built between them as he tried to absorb the suggestions and plans she had for the staff and the overall changes she planned to implement. He wasn't so mesmerized by her now. The headache that had started shortly after Rachel left his classroom had pestered him for the remainder of the day.

Liam was glad work was over and decided he would try to let a lot of what Rachel said roll off his back. He knew how to teach his students and was confident that he was good at his job. He swallowed some aspirin and gathered his backpack to head home.

***

## Rachel

Rachel's feet ached as she stepped toward her car, but she overlooked the pain as the rest of her day had been pretty great and she was still riding on the leftover adrenaline. She'd met all the teachers and students, and popping into each classroom throughout the day had been fun and reminded her exactly why she had wanted this position.

Some of the staff seemed to welcome her and her ideas, but she faced opposition from a few others, and one of the fourth grade teachers in particular. His name was Liam O'Brien, and Rachel couldn't explain the feelings that erupted inside her when she entered his domain. His students were by the far the politest group of children she had ever encountered, and the classroom was bright and colorful, yet unmistakably masculine. Large posters of important historical figures graced the walls, neatly arranged bulletin boards filled with memos and assignments stood proudly near the entrance, and the students' desks as well as the cubbies that lined one wall were tidy and well organized. She could tell the children adored him and followed his every move and word, and Liam seemed just as wrapped up in them.

Perhaps it was Liam's tall, lean, but muscular body as it leaned against his desk that had driven Rachel into an unexplained frenzy. He looked good dressed in comfortable jeans and a dark brown sweater, and his sandy-brown hair was in desperate need of a cut. Her stomach clenched as she recalled the relaxed way his mouth moved into a sexy smirk when she'd discussed some of her ideas with him. But she was most concerned by the jolts of electricity she felt when she looked into his green eyes. Reprimanding herself for having such thoughts about one of her staff members, Rachel decided she needed to keep her distance from Liam O'Brien.

***

## Liam

Liam was sitting on his couch working on a cold bottle of beer when his phone rang.

"Hello?" he said after swallowing a mouthful of beer.

"Hi, dear. I wanted to see how work went today," his mother said.

Liam decided he needed to answer this question carefully. "The kids were pretty happy to share everything they did over the holidays. Guess what? Mr. Anderson held a staff meeting today with some pretty exciting news."

"Oh? What was the big announcement?"

"He's retiring, if you can believe it."

"Wow. I have to say, though, I'm not really that surprised, to be honest. When will he be leaving the school?"

"That's the strangest thing. He had this planned out for a while. He will gone by the end of the week," Liam answered as he thought of Rachel Montgomery, his new boss.

"No way. So they already found a replacement, then?" His mother's voice raised with surprise.

Liam wasn't certain he should tell her who the replacement was after how much she had pestered him about the newcomer during the holidays. He decided to be as vague as possible. His mother would find out soon enough, anyway, and he simply didn't feel like hearing any more about Rachel right now.

"Yeah, the district apparently did some interviews, so the new principal will be taking over by next week." Liam tried to sound as casual as possible.

"Well, I'm stunned Karen didn't mention anything to me." His mother sounded puzzled. "Funny too, because I just ran into her when she was at the grocery store the other day."

"Apparently she didn't know anything about it. I guess Mr. Anderson decided to keep it all pretty quiet," Liam replied.

"That explains that, I suppose. That darn man

has been at that school forever. Still, I'm quite shocked he didn't say anything, at least to Karen."

Liam knew full well why Mr. Anderson had kept his plan to himself. If he had told Karen, then she would have shared that information with Mary O'Brien, and in no time the entire town would know everything down to the very last detail.

"I guess he didn't want everyone to make a big fuss. But it's too late for that. Karen is now fully planning a retirement party for him. I bet she will be calling you today, Mom," Liam added before he took another swig of his beer.

"Oh, well, that will be fun. Maybe I should give her a call and volunteer. Okay, dear, I better let you go. Love you." His mother hung up before he could respond.

Liam spent the rest of the evening going over his lesson plans and flipping the channels on his TV. He found concentrating difficult as his brain kept sending him glimpses of Rachel. The blueness of her eyes as she had stared at him as if trying to read his thoughts, the soft flesh of her lips as she bit down on them in nervousness, and the way her slacks fit against her petite body. He didn't understand why he felt an attraction to her. She wasn't his type at all. Not that he had a type lately, but he knew a snotty Californian definitely was not what he had in mind. He was just glad his mother didn't know about the new so-called principal. He was having a hard enough time trying to wrap his own mind around her.

\*\*\*

## Rachel

Dressed in her warmest pair of sweatpants and a fuzzy pair of socks, Rachel stretched out on her couch and wrapped her throw around her as she turned the page of her book. She stared at the words, not comprehending any of them, as her mind kept drifting back to the events of the day. Her house was so still and quiet, and she wasn't used to complete silence. Back home, she would hear cars passing by on the busy boulevard or the random thumping of neighbors living their lives next door. She skimmed over the page a second time before she laid the book down in her lap. Her phone buzzed loudly, the vibration startling her, and she felt underneath her legs for it. Her couch was always swallowing her phone.

As Chelsea's image popped up on the screen, she felt an overwhelming desire to tell her best friend all about her first day.

"Hi, Chelsea," Rachel chirped.

"Hey, lady, I wanted to see how today went," Chelsea said.

"It went pretty well, actually," Rachel said as she sat up on the couch. "The school's a little older but has this beautiful mural when you walk in. There is also this awesome secretary named Karen, and she's really sweet and nice."

Chelsea listened intently as Rachel told her about meeting the soon-to-be former principal and the rest of the staff.

"So you liked it, huh?" She sounded a little disappointed.

Rachel frowned, knowing her friend had hoped her first day at work was a major disaster so that Rachel would move back home.

"I did. There is so much I think I can do at this school. But one of the fourth grade teachers didn't seem to be too interested in some of my ideas," Rachel said cautiously, hoping Chelsea wouldn't pick up on anything odd in her tone.

"Really? What is he, some kind of old jerk or something?" Chelsea sounded annoyed.

"Well, I wouldn't go as far as saying that. Maybe he just needs to warm up to the idea that I will be taking over. Apparently, the guy who is the principal now has been there forever. So everyone is pretty used to him, and I think they were a little shocked that he's going to finally retire. He didn't even tell anyone he was leaving, let alone that he hired me."

"Wow, no way! Yeah, maybe they all just have to adjust to the new sheriff in town." Chelsea laughed, causing Rachel to giggle "So what's this teacher like, the one giving you a hard time?"

"He's not giving me a hard time—well, not yet anyway. His students seem to love him, and he's great with them. All the teachers are real fond of him too. I guess he grew up here, and so his family lives here and whatnot. Karen, the nice secretary, speaks highly of him, so I'm sure we'll learn to get along fine," Rachel assured her friend, even as thoughts of Liam curled into the deepest parts of her mind, sending an odd tingle down her spine.

"Your voice sounds weird, Rachel. Oh God, is he, like, super-hot?" Chelsea asked suspiciously.

Rachel gulped. "Um, he's fairly good-looking. He could really use a haircut, though. He's one of those super-laid-back types, a 'wears jeans instead of dress slacks' kind of teacher."

"Okay, yeah, that's why your voice got all weird," Chelsea teased.

"Good grief, my voice didn't get all weird, Chelsea. You'd probably think he's cute, but he's part of my staff, and honestly the guy was a little annoying."

"Whatever. I bet he's hot, and I hope you'll introduce me when I come up for a visit," Chelsea said, and Rachel felt a sliver of jealousy she couldn't understand.

"Sure, of course I'll have you meet him. I don't even know if he's single or anything about him. So how's the weather there?" she asked, quickly changing the subject. "It's pretty cold here, but it didn't snow yesterday or today."

"It was gorgeous today. I got in a good run down by the beach. Are you able to run or anything there? Do they have a gym?"

Rachel was relieved when Chelsea didn't press her any further about Liam. "My house is right across the street from this little park, and so when the weather is better, I think I'll run there. But yeah, they do have this small gym, not too far away from my house, so I'll probably join eventually. I haven't even been here a whole week and have been so busy unpacking."

Chelsea let out a loud sigh. "Well, you should have hired someone to help decorate and unpack. I don't understand why you feel the need to do everything yourself. As for working out, girl, please don't let yourself go."

Rachel rolled her eyes. Chelsea was extremely self-conscious and spent most of her free time grooming or working out to perfect her already amazing body. Chelsea, however, sculpted her body with liposuction, implants, fillers, and injections, all of which were commonplace for where they lived. She was also constantly encouraging Rachel to try one of the latest diet fads she'd read about. Rachel couldn't understand why Chelsea was in constant pursuit of changing herself. She looked great, and judging by the obvious stares and gawking she got from the opposite sex, they would agree. As for herself, Rachel tried to eat right, and she enjoyed jogging and hiking, but she didn't feel the need to constantly buy in to the whole "workout routine and gym membership" nonsense. Luckily, Rachel was naturally thin with an athletic, petite build, but she lacked curves.

Right now, she couldn't help but wonder what Liam would think of her best friend. Shooing away those thoughts, she returned her attention to their conversation.

Her friend chattered on, going into detail about a lunch she had shared with a mutual friend, and Rachel strained to remain focused. Feigning exhaustion, she told Chelsea she would give her a call the following day, and they hung up shortly thereafter.

Nightfall draped across the little town of Birch Valley, and the air was cold beneath the star-studded, clear sky. A bright moon spotlighted the snow-capped mountains that surrounded the area.

*** 

Snow had formed into hardened, sparkling white mounds overnight, which the early-morning plows had shoved to the sides of the roads in dirty, black piles. Rachel was not impressed with the ugly sight as she drove to the school, but it wasn't going to dampen her mood. Today, she was feeling more confident and self-assured. She'd opted for pants again, this time deep mocha slacks paired with a soft, cream-colored, cashmere sweater. Finding she had extra time this morning, because her alarm had actually gone off at the correct time, she put a little more effort into her makeup and hair. Still, she wasn't sure why she fussed with her appearance today. She had no plans to engage in any type of personal relationship, let alone with one of the teachers. Maybe the talk with Chelsea the night before had left her feeling a little insecure. Either way, she felt great now, and after locating a parking spot near the front of the school, she got out of her car and walked inside with a sense of purpose and high hopes for the day.

*** 

**Liam**

While driving to work, Liam drummed his fingers on the steering wheel in time with the song that shouted from the radio. Feeling well rested and ready for the day, he noticed a group of Canadian geese flying in formation in the pink sky as the early-morning sun feathered its soft colors across the horizon. He pulled into the partially full parking lot of the school and zoomed toward his usual spot, only to find a silver BMW obnoxiously parked in it. Worse, the car was straddling two parking spots, making it virtually impossible for anyone to park next to it.

He circled around the lot to another location farther away from the doors, feeling the same irritation he'd experienced when she'd cut him off that morning at Herrick's. Now how would his mother explain this one, he wondered. Mary would probably say too much snow was covering the paint on the asphalt, and the poor lady couldn't decide which spot to take. Liam grunted as he got out of his truck.

"Good morning, Liam," Karen called as he stomped into the lobby.

"Morning," he answered when he rounded the counter to check his mailbox.

"Oh, did we wake up on the wrong side of the bed this morning? You don't seem your usual chipper self," Karen commented as she punched holes in several documents she had stacked in front of her.

"I'm fine. Someone just parked in my space this morning." He tried to hide his irritation.

It wasn't as though he owned the spot, but the teachers all sort of knew where everyone liked to park, and not taking someone else's spot was an unspoken rule.

"Oh, I see. Well, dear, it isn't like she knew." Karen had apparently guessed the culprit's identity.

"I know. It's just that a couple days ago, I went to have breakfast with Daniel and Patrick at Herrick's, and she pulled into the spot I was waiting for. Now, today, she hogs two whole spots," he complained as he went through his mail.

"Well, would you like me to ask Rachel to move?" Karen offered as the woman in question strolled past.

"Good morning. Move what?" Rachel asked firmly with a tight, professional smile.

Liam looked at her, noticing the softness of the cashmere sweater against her tan skin.

"Nothing," he replied as he gathered his papers before heading toward the teachers' lounge next door.

*** 

### Rachel

"Wow." Rachel lifted her brows and frowned at Karen.

"Oh, well, it seems you parked in Liam's spot. The teachers sort of have this thing, where they each kind of know where the other likes to park. A lot of it is based on seniority," Karen explained carefully.

"Well, I'd be happy to move my car if he has such an issue with it," Rachel offered, not understanding why Liam would make such a huge deal out of a parking spot. It wasn't as though he had no others to choose from. Back in Newport Beach, at her old school, they were given assigned parking, but usually a parent or someone else would snag the spot, so the system didn't do a whole lot of good.

"He's fine. Liam likes things to go on as they always have. He isn't the biggest fan of change. But once he has his coffee, he will be right as rain, so don't you worry about him," Karen soothed as she reached for another stack of papers.

Rachel smiled. There wasn't a whole lot she could say to that. Maybe he was just a creature of habit. Perhaps that would explain his annoyance with her suggestions yesterday.

A curvy brunette sashayed toward them. Rachel knew the woman was another fourth grade teacher but struggled to remember her name.

"Good morning," Rachel offered politely.

The teacher flashed a perfect set of white teeth against heavily lipstick-stained lips. "Why, hello. Rachel, right?" Her voice was high as she stepped past Rachel to get to her mailbox.

Rachel was about to answer when the teacher cut her off. "I'm Megan Patterson, fourth grade. We spoke briefly yesterday, but I'm sure it's hard to recall all people you must've met already." Adjusting her tight tweed skirt and equally tight red sweater, she continued, "So what do you think of our little school so far?"

Restraining her irritation, Rachel offered her a warm smile. "It's quite nice. The students are wonderful."

Liam was walking past them, and Rachel watched Megan as she seem to drink him in. As Liam waved and gave her one of his sexy, lazy grins, Rachel felt a pinch of jealousy.

"Well, I better scoot off to class. I would love to get a coffee with you sometime," Megan said as she hurried in Liam's direction.

Karen huffed, "I'm sure she's anxious to get to her classroom."

Realizing Megan was the same teacher whose classroom was next door to Liam's, Rachel rolled her eyes, causing Karen to let out a little laugh.

"Good morning, ladies," Mr. Anderson announced loudly as he entered the room.

"Good morning," they replied in nervous unison, worried they had gotten caught gossiping.

\*\*\*

## Liam

As Liam walked to his classroom, he heard the heavy tapping of heels behind him.

"Liam, wait up," Megan hollered as she quickened her pace.

"Morning, Megan," he said as he unlocked the door to his room. He then turned around to face her, feeling a tad irritated.

"Hey, I noticed our new little principal decided to park in your spot—well, actually two spots," Megan commented, crossing her arms across her chest and causing her cleavage to bulge a little from her snug sweater.

"Yeah, well, like Karen said, it's not like she knew," Liam replied, feeling an odd need to defend Rachel, especially from Megan.

"So I assume she came into your class yesterday too. She sure does have a lot of plans, doesn't she?" Her tone was rich as she inched closer to Liam's tall body. She smelled like flowers, and he wasn't sure if it was her perfume or shampoo. He tried not to focus on the formfitting skirt that outlined her curvy hips and rear. Megan always seemed to dress for attention, and he was having to train his eyes to avoid looking into hers. That was his best bet to keep her at bay.

"She popped in yesterday. The kids seemed to like her, though, so that's a good thing, I suppose," Liam answered, trying to break away from her. But she followed him into his classroom and leaned against one of the student desks. Liam could feel her chocolate-colored eyes stalking him with desire and interest, but he ignored them as he walked to his desk and busied himself with pulling out his lesson plan.

When Megan cleared her throat, Liam looked up to find her licking her glossy, red lips and wrapping her arms around her generous chest again. "My students are so sad Mr. Anderson will be leaving." She pouted her full bottom lip out.

"Yeah, it was sort of surprising, yet kind of expected, you know? He was the principal when I was a kid, so it does feel a little strange that he won't be here. But at the same time, I'm sure he's ready to retire," Liam said as he stood behind his large desk, waiting for her to leave. When she didn't take the hint, he continued, "Well, I have some last-minute things I need to do before class starts. I'll catch up with you later." Instantly, he regretted his words, as they had just given her ammunition to pursue him.

"Sure, Liam. I was thinking maybe we could go over some of my lesson plans over lunch or dinner sometime. I need a little help on some of the coursework they have outlined for the state testing," she said with a slight flare of seduction in her voice.

Liam swallowed. "Yeah, I better get this stuff done before my kids are here." He tried to ignore her stare as he looked at the large clock on the opposite wall.

"Well, I'll leave you to it. See you a little later," Megan said as she sauntered out of his room.

With a sigh of relief, Liam fell into his chair. Good grief, it was hard to say no to such an attractive woman, but the way she kept throwing herself at him was a huge turnoff, especially when she did it at their workplace.

The bell rang, and students poured noisily into the classroom.

\*\*\*

## Rachel

Rachel spent most of the morning poring over information about her new position with Mr. Anderson and Karen. After a few hours, she was feeling as if her head were going to explode and craving a cup of coffee. Karen must have sensed her need for caffeine, because she suggested a reprieve.

"It can be a little overwhelming, I'm sure," Karen said as she poured some of the warm liquid into her own mug, which was emblazoned with the words *World's Best Grandma*.

Rachel wondered if she would ever have children and what her mother would be like as a grandmother. Would she be warm and loving, as Karen appeared to be, or would she continue being cool and distant, as she had always been with her daughter? Rachel hadn't heard from Evelyn since she'd left for Washington. After sending her several text messages with no replies, she couldn't help but feel a little disappointed and sad that her mother wasn't interested in her daughter's new life here in Birch Valley.

"Rachel, you doing okay, hon?" Karen asked softly, breaking Rachel away from her thoughts.

"Yes, it's just a lot to process. The school is run a tad differently than the charter school I came from. But you guys are doing an amazing job, and I really feel like I'm learning so much."

"You'll be fine, and once that old goat is gone, you'll find your way. I'm sure you might want to change some things or implement some of those new ideas I heard some of the teachers discussing." Karen nodded happily as she savored her coffee.

"You're completely right, Karen. I'm so glad you're here. I hope you don't decide to retire anytime soon." Rachel laughed as she filled her travel mug and added some sugar and creamer to it.

"Well, I can't promise I won't retire eventually, but one thing's for sure: everyone will know when I do. It won't be a big secret. Speaking of which, we are thinking of throwing Mr. Anderson a retirement party. I was wondering if you'd be interested in helping me, some of the staff here, and a couple of my friends with decorating and whatnot," Karen asked, giving her a pleading look.

Rachel paused to consider. She wasn't sure it would be a good idea for her to help with this man's sendoff, considering she was his replacement. Yet at the same time, Rachel was becoming seriously stir-crazy. She had already unpacked everything at her house, and she was having a hard time finding stuff to do. She didn't want to step on anyone's toes, but perhaps by helping out she would get to know the staff and possibly make some new friends. She had been somewhat close with her old coworkers, and they would occasionally go out for drinks or dinner to celebrate one another's birthdays or to blow off a little steam after surviving state testing or report cards.

"You know what Karen, that sounds like fun. I'd be very happy to help," Rachel answered.

"Great. I think we're getting together tomorrow evening at Herrick's to go over some plans. Maybe you'd like to join us for dinner?" Karen casually asked.

"Um, yeah, that'd be nice. I've been wanting to try the diner out. I had a coffee there my first day in town, and it was wonderful," she said as she lifted her own mug.

Karen smiled. "Well, you are in for a treat, then, my dear. Their food is delicious."

The lunch bell rang, and the students began

trickling past the room on their way to the cafeteria. Rachel had brought a small salad and some fruit from home and felt her stomach gurgle with hunger.

"Well, duty calls," Karen excused herself as she hurried toward two children who were about to get into a fight.

***

After entering the teachers' lounge, Rachel waited by the fridge as a teacher retrieved his lunch. "Good afternoon," she said with a smile.

He simply nodded as he strode past her on his way out. Rachel opened the refrigerator door and found her lunch tucked neatly in the back corner on the top shelf. When she sensed someone's presence, she hurriedly shut the door and looked up.

Liam was standing next to the fridge, his tall frame towering over her. Looking up to meet his emerald eyes, she nervously excused herself and quickly took a seat at one of the three tables.

Grabbing a juice and a small cooler from the fridge, Liam then quietly took a spot at a table directly across from her.

Rachel looked away as she forked a mouthful of salad, then sensed Liam staring at her.

Clearing his throat, Liam broke the tension filled-silence. "So how are you liking it here?" he asked as he unwrapped his sandwich.

Rachel looked up. The cool and relaxed way he sat there, provoking her by doing nothing at all, made her nerves tighten. "It's been great so far," she said, her voice quiet and unsure. She felt as though this was the start of a game of chess with each player watching and waiting, trying to size up their opponent.

Liam smirked. "So how long have you been up here? What made you want to take a position so far away from your home and family?"

Rachel sucked in a breath of dry air. "I came up a couple days after Christmas, actually. I know it's quite a change in scenery for sure, but it's lovely here, even though I've been mainly a shut-in, just unpacking and getting settled." Her mouth turned sticky and dry as she rambled, and she reached for her bottle of water.

"So why Birch Valley?" he pressed. "I mean, I'm sure you could've had your pick of any school, especially being from such a prestigious school and area."

Rachel felt as though he was getting ready to attack, so she chose her words carefully. "Why not Birch Valley? Seems like as good a place as anywhere else," she retorted.

Liam casually leaned back in the plastic chair. "I suppose you're right. Just seems a little odd, a 'large fish in a small pond' kind of thing, you know? Obviously, you have the skills to go probably anywhere you'd like."

"Well, this opportunity came, and I decided it was the one I wanted." Rachel was steaming. Why did he feel the need to question her motives for taking this job? What did it matter to him? And why did his eyes have to twinkle when he talked?

She glanced at her watch, praying silently that the bell would ring and she could excuse herself.

She refused to get up before he did. She didn't want him to think he was going to win this battle.

Liam swigged his juice. "So have you come up with any more *ideas*?" His tone was smug.

"About that, I shouldn't have come into your classroom and ambushed you the way I did. I now realize it was a little too soon for that. I suppose I'm anxious to get everyone on board. We have testing in a couple months, and I'd really like to see this school rise above its current standard," Rachel answered calmly, and Liam nodded, giving her his full attention.

She knew she had probably come off as a little abrasive yesterday, and maybe she should have waited a while before telling the staff she was going to make changes. She'd just been so excited about all her ideas that could change the school for the better. Rachel wasn't trying to step on anyone's toes or make them feel as though they weren't doing a good job, but she wanted to show she wasn't a doormat and that she needed to be respected and taken seriously. Charting the course for change wasn't easy, and those who did almost always faced opposition. But Rachel thrived on challenge, and as she glanced at the man across from her, she realized he might be her biggest one yet.

# *Chapter Nine*

As her day came to a close, Rachel felt as though the week was steadily moving forward and she was making progress. Some of the teachers were finally warming up to her and trying to make conversation with her, and she was beginning to feel more comfortable in her new position. In fact, the only time that her newfound self-confidence wavered was when Liam was in her presence. Rachel hoped these feelings would pass. She couldn't quite wrap her mind around why her body responded the way it did when Liam was near. She wondered if he also felt the blistering connection, the same crackle and burn that would suddenly erupt inside her. She was thankful when the final bell rang, emptying the school of its students.

\*\*\*

Planning to head home to change before meeting up with Karen and her friends at Herrick's for dinner and to discuss Mr. Anderson's retirement party, Rachel started to have second thoughts. Once inside her car, she decided to call Chelsea to get her opinion.

Chelsea picked up on the second ring. "Hello?"

"Chelsea, what are you up to?" Rachel asked as she pulled away from the school.

"Nothing much. School just let out?" Chelsea sounded slightly out of breath.

"You doing okay? You sound a bit winded."

"Yeah, was out for a run. It's supposed to rain tonight, and I wanted to make sure I got one in before it started. But keep talking. I'm doing my cooldown now," Chelsea panted.

Rachel was already turning onto her street. "It's so wild, Chelsea. You wouldn't believe how close I live to work. I literally called you as I was pulling out of the school, and I just got home."

"Wow, that is crazy close. So why are you even driving? I would totally be walking or jogging home."

"Well, I hope to do that when the weather warms up. It has been, like, in the thirties this week. Everyone is teasing me that this is actually warmer than usual for this time of year." Rachel laughed, scared to think of how cold it could actually get.

"Wait, you said in the thirties. You mean like at night, right?" Chelsea asked, sounding confused.

"No, you heard me right. That is the daytime high. Crazy, huh?"

"Why are you even living there? Are you nuts?" Chelsea screamed. "I couldn't imagine dealing with that kind of weather. No thanks, I will keep my lovely eighties we are rockin' over here."

"Don't make me jealous. I'm trying desperately to adapt to this temperature. Actually, I'm going shopping in Spokane soon for some warmer clothes for work. I have worn pants every single day this week so far," Rachel said as she headed into her house and immediately switched her heater on high. She shivered as Chelsea went on about some ideas for outfits Rachel could buy.

"Oh hey, I remembered why I called in the first place," Rachel interrupted her. "I got invited to help with the retirement party for the man I'm replacing. I think it's sort of awkward for me to be involved. What do you think?"

"Hmm, I don't know. What are they wanting your help with?"

"Well, I don't know exactly, but the secretary— Karen, the nice lady I was telling you about the other day—she's the one who invited me. She asked me to meet her and her friends, as well as some of the other teachers at this diner here for dinner tonight."

"Sounds okay to me. I don't think you are stepping on anyone's toes or anything. After all, she invited you, and obviously you won't be trying to, like, host or run this party. I would tag along for dinner. At least it would get you out of the house."

"See, that is kind of what I thought too. I figured if they want me to help decorate, I'm totally willing to, but I just felt weird." Rachel kicked her shoes off as she headed to her bedroom to undress.

"Yeah, I think you're fine. I wouldn't worry too much about what people say. That's not the Rachel

I know."

Rachel smiled. "Uh, yeah, right. I appreciate the vote of confidence, but it's just so different here. I do feel like an outsider. These people all sort of grew up together and have this bond. I want to make friends here and get to know everyone."

"You will make friends. Just got to give it a little more time. Hell, you have only been working for what, three days or something?" Chelsea said.

"You're right. So I guess my next question is, what should I wear tonight?" Rachel asked, hopeful that Chelsea would steer her in the right direction.

"That I can help you with," Chelsea sang out.

Rachel sent pictures of various outfit choices to Chelsea so she could decide what pieces worked well together. They went over nearly every article of clothing Rachel owned until they found the perfect cross between casual, yet pretty: a dark-wash pair of skinny jeans, her brown leather riding boots, and an oversized, apricot sweater with a shiny brown belt. The tone of the outfit brought out the bronze and pink tones of Rachel's skin, and her short, blonde hair looked lighter against the apricot.

Pleased with the outcome, Rachel said her good-byes and promised to fill her friend in about how dinner went. She then dressed and stared at her reflection in the floor-length mirror. She added a little gloss to her already-pink lips, spritzed on a little floral body spray, and headed out to meet Karen.

Rachel felt nervous as she drove the several blocks to the diner. As she parked outside Herrick's, she saw the place was packed with patrons, nameless faces sitting in booths by the large windows, which were only partly covered by small, checkered curtains. Rachel spotted Karen's car driving in and waited patiently for her to get out so they could walk in together.

Karen greeted Rachel with a wide smile as she emerged from her car. "Wow, I love that color on you," she said as she examined Rachel's outfit.

"Oh, well, thank you," Rachel replied, swinging her large designer bag over her shoulder and trailing behind Karen, who led the way.

A tiny bell on a dirty, weathered piece of yarn chimed as they entered. Rachel's senses were instantly bombarded with the scents of the diner, and her stomach growled. She hadn't realized how hungry she was until a waitress carried past a burger that was practically toppling onto the heap of French fries next to it on the plate. Karen scurried toward a large booth in the corner, and Rachel recognized a few of the teachers from the school, but some of the faces were new to her.

Karen stood before the table and pulled Rachel close to her. "This is Rachel, everyone."

A short, round woman with auburn curls smiled broadly. Her eyes were warm and kind. "Why hello, dear. So very nice to meet you. I'm Mary." She stood carefully and extended her hand.

Rachel shook it. "Nice to meet you as well," she said before sitting down next to Karen. The booth was rather large and could have easily seated more than the six or eight people gathered around it.

"Karen, do you know if more of the teachers are coming to help plan this shindig?" Mary asked politely.

"You know, I asked a couple more, but I figured this would pretty much be my dream team," Karen replied, bringing a smile to Mary's lightly wrinkled face.

A waitress came to their table and proceeded to take everyone's order. She then left and returned shortly with water and promises that their meals would be ready soon.

Rachel sat quietly, taking inventory of the older women sitting at the table with her. They all looked as though they were in their sixties or so, about the same age as Karen, she figured. She was by far the youngest.

She listened as Mary and Karen chatted about people whose names she didn't recognize. The others commented here and there but mainly participated in their own conversations. Rachel felt a little out of place as she sipped on her water, twirling the straw between two ice cubes.

"So, Rachel, my dear friend Karen here tells me you are going to be replacing Mr. Anderson," Mary said, smiling directly at Rachel.

"Uh. Yes, that's right. I started on Monday," Rachel responded as the other women turned their attention to her. She instantly felt as though they had placed a spotlight on her.

Karen patted Rachel's arm, as if sensing her nervousness. "I was quite shocked when Mr. Anderson brought her in and decided to drop this bomb on me. I had no clue he had decided to retire, let alone had hired a replacement," Karen addressed the group. "But he did a fine job, and we're all very thrilled to have Rachel with us now. The students seem to really like her too."

"That's wonderful," Mary said, then turned to Rachel. "You know, my dear, all of my children attended that school. In fact, my son Liam is a teacher there."

Rachel felt her stomach bottom out. "Oh wow, really? Liam's a fantastic teacher, Mary. His students just love him." She figured it was best not to mention how stubborn her son seemed to be.

"So where did you move here from?" another woman asked.

"I'm a California transplant."

A few of the women sighed in longing, and one said she wished she lived somewhere nice and warm like California.

"Oh dear, it just dawned on me. My friend Janice—she works at the real estate office with Cheryl—mentioned a gal had moved into Bob Flannery's old home, near the park," Mary said, her eyes wide as she looked at Karen.

Rachel nodded in confirmation, and Mary went on to tell her stories about Liam mowing the lawn at what was now Rachel's house. She also shared other tales about her children, which seemed to captivate the other ladies. No one seemed to notice when the waitress brought their dinners. Mary apologized for rambling, but Rachel loved the soft tones of her voice. There were moments when she could have sworn she'd caught bits of an Irish brogue.

Biting into a perfectly cooked, golden French fry, she listened as Karen and Mary continued to swap stories about the school and Mr. Anderson. During the course of the meal, they also planned the party, deciding to hold the event in the school cafeteria. Mary and some of the other women offered to cook, and Rachel and the two teachers said they would help with decorating. Karen felt satisfied with the arrangements and thanked everyone for their support.

Rachel would have never imagined feeling so comfortable around this group of women, especially in a diner that was clearly a throwback to the previous century. But its decorations were charming, the food was scrumptious, and Rachel was full and content as she replied to Mary's questions. The older woman genuinely seemed to want to get to know her and make her feel included.

Karen and Mary were so much alike, both kind and warm, that Rachel could tell they had been good friends for a long time. Mary was such a lovely, down-to-earth person that Rachel found it hard to believe Liam was actually her son.

After they finished their dinners and had a cup of tea, Rachel was a little sad to say good-bye to the women. Mary, of course, demanded that she come by her house for a home-cooked meal, and Rachel accepted her offer. When she explained that her culinary skills were very limited, Mary insisted they turn dinner into a cooking lesson and seemed thrilled at the opportunity to teach her new friend some of her famous dishes. Rachel could honestly say she was looking forward to it.

Driving home, Rachel felt a sense of community that she hadn't felt in a long time. Perhaps moving to Birch Valley was indeed the right call.

\*\*\*

## Liam

Liam lay in bed, staring up at his ceiling. He had just gotten off the phone with his mother, who had told him all about her lovely dinner with the new principal. Apparently, Rachel was going to be assisting Mary and a few other ladies with Mr. Anderson's retirement party. Mary couldn't seem to stop praising Rachel and saying what a wonderful girl she was. He rolled his eyes, annoyed that his mother didn't see what a real pain Rachel really was. He decided he would do his best to keep out of her way and only hoped his mother would quit her meddling.

# Chapter Ten

## Rachel

The rest of the week scooted by without incident. Rachel noticed Liam was keeping his distance, which was fine by her. She was able to concentrate a whole lot better when he wasn't around. Hearing him laugh at something that someone was telling him and seeing him smile at the students who raced around him was hard enough. Regardless of how much he seem to irritate her, he had an odd magnetism, and it kept drawing her in.

On Friday, she filled her favorite mug with the last remaining coffee in the pot, only to turn and find Liam standing nearby, mug in hand, looking irritated.

"Oh, I'm so sorry. I can get another pot started," she said as she held the empty coffeepot out.

"No, it's fine," Liam replied, but Rachel could tell it was anything but fine.

She set the empty pot down and slipped past him as she inhaled his masculine cologne—spices mixed with notes of pine.

Megan brushed past Rachel, giving her a sickly sweet smile as she reached out to Liam.

"Oh no, we're out of coffee. I know how much you love that, Liam." Megan pouted, her full lips curved downward.

"Yeah, it would seem so. Oh well," Liam replied before refilling his water bottle instead.

"You want me to start another pot?" Megan said in a sugary voice as she batted her lashes.

Rachel mentally rolled her eyes as she escaped the room. That woman annoyed the crap out of her. The whole sweet-and-sexy bit was getting pretty old. Maybe Rachel should have Karen draw up a memo about implementing a new dress code policy, she thought and smiled to herself.

***

The day had ended, and as the last of the students went home for the weekend, Rachel wandered the halls, looking for any stragglers and securing the exits. Along the way, she strolled down a hallway that housed the third, fourth, and fifth grade classes. As she passed Liam's classroom, she glanced through the half-open door and spotted him erasing the large green chalkboard with his shirt rolled up to his forearms. She peered in, watching him swirl the eraser as the chalk dust floated lightly around him like a mist. He seemed to be deep in thought as he scrubbed the board, and she was mesmerized by the strokes of his well-toned arms, his fixed gaze, and the shadow of stubble covering his strong jawline.

Pulling herself away, she picked up her pace in hopes he wouldn't catch her staring at him. Not looking where she was headed, she collided into someone.

"Oh God, I'm sorry," Rachel stammered, turning to the person she'd just run into.

"That's okay." The high pitch of Megan's voice seared Rachel's ears.

Of course she would run into Megan of all people, Rachel thought as she tried to excuse herself.

Megan moved in front of Rachel, holding her hostage in conversation. "So how are you getting on here? Sure is a great school, isn't it? Filled with all sorts of wonderful students and *people*."

"Yes, everyone has been great," Rachel answered, running her fingers nervously through her cropped hair. She had cut it short after a terrible breakup a couple of years ago and now felt very aware of the missing tresses while looking at Megan's brown hair that cascaded in waves past her squared shoulders.

Megan placed a hand on her curvy hip and pointed to Liam's classroom. "I'm so lucky to be on the same fourth grade team as Liam. The kids love him. He's going to help me with some of that state testing curriculum you outlined for us." Her voice continued to grate on Rachel's nerves.

"Oh, that's awesome. I'm glad to hear he's going to start following the curriculum, especially as I know he wasn't a big fan of some of the ideas I had." Rachel was a little jealous that Liam was going to be spending his time with Megan, who, she imagined, had plans for him that did not include going over the new testing pamphlet Karen and Rachel had handed out the previous day.

"Yeah, I look forward to really going over the material with him." Megan's eyes sparkled mischievously.

*I bet you are*, Rachel almost said. Catching herself, she asked, "So will you be attending the retirement party this Saturday?"

"Of course. Mr. Anderson has been such a great principal here. We all just adore him, especially Liam," Megan added, smoothing her taut skirt.

"Well, I look forward to seeing you there this weekend. I'll be assisting Karen and Mary O'Brien at the party," Rachel said, hoping Megan would pick up on the slight dig. She didn't know why she felt the need to drag his mother into this little spat, if you could even call it that, but Rachel wasn't stupid. She knew Megan's intent was to get under her skin—to mark her territory, so to speak. Rachel mentally kicked herself for getting drawn into her scheme.

"I see. Well, that's nice. When did you meet Mary? Isn't she just the loveliest woman? So much like Liam, isn't she?" Megan's voice became pitchy.

"Yes, she's great. She and I have some plans to get together soon." Rachel didn't elaborate. She just wanted to plant that little seed of worry in Megan's mind.

Megan's face contorted in confusion. "Oh, really? That's thoughtful of her. She must have felt bad that you don't really have any friends here," she said sweetly as she stared directly into Rachel's eyes.

Rachel's jaw tightened. "Well, I better let you go. I need to lock up the exit down here." She pointed to the end of the hallway. Megan's last comment had stung a little, and she wanted to go lick her wounds.

\*\*\*

## Liam

Liam heard talking outside his door and realized he had forgotten to shut it after one of his students had returned to fetch their backpack. He finished wiping down the board, then rubbed his hands on the front of his jeans, leaving a trail of chalk dust on the denim. He grabbed his coat and backpack, turned off his light, and shut the door. As he locked up, Megan sprung out of what appeared to be nowhere.

"Hi, Liam, finally getting out of here?" she asked as she moved in uncomfortably close, making it hard for him to concentrate.

"Yeah, you too?" he replied. As he tried to put a little space between them, Megan inched closer, not allowing much air to pass between their two bodies.

"So what do you have planned tonight?" her voice turned breathy. They were almost touching now.

"Actually, I need to stop by my brothers' shop before they close. Sorry." Liam was thankful his brain had enough sense and blood flow to come up with an excuse.

"Well, if you want to maybe hang out later, give me a call." Megan licked her already moist lips, adding to their sheen.

"Yeah, for sure. Thanks, though," Liam said politely as he maneuvered away from her.

Liam practically jogged to his truck and was tempted to lock the door once he was inside the cab. Good grief, that woman came on strong. He turned the key in the ignition and drove over to the O'Brien Construction shop to see if his brothers were around.

As Liam pulled up to the large metal building, which was just off Main Street, he saw that the work truck was outside. He parked on the street and walked into the shop.

"Hey, guys?" he called.

The large shop was divided into several sections. The front had a counter and behind it a small desk their receptionist used during the day. There were two fairly small offices to the side of it, one for each of his brothers. The bigger of the two was Patrick's office and used to be their father's. A larger part of the shop housed some of their supplies and tools, and an additional but smaller garage outside stored more equipment.

Liam heard someone coming and smiled as Daniel entered from the shop, wiping his hands on a work towel. He had a smudge of dirt on his cheek.

"Liam, how's it going, buddy?"

"Pretty good. You guys about to close up? Was thinking maybe we could grab something to eat or maybe a beer," Liam offered as he leaned against the counter.

Patrick rounded the corner right as Daniel was about to answer. "Hey, haven't seen you in a while," he said. "How did the first week back at school go?" Patrick had a grin on his long face, as though he knew a secret he was dying to share.

"It was a 'thank God it's Friday' kind of week, I guess you could say. Anyway, I was seeing if you guys wanted to grab a beer or something to eat," Liam said, steering the conversation away from his job.

"I hear ya. I could go for a beer," Daniel said as he continued wiping the grease off his hands.

"I'll call Mom and let her know and see if she minds keeping the boys a little longer," Patrick added, pulling his cell phone from his pocket.

Liam was glad he could spend some much-needed time with his brothers. And an ice-cold beer and maybe a good ol' bacon cheeseburger with it would hit the spot.

After Patrick confirmed that Mary would love to keep the boys a little longer, the three men ventured out for dinner. They decided the best place for beer and a burger would be Antlers, a rustic bar and grill that got its name from the moose and elk antlers covering its walls. The hole-in-the-wall restaurant was located just off the main street, near both the community radio station and the O'Brien shop. The lighting was low, and the booths were shielded by darkened windows, and overall, it was a great place to go to seek refuge from your troubles.

Antlers was fairly busy, as it usually was on Friday night. All the pool tables were occupied and most of the seats at the bar were taken when the three brothers walked in. One of the bartenders waved at them, and Liam and Daniel returned the wave as they led Patrick to a booth at the rear of the bar, away from the pool tables and dart area. Daniel let Liam scoot in first, then slid in next to him while Patrick sat opposite them.

Daniel inhaled deeply and said, "Smells good in here tonight."

"Yeah, I'm starving. What are you guys getting?" Liam asked as he scanned over the simple, laminated, double-sided menu.

Patrick looked thoughtful. "I think I'm going to go with the halibut, actually. Maybe some rattlesnake skins too." Rattlesnake skins were onion rings with a spicy batter, and they came with an even hotter dipping sauce.

"That sounds good, but I think I'm more in the mood for their bacon cheeseburger," Liam said as he sat his menu down.

"Dang, both sound really good, but I think… hmm…" Daniel was lost in deciding what to eat when a waitress approached.

Daniel ordered the bacon cheeseburger as well, after making Patrick promise to give him a bite of his halibut. Once the waitress wrote down everything the guys wanted, she left them with a pitcher of beer to start working on.

"So I hear you guys got a new principal," Patrick said nonchalantly, fiddling with his paper napkin.

"Yeah, Mom tell you?" Liam replied before taking a swallow of the cold beer and enjoying the sensation of the foam trickling down his throat.

"She mentioned it. She also mentioned she's quite pretty." Patrick grinned.

Daniel seem to perk up. "That's so weird that Mr. Anderson's going to finally retire." He turned toward Liam. "So what's up with this new one?"

"There's really not a whole lot to tell. She's okay, I guess, but she's only been here a week and she's already trying to change everything." Liam then explained how Rachel had visited each teacher on her first day to explain her plans, then gave the staff a thick pamphlet of material to go over a few days later.

"Wow, so she's pretty hardcore? Wonder why she wants to change so much stuff there," Daniel said.

"Money, numbers, you know, everything besides actually teaching the kids," Liam said hastily. He suspected her emphasis on state testing and improving the school's ranking was one of the reasons the district had hired her.

"You know, it's hard being in charge, and she's probably trying to get everyone to take her seriously," Patrick said. "Especially with her being a woman, and a young, attractive one at that. But it's hard coming into a new place and having to set the rules."

"Oh good God, not you too," Liam blurted." Mom already said the same crap when I complained to her. You know, she's the same one that cut me off when I came to meet you guys for breakfast."

Both Patrick and Daniel stared at him, clearly surprised by his outburst.

"She *is* cute, then," Daniel confirmed playfully

as the waitress carried their food over.

"Yeah, also heard she took your parking spot at the school too," Patrick said, adding insult to injury.

"No way," Daniel exclaimed as he took apart his burger to add some salt and pepper to the patty.

"She didn't know, I guess. Just like she probably doesn't realize I was the one she cut off at Herrick's. But something about her just irritates me." Liam reassembled his cheeseburger after adding some ketchup and mustard to it.

Patrick dipped his beer-battered halibut into the restaurant's famous homemade tartar sauce, letting out a sigh of approval. "This fish is awesome."

As the brothers enjoyed their meal, they shared some laughs, ordered another pitcher of beer, and soon moved on from the subject of Rachel. As more patrons trickled in, Patrick excused himself to go and get his boys, and Daniel and Liam decided to stick around and wait for one of the pool tables to open up. Liam wasn't ready to head home yet. He needed a distraction, anything to get Rachel out of his head, even if for just a little while.

*** 

## Rachel

Rachel woke up early on Saturday. Now that she was settling into the routine of her job, her body was starting to act as its own alarm clock. She put on a pot of coffee and went to peek out the sliding back door while she waited for her precious caffeine to brew. To her surprise, two deer were standing in her backyard. Rachel grabbed her cell phone and snapped a picture to send to Chelsea before the deer sensed her watching them and bolted off.

Her cell phone buzzed in her hands. "Hello?" she answered.

"Oh my God, are those deer? Where at?" Chelsea practically screamed with delight and wonder.

"Yup, in my backyard. Isn't that crazy?" Rachel asked as she continued to peer through the glass door, trying to see if any more were in the yard. They'd had a break from the bad weather for a couple days, and some blades of yellowed grass poked through the melting snow.

"That's pretty cool. So how's it going?" Chelsea asked.

"I'm meeting with those ladies later this morning to decorate for the retirement party tonight."

"That's right, I forgot. What are you going to wear? Something cute, please. What if you meet some hot, single guy there?" Chelsea sounded excited.

"Oh, please!" Rachel answered, instantly thinking of Liam. She pushed the images away. "So what about you? What do you have planned for this weekend?"

"I actually have to go out with some guy my dad met." Chelsea groaned. "The upside is he's also a plastic surgeon. I guess they met at some conference or something."

"Well, it's nice your dad thought about fixing you up, right?" Rachel said cautiously.

"I think he's trying to find someone to take the

load off him, financially speaking."

Rachel wanted to tell Chelsea that she didn't have to rely on her father for support. In the past, Rachel had tried encouraging her friend do something with her life so she could support herself, but like Rachel's own mother and Chelsea's mother, Chelsea figured she would eventually marry someone rich, and that would take care of everything.

"So when are you meeting this guy?" Rachel asked, noticing her coffee was finally ready to pour.

"I guess we're going to dinner tonight. I'm not sure I even want to deal."

Rachel frowned. Chelsea was sounding a bit like a spoiled brat. "What could dinner hurt?"

"That's funny coming from someone who, like, never goes out and never wants to meet anyone," Chelsea sprang back playfully.

"I know, and I guess I'm at a point right now in my life where I want to put my career front and center. Not that I don't want to meet my Prince Charming, get married, and have children, but not right now, you know?" Rachel stirred cream into her coffee, watching the white swirls dance against the dark brown liquid.

"You're impossible, that's all I know. Give me Prince Charming and the big castle, and I'd be a very happy girl. You know, Rachel, we're in our thirties now. I looked in the mirror the other morning as I was using my cleanser, and I saw several little wrinkles I have to go in and get fixed," Chelsea complained. She sounded like Rachel's mother.

Rachel spied the time on the clock above her fireplace. "Well, try and have a good time. I'll check in with you later. I need to hurry and get ready to meet the ladies to decorate for that party." Rachel hung up and chugged her coffee.

\*\*\*

Karen was unloading several large plastic bags from her car when Rachel parked next to her.

"Good morning, let me help you with some of those," Rachel offered as she climbed out of her car and quickly moved to grab some of the sacks.

"Oh, thanks, dear. Some of the other ladies just got here too. I'm so glad you decided to help."

"I have been looking forward to it since you guys invited me," Rachel said as they hurried inside. Even though it hadn't snowed in a few days, the air remained chilly, and the sky this morning had been purple and gray with storm clouds.

Inside, the other women greeted Rachel and brought her attention to a platter of homemade muffins at the end of one of the tables.

Mary smiled at Rachel. "Please help yourself to one of my muffins."

"You know, these muffins are pretty famous," Karen explained as Rachel grabbed one that was glazed with honey and nuts. "Everyone in Birch Valley just gobbles them up. The bakery keeps begging Mary for the recipe or at least for her to bring them in so they can sell them."

The weather needed to warm up soon so she could start running again, Rachel thought. It seemed as though every time she got together with these ladies, she ended up eating. As she bit into the muffin, she discovered it was banana nut, but unlike any banana-nut muffin she had ever tasted. It was dense and rich but tasted healthy and hearty.

"My God, Mary, these are amazing," she exclaimed. "You seriously need to consider selling these."

Mary's eyes twinkled with a quiet pride. "That's nice of you, dear, but I just enjoy making them for friends and family every now and again," she said humbly.

"Well, I think you're sitting on a goldmine. This is wonderful," she mumbled with her mouth full of the delicious treat.

Mary playfully shooed her away. "You are too sweet, honey. Perhaps when I bake again you can come over and we will make them together."

"Oh, that would be fun. But I can't promise I won't try to convince you to sell these."

Both women laughed, and Karen started laying out the decorations she had purchased for the affair. Over the next hour, the women hung party lights and streamers and laid out table cloths to get the cafeteria looking festive. They also placed bouquets of balloons around the room and hung a huge banner on the wall had been made by one of the classes. It read in bright, colorful letters:

### *Best Wishes, Mr. Anderson.*

After saying good-bye, Rachel headed home to wash up and get ready for the festivities.

\*\*\*

After showering, Rachel decided to take Chelsea's advice and dress to impress. The short dress she pulled from her closet was completely out of season for the blustery winter weather, but the aqua chiffon material called out to her and begged to worn. Shoes, however, were a whole different matter. Rachel debated between shiny black pumps and a tan pair for a while without making a decision. At one point, she stood in front of her mirror wearing one of each color. Both gave her legs some length, but the black pump added a fun nighttime flare to the outfit while the tan pump kept the dress classy and understated. She wasn't too sure which look she was going for. She knew the party was semiformal, but it was also being held in the school cafeteria—not a semiformal location at all. Rachel decided to keep things simple and went with the tan high heels. With hair and makeup complete, she felt like Cinderella ready for the ball.

\*\*\*

### Liam

Liam was adjusting his tie when his phone rang. "Hello?" he answered, balancing the phone between his chin and shoulder while he manipulated the knot on the tie.

"Oh, hello, dear. I wanted to see how your outfit for this evening was coming along," Mary's soft voice replied.

"Hi, Mom. I'm getting my tie on as we speak, but I'm pretty much ready to go. Did you want me to meet you guys at the school or at the house?"

"Actually, at the house would be perfect, but only if you don't mind. I have a couple of dishes I made for the party and could use a little help carrying them." She sounded thankful.

"Sure, not a problem, Mom. Are Dad and Grandpa Paddy tagging along?" Liam asked as he finally got the knot into position.

"Yes, but I had to bribe them. I figured we could all ride in our car, if that's okay?"

Liam agreed and said good-bye after promising he'd be there shortly.

\*\*\*

As Liam entered the house, he saw his father and grandfather waiting patiently like overgrown children on one of the leather couches in the living room.

"Oh, there he is," Grandpa Paddy exclaimed with a grin.

"Hi, son. I see you got roped into going too, huh?" Pat said.

"Didn't have much choice since I work there," Liam said with a laugh as he heard his mother's heels clicking madly against the wood flooring.

"Oh good, you're here." She handed him a foil-covered dish and spun around to retrieve another from the kitchen. "You look quite handsome, son," she gushed as she motioned for her husband to get up and help.

"You look pretty tonight too," Liam called after her.

Once all the food was loaded, the family piled into their sedan and set off for the school.

\*\*\*

The O'Briens arrived a little earlier than the guest of honor and the rest of the guests so Mary and the other ladies could set up the food. When they pulled into the school parking lot, several other cars were already there. When Liam spotted Rachel's silver BMW, a twinge of nervousness developed in his gut.

Pat held the cafeteria door open for Mary, Grandpa Paddy, and Liam, whose arms were fully loaded. As he headed for the buffet table, he was amazed at how the women had transformed the cafeteria.

As Mary, Karen, and a few other women scurried around, unwrapping food and putting out serving utensils, Liam saw Rachel out of the corner of his eye. As he turned to look at her, he noticed her dress. The aqua color boldly contrasted her sun-kissed skin and drew his attention to the exposed flesh of her arms and calves.

Liam's father and grandfather also seemed to have noticed her.

"Who's the lass?" Grandpa Paddy asked as he elbowed him softly in the ribs.

"That's Mr. Anderson's replacement, the new principal," Liam answered, having a hard time taking his eyes off Rachel as she rushed around helping the women with the flurry of last-minute details. She was clearly unaware the O'Brien men were staring at her.

"Wow, she's quite pretty," Pat said.

"Yeah, she's also my new boss, Dad," Liam added, wondering why he felt a twinge of regret.

"I'd like her to be my boss," Grandpa Paddy added with a chuckle.

*Good grief*, Liam thought as he led his grandfather to a table and his father went to see if Mary needed any help. When Liam looked back at Rachel, she quickly turned away, busying herself with arranging some plastic cups near a large punch bowl.

He suddenly felt thirsty.

"Hi," he whispered as he approached, so as to not scare her as he reached out to pick up a cup she'd dropped.

\*\*\*

### Rachel

Rachel's skin had started tingling the moment Liam arrived. It was as if some internal magnet drew her to him no matter how hard she resisted. When she turned around to look at him, she almost gasped. Fitted slacks encased his muscular legs, and the brown dress shirt brought out both his trim waist and hues of green and gold in his eyes that she had never noticed before. She watched as he gently led an elderly man with the same bright green eyes, and who seemed to have difficulty walking, to a nearby table. He then turned to her, and electricity fired through her as their eyes met.

She turned away to stir the punch bowl, and his cologne tickled her senses as he neared her. Feeling clumsy, she knocked over an empty cup. As she reached for it, his warm, firm hand covered hers. It was so much larger than her own. He stood the plastic cup upright on the table and tried to calm her obviously disturbed nerves.

"Wow, you ladies did an amazing job," he offered in a soft, husky voice as he scanned the room in wonderment.

"Thank you. Karen was the brains behind the operation. Also, your mother," she stammered as electricity coursed through her, along with a fleeting thought of what his lips would feel like on hers. She pushed it away, chiding herself for acting like some lovesick schoolgirl.

"Yes, my mom loves doing events. She gets a kick out of it. She also enjoyed meeting you. Apparently, you made quite an impression on her," Liam said as his green eyes drank her in.

"She is such a lovely woman. I really like her, Liam. Is that your grandfather I saw you with earlier?" Rachel questioned as she attempted to gather her wits about her while trying to disentangle one of her silver, dangly earrings from her hair.

"Here, let me help you." Liam moved her small hands away from her ear and worked the earring loose.

Rachel struggled not to shiver at his touch and tried steadying herself as a wave of emotion flooded her.

"Yes, that's Grandpa Paddy. He's my dad's father," Liam answered as he moved to grab a cup, which he then filled with bright red punch from the bowl.

Rachel opened her mouth to speak.

"Hi, Liam," a flirty, high-pitched voice interrupted as Megan pranced up to them. Her gaze turned cool as she scrutinized every inch of Rachel. "Hello, Rachel," she said, her tone much chillier.

"Hello, Megan. It's so wonderful you made it," Rachel replied politely before excusing herself to go help Mary and Karen. Unable to think of anything else to say, and completely aware why Megan was so drawn to Liam, Rachel felt the need to run away. She couldn't compete with someone like Megan, she thought. Her eyes felt watery as she quickened her pace.

***

## Liam

"Don't you look handsome, Liam." Megan's tone turned breathy.

"You look great too, Megan," Liam politely responded. She did look great in the red and black dress that fit snugly around her voluptuous body and the gold jewelry glittering invitingly against her skin. It just didn't mix up Liam like Rachel's outfit had.

"I see they set up an area for dancing. Promise me you'll dance with me later," Megan practically begged as she reached for his arm.

Liam saw Mr. Anderson entering through the doors with his wife. "Look, there's Mr. Anderson. If you'll excuse me, Megan." As he turned to walk away, he noticed Megan looked slightly disappointed but definitely not defeated.

\*\*\*

## Rachel

Rachel watched the interaction between Megan and Liam and felt her heart sink. The way Megan kept touching Liam made her want to gag. It was just too much. Completely lost in spying on Liam, she didn't notice that Karen and Mary had joined her at the buffet table until they started speaking.

"Boy, she tries so hard to get her claws into Liam," Karen said with a hint of anger. "He's such a nice man. I'd hate to see what she would do if she succeeded."

"I thought she was such a doll when I first met her, but she does come off a little strong," Mary said just as Mr. Anderson and his wife walked in. "Oh look, he's here."

Everyone clapped as Mr. Anderson smiled and waved bashfully to the crowd.

"You guys are making too big of a fuss for an old guy like me," he said in his booming voice. "But since you went to all this trouble, let's party!"

As Karen went to take Mr. and Mrs. Anderson to the buffet table, Rachel searched for Liam and found him sitting at a table, laughing with his grandfather and a man who must have been his

161

father.

"They have such a great time when they all get together, you know," Mary said, leaning in close to her. Feeling guilty for having been caught staring at Liam, Rachel immediately turned her attention to a fruit salad that was in front of her, taking the large metal spoon and giving it a stir.

"Liam has a sister and two brothers, and when those O'Brien men get together, Lord help me." Mary laughed. "Do you have any siblings, dear?"

"I have a brother, Ethan. He's a doctor back in California," she answered proudly.

"Oh, that's nice. Is he older than you? Are the two of you close?" Mary questioned.

"He's a little older, and I'd say we're fairly close. Ethan's obviously very busy, but we try to keep in touch when we can." Rachel couldn't help but feel a bit sad as she thought about her brother and wished they were more connected. In fact, she wished her whole family shared a deeper connection, but everyone was so focused on leading their own lives, they didn't have time to share or be a valued part of one another's. That was one the reasons Rachel had left. She'd felt as if she were slowly being vacuumed into a vortex of shallowness.

When Mary excused herself to say hello to Mr. Anderson, Rachel felt like an outsider as she watched the warm interactions between the members of this community. Feeling alone and awkward, she considered leaving. Maybe she shouldn't have included herself in this event after all. Did she have a right to be here when she was replacing this well-respected and beloved man? Did she even belong in this community? Rachel hadn't really known what to expect when she came to Birch Valley. She certainly didn't expect to be scooped up into a collection of old women who happened to take a shine to her, that's for sure. Earlier in the evening, one of Karen's friends had even invited Rachel over to play with her Bunco group. Rachel had wanted to make friends, but had assumed they would be women her own age. Now she found herself feeling like a child among these women.

Rachel had convinced herself that she should probably say good-bye to the guest of honor and head home when she felt Liam standing next to her.

"Sorry, I didn't see you," she said nervously.

"That's okay. You seemed a little lost in thought," Liam replied as he searched her face.

"Yeah, I was thinking about how great it is that they threw this party for Mr. Anderson." She shrugged. "So have you had a chance to review that pamphlet I handed out? Megan mentioned you guys were going to start studying it together." She tried to sound professional and not petty but was pretty sure she failed at it.

Liam rolled his eyes. "Let's not talk shop tonight," he pleaded.

"Why? We work here. If anything, this is the perfect place." Rachel motioned around them.

"No, it's not. This, Rachel, is a party, if you hadn't noticed. And usually at parties, people eat, drink, dance, and have a good time. Talking about some annoying program, that I have no intention of following, is not really what I do at parties."

Liam was obviously irritated with her, and Rachel recoiled, her blood starting to simmer with anger. "I see. Well, I guess there's really nothing for us to discuss then. But as far as that new curriculum guideline is concerned, you will be following it."

Liam hovered over her and rubbed his chin. "You know, you weren't even here for a full day before you started bossing everyone around."

"Well, in case you weren't aware, that's exactly what I am—your boss," she snapped, squaring her shoulders defiantly.

"Oh come off it," Liam said, raising his voice slightly. "You could have waited, let everyone warm up to the idea of Mr. Anderson leaving first. You didn't have to rush right in, guns blazing, shooting off orders about how you want to change everything. Oh, and for the record, everything was just fine before you got here."

"For the record, everything was not 'just fine,' and that, Liam, is why the district hired me. They know what I can do for this school. So, obviously, whatever you're doing isn't quite enough. At least according to the state's standard."

Rachel stopped, wondering if she had crossed the line. After all, Liam wasn't the only one responsible for the school not quite being up to par.

But that regret vanished as Liam furrowed his thick brows at her. "You think you're better than us because you come from California," he said, his eyes darkening with anger. "But let me tell you something, we are tons better than you."

His words stung. Rachel knew she had hurt him,

but insulting her because of where she came from was ludicrous. Without another word, she stormed away, making a beeline for the principal. Calming herself, she congratulated him again on his retirement and wished him the best. She also made sure to thank him for handing over such an amazing school that he had cultivated during his tenure.

Rachel then left through the double doors, fighting the urge to go back and apologize to Liam while chastising herself for having let her guard down even a bit. Earlier in the night, she'd thought she felt a spark of attraction between them. Now she wanted nothing to do with Mr. High and Mighty.

# *Chapter Eleven*

A couple weeks had passed since the retirement party, and things between Liam and Rachel remained awkward. They would give each other a curt nod or a brief glance when passing in the halls, but they didn't speak. Instead, Rachel went about focusing her attention on her new job, paying no mind to what Liam O'Brien was doing—well, she tried not to, anyway.

The school would be testing at the end of the following month, and she planned on getting together with the staff to see how her curriculum change was going. She'd recently met with the superintendent, who had harshly reminded her about the importance of her position and the need to get the school on track. She'd walked away from the meeting a little shaken up, knowing she needed to get the school in line if she wanted her contract renewed for the following school year.

One Thursday evening, Rachel was at home going over a mock skills test for the students when her phone rang.

"Hello?" she answered.

"Hello, Rachel, dear," Mary O'Brien sang out. "I was thinking about baking some of those muffins you loved. My daughter and my adorable granddaughter are coming out for a visit this weekend. They live in Seattle and just called me a little while ago, saying they're going to be here Saturday."

"Oh, that's nice that they're driving over. How will the pass be with that snow we just got?" Rachel asked, remembering the fiasco with the moving truck a month earlier.

"Maggie, my daughter, says it's pretty clear. Anyway, I know I promised to show you how to make my muffins."

Rachel appreciated Mary's thoughtfulness, and she was itching to get out of the house. Since the meeting with the superintendent, she had pretty much left her home only to go to work and get groceries so she could keep her mind on business.

"Also, I was thinking we could throw in a little cooking lesson perhaps," Mary suggested warmly.

"You know what, that sounds great, Mary. When would you like to get together?" Rachel asked, throwing caution to the wind. She deserved a little downtime, and she couldn't refuse a chance to eat some more of those scrumptious muffins.

"I was thinking perhaps Saturday morning if you are available. My daughter could use a lesson in the kitchen as well, and I think she will just love you," Mary added with a hopeful sigh.

"Sounds good. Can I bring anything?"

"Nope, only yourself, my dear."

\*\*\*

## Liam

That Friday night, Liam had his feet propped up on his rustic coffee table as he enjoyed a beer. Snow had started to spill from the sky on his way home from work, and he was glad he'd had time to carry a bunch of firewood into his house before the storm really got going.

The log in his fireplace fell and loudly groaned as the heat split it, and Liam slowly lifted himself out of his comfortable position to add another to the dying fire. He was nearly finished stoking it back into a roaring blaze when he heard the familiar ring of his phone.

Pushing himself off the ground, he sprinted to answer it. "Hello?"

"Hi, sweetheart. How was work today?" Mary sounded delighted and upbeat.

"Good. Was getting the fire going here. You guys doing all right with this little storm we got going on?"

"Oh yes, handling it just fine, dear. I only pray this doesn't hinder Maggie coming over the pass. She was going to leave this afternoon but decided to come tomorrow morning instead."

The pass could be dangerous this time of year, so Liam was glad his sister was being cautious. "That was a good idea, Mom. Better to be safe than sorry. How come she doesn't fly in more?"

"Heaven knows I'm deathly afraid of planes, and I hate to admit it, but I think she inherited her hate for flying from her dear old mother," Mary added, her tone worried.

"Ah, it's not that bad, and Michael does it all the time."

"Well, my daughter prefers keeping both feet on the ground, just like me. Anyway, I wanted to make sure you were going to come over tomorrow for dinner and to see them."

"Of course, Mom. How is Maggie doing, by the way? She seemed way happier when she left with Michael on New Year's Day," Liam said, planting himself back on the couch.

"Maggie is doing okay, though I fear they've had a spat recently. She seemed a little upset this morning when I spoke with her."

"Well, she probably misses everyone. You know how she loves being out here. Funny too, because she couldn't leave fast enough after high school." Liam laughed.

"I suppose you're right, dear. We miss her terribly too. She has to feel so lonely with how many hours Michael has been putting in at the office. Poor man, working himself to death," Mary added, sounding concerned.

"It's good she tries to come out for visits. You should go over there soon, Mom. I bet she would really enjoy that," Liam suggested, thinking he might have to visit her himself soon too.

"I prefer being here, but perhaps I will. Well, sweetheart, I look forward to seeing you tomorrow."

Mary hung up, leaving Liam alone in the quiet of his house with only the sound of the crackling wood for company. Liam usually enjoyed the serenity of his home. He got enough chaos and loudness in class during the week and at his parents' home at Sunday dinner. He liked being able to decompress and meditate, but after having that argument with Rachel at the retirement party, he had a hard time being alone with his thoughts. He replayed their conversation over and over again in his mind, trying to see how he could have handled it differently, but at the same time, he was still angry with her because he didn't care for how she'd diminished his teaching and practically blamed him for the students' mediocre performance on standardized tests. He also hated how Rachel invaded his sleep. He kept dreaming of them being together, mainly in a physical sense, and they were doing a lot more than holding hands.

Why was he plagued by her? He knew a relationship between them could never work out. They were polar opposites, and he refused to believe the saying about opposites attracting.

\*\*\*

### Rachel

Rachel woke up Saturday and dressed for a day of baking and cooking in her most comfortable jeans and a faded, old T-shirt featuring her college mascot. She decided to pack another shirt in case she stayed for dinner, as she wasn't sure how messy this whole baking adventure was going to be. The last time she'd tried to make anything in the kitchen, she and Chelsea had drunk a bit too much wine before attempting to bake brownies, and Chelsea's fabulous kitchen had quickly turned into a chocolate-covered disaster. Neither woman had any clue about how to cook, having grown up relying on their nannies or their parents' personal chefs to feed them. Rachel had learned how to make coffee, which was essential for survival, and she could nuke a frozen dinner pretty darn good. But after that awful experiment and a couple others she would prefer to forget, she'd realized she had no business being in a kitchen. Thank God for takeout.

*** 

Several inches of new snow covered her car as Rachel left her home, suited up to face the cold weather. The snow brush her neighbor Sue-Ellen had gifted her made easy work of clearing the white, icy powder off her car. Rachel was acclimating to the cold temperatures, but she still wasn't a fan of snow. It got in the way, complicating travel to work and to the grocery store, which were the only places she had been in weeks. She wanted to invest a little time in checking out the adorable businesses that lined the gorgeous main street. Each storefront looked friendly and inviting, and Rachel longed for warm and sunny days like those back home, where she could enjoy lazily window-shopping while sipping her gourmet coffee.

As the thoughts of warmth and sunshine penetrated her mind, Rachel stopped at the grocery store, where she perused the small floral department for something cheery to bring Mary. She decided on a lively bouquet of sunflowers in different shades of yellow and sprigs of greenery, then carefully drove the several blocks to Mary's street, where she admired the similar homes with matching front porches until she located Mary's.

After parking on the street, Rachel gathered the flowers and her purse. As she trudged up the snow-filled walkway, a man exited through the bright red front door carrying a snow shovel.

"Hello, can I help you?" he asked, smiling broadly.

"Hi, I'm here to see Mary," Rachel cautiously answered. Perhaps she was at the wrong house.

"Oh, you must be Rachel?" The man extended a large gloved hand. His cheeks were already rosy from the few seconds he'd spent out in the cold. "I'm Daniel."

"Hi, Daniel, nice to meet you." She shook his hand.

"Mom's been expecting you. Sorry, I was meaning to shovel the path before you got here." He stabbed the snow with the bright red plastic shovel.

"It's okay, really," Rachel said. If this was Liam's brother, he didn't really look anything like Liam at all, and he was definitely cheerier than Liam, but he did have the same remarkable eyes.

"Mom's going to love those," Daniel said as he eyed the bouquet.

"Oh good. You know, some people hate getting flowers brought to them, but today I was thinking about spring, and how warm it is back home in

California, and I suddenly felt like flowers," she rambled, feeling nervous.

"Well, let's get you and those pretty flowers inside." Daniel led Rachel through the front door, while loudly announcing her arrival to his mother.

The O'Brien home was older and had a distinctive style, much like the home she was renting, with arches and shelves built into the walls and unexpected surprises. The comfortable and soft decor had a modern, rustic flare. A fire was burning in the brick fireplace in the living room, where two soft, brown leather couches with bold-patterned pillows sat across from each other on a beautiful thick rug that covered the dark wood floor.

Mary stepped from a hallway into the room, wearing a floral apron over her blouse and pants. "Oh Rachel, so glad you could make it. Welcome to our home."

"Thank you so much for inviting me. These are for you," Rachel replied as she handed Mary the flowers.

"These are beautiful. I simply adore flowers."

Rachel smiled. "Yeah, I was telling Daniel how I was missing the warmth of the sun back home and needed a little dose of spring."

Daniel returned her smile with a broad grin, his cheeks still rosy from the cold. "Well, I got a sidewalk to shovel, especially if I want to get one of those muffins you guys are going to be baking."

"Son, you better get out there, then," Mary teased as she playfully swatted at Daniel, who was already heading back outside.

Before Mary could lead Rachel to the kitchen, a

little girl with thick, bouncy, auburn hair cut into a bob rammed into Mary.

"This, Rachel, is my prettiest little granddaughter, Melanie."

Rachel leaned down to greet the child, who was, indeed, quite pretty. Her skin was milky, her cherub lips were pink like little rosebuds, and her eyes, though a different shade than Liam's and Daniel's, were green with flecks of amber and sheltered behind thick lashes.

"Melanie, this is Rachel." Mary peeled the little girl from her waist and led her closer to their visitor.

"Hello, Melanie, it's nice to meet you. And your grandmother is right. You are such a pretty girl," Rachel said in a soft voice, trying to sound soothing and gentle.

"Thank you," Melanie whispered as her eyes twinkled and her chubby cheeks rounded into a sheepish grin, much like Daniel's.

Rachel went on to ask Melanie several questions: how old she was, what grade she was in, her favorite animal, and other simple icebreakers to get the child to open up, which she quickly did.

After they got acquainted, Mary led them down a hall, where Rachel spotted an archway to her right that led to what appeared to be a den. Two older men sat inside, engrossed in newspapers, one puffing on an old pipe. As the sweet, tantalizing tobacco smoke reached Rachel's nose, Mary knocked softly against one side of the archway.

"We have a visitor, gentlemen," Mary announced, pointing to the younger of the two men. "Rachel that is my husband, Pat, and his father, who we all call Grandpa Paddy. My friend Rachel is here to do a little baking with me," she said proudly.

Rachel emerged from behind Mary and gingerly waved at them. "Good morning, I'm Rachel. Very nice to meet you both."

"Ah, you're the new principal down at the school where my grandson teaches?" Grandpa Paddy asked in his thick brogue as he looked at her over the rims of the glasses perched on the bridge of his nose. He too had the famed O'Brien eyes, which danced with mischief.

Rachel loved the sound of accents, especially Irish, Scottish, or English ones. The way words rolled off their foreign tongues gave every word an unusual, almost fairy-tale-like flare. "Yes, that would be me." Rachel smiled back.

Liam's father congratulated her and told her what a fine place Birch Valley was, then asked Rachel to tell him more about her background and family history. Mesmerized by his charm and his accent, Rachel enjoyed talking to him. After a few minutes, Mary took her arm and escorted her out of the den, telling her husband and father-in-law they could visit with her at dinner.

"If I didn't steer you away from that old goat, you would've been talking to him for hours," Mary explained.

"I didn't mind. Your father-in-law is a delight. His accent is so charming," Rachel gushed.

"Well, charming or not, that man is usually busy trying his hardest to get on my last nerve, or anyone's, for that matter. He's quite the character, but he seems to have taken a liking to you as well,"

Mary said as she gave her a kind smile.

***

The large, open kitchen was several feet from the den, and had an array of baking ingredients were lined up along the island inside. As they entered, a slender young woman whom Melanie was now hugging looked up from donning an apron like Mary's and gave Rachel a slight, unsure wave.

"This is my lovely and only daughter Maggie," Mary said, giving Melanie a tickle when she passed by them, causing the girl to squeal.

"Nice to meet you," Rachel said politely as she took Maggie's hand.

"Same here. I've heard so much about you from Mom. Looks like I'm also getting a much-needed cooking lesson," Maggie said with a slight, nervous laugh.

Maggie had a plain sort of beauty with pale skin and chestnut hair bound up in a high ponytail from which a few strands had escaped to fall down her neck. Those incredible O'Brien eyes dominated her face. Though polite, she didn't come off as warm and friendly as Daniel had. Rather, she seemed unsure of their visitor. Rachel didn't take offense, though. She understood that Maggie was sizing her up, attempting to understand why her mother had invited this strange woman into her home.

"I'm here because those muffins your mom makes are out of this world. I'm pretty awful in the kitchen," Rachel added lightheartedly.

"Yeah, we do a lot of takeout too, which I know

is terrible. I'm spoiled in Seattle. We have so many options for dining out," Maggie commented while her mother turned on the double oven.

"You ladies ready to do some baking?" Mary asked cheerfully as she began setting out several large, glass mixing bowls.

Rachel watched Mary flutter around the kitchen, a domestic butterfly, completely in her element.

"I don't know how she does it," Maggie said as she watched her mother.

"Me either, and she looks so happy about it too." Rachel looked on as Mary pulled out different ingredients from the cupboards. "Oh wow, so is this like from-scratch type of baking?"

"Nothing comes out of a box when it comes to my mom cooking."

Mary placed her hands on her plump hips. "Let's get started."

The women had baked several batches of muffins when two little preschool-age boys ran into the room. Rachel raised her eyebrows in surprise when she realized they were identical twins.

The man who entered calling after them had the same green O'Brien eyes, but he looked different from the rest of the family. He was tall like Liam, but his dark hair and features gave him a sense of mystery and sex appeal that was completely different than that of his brother. The beginnings of a beard peppered with gray outlined his strong jaw, and he parted his sensual lips to greet his mother as he locked eyes with Rachel.

She'd thought Liam made her feel nervous. This man caused a whole array of emotions to rush through her.

"Patrick, love, this is Rachel." Mary grabbed his hand and pulled him over. "Rachel, I present to you my oldest son, Patrick," she announced playfully.

"How do you do?" He extended his long arm. His sleeves were rolled up, showing muscles rippling under a light spray of fine, dark hair.

"Nice to meet you." Her palms turned sweaty, and she used a nearby dish towel to wipe them.

"Come on, boys, let's go see where Uncle Daniel's hiding," Patrick said, corralling his children.

Mary eyed Rachel, who felt a little flustered. "Aren't Patrick's twins the cutest little guys?" she asked.

"Adorable. I love their matching overalls. Too cute," Maggie said.

"They are really cute. How old are they?" Rachel asked, shaking off her stupor and taking a dirty mixing bowl to the sink.

"Those sweet little things are three years old. I get to watch them while Patrick is at the shop," Mary explained as she reached into the oven to check on another batch of muffins.

"Oh, what does Patrick do?" Rachel asked, trying to sound casual. She was still recovering from how incredibly handsome he was. She could only imagine what Chelsea would think.

"He and Daniel run my husband's old business that his father, Grandpa Paddy, started. It's the construction company here in town. That large metal building just off Main. You probably have driven past it." Mary brought the warm muffins to the kitchen island to cool.

"God, those smell amazing." Rachel inhaled deeply.

"And now you both know how to make them," Mary added, stacking the muffins that had already cooled onto a glass platter.

Next, Mary told them the basics of a pot-roast dinner. Rachel learned how to make homemade biscuits as well.

The aroma of the cooking meat simmering in veggies and its own juices made Rachel's mouth water, and apparently, she wasn't the only one, as each member of the family kept coming into the kitchen to ask when dinner was going to be ready.

Rachel was helping butter some biscuits Mary had pulled out of the oven when she felt Liam enter. She could somehow smell his cologne through the thick scent of the cooking dinner. Trying to keep her back to him as Liam talked to his mother and sister, she lost her grip on the butter knife and sent it clattering to the floor.

"I'm so sorry," Rachel said, quickly bending down to grab it.

"Oh, that's quite fine, dear," Mary assured her as she got Rachel another butter knife.

Maggie laughed when Liam retreated from the kitchen, and Rachel realized how painfully obvious her reaction to him had been.

"Good grief, what was that about? I just have to ask," Maggie teased. Though she had started off wary of Rachel, the two had bonded over their lack of cooking skills and found they had quite a bit in common, especially the time they'd spent living in large cities. Rachel could see herself becoming good friends with Maggie, and she adored Melanie, who had had enough of baking and was off playing with her cousins.

"Oh, it's nothing. Liam and I work together, as you probably know." Rachel shot Mary a look.

"I may have mentioned it to Maggie, yes," Mary confirmed.

"Yeah, I know you're his new boss, but what gives?" Maggie pestered as she walked just a few feet away to get a stack of dishes from the hutch in the dining room.

"Nothing really. We just don't see eye to eye on some stuff at the school," Rachel tried to explain while remaining as vague as possible.

"It doesn't look like nothing. You could cut the tension with a knife, it was so thick. Well, or drop the knife," Maggie teased as she proceeded to set the table.

"I think you and my son need to sit down and really come to some sort of agreement on this whole matter," Mary continued as she gathered glasses from the cupboard above the sink. "I know about the whole testing thing. He ran it down for me, and so did Karen. Personally, I think change can be a good thing. I know you are just doing your job, and ultimately you want what you think is best for the students and the school. But so does Liam. He doesn't like having to grill those kids on filling in bubbles and worrying about a bunch of tests. So you both need to meet in the middle."

"But Mary, Liam flat-out refused to use the guidelines I created." Rachel was starting to feel defensive.

"Mom, Rachel's right. Liam's being a little stubborn about the whole thing, and Rachel is his boss," Maggie said from the dining room.

"I know. He's been acting a bit odd since you came here, to be honest, Rachel. Liam's normally so easy-going and lets things roll off his back without making too much of a fuss," Mary said as she brought several glasses to the table.

"Well, I need his support. The other teachers are hardly wanting to comply, and they seem to look to Liam for what to do. They take his lead."

"Maybe I can talk to him," Mary said.

Rachel shook her head. "No, we're having a staff meeting next week. I'll try and sit down with him and hammer this out before then."

Maggie cleared her throat and motioned to Rachel that Liam was entering the room.

\*\*\*

## Liam

As Liam walked into the dining room, Rachel quickly ducked back into the kitchen. He'd been surprised to see her in there when he'd arrived earlier. His mother had conveniently failed to mention she would be coming to dinner.

Rachel was all Daniel and Patrick had been talking about for the last hour. Patrick thought she was great and couldn't understand why Liam had a problem with her. Daniel thought she seemed nice and was gorgeous. He then suggested Liam should try to get to know her better on a way more personal level.

His brothers didn't realize that Liam had been struggling to keep his thoughts about her professional. Seeing her in the kitchen, mingling with his family and doing a great job of making everyone fall in love with her, possibly even him, didn't help. She acted as though she wanted nothing to do with him, and that bothered him a great deal, but he wasn't about to let his brothers know that.

Mary declined Liam's offer to help her set the table and told him to round up the rest of the O'Briens because dinner was almost ready.

"Hey, Liam, so what's up with you and Rachel?" Maggie asked as she trailed after her brother.

Liam huffed. "Nothing, why?" He had heard her chatting and laughing away with Rachel as though they were long-lost friends and was curious to know what Rachel had said to her.

"You guys didn't really acknowledge each other a little bit ago, and I just thought that was kind of weird, considering you work together."

"I don't know," Liam said, softening to her questions. He had always been close to Maggie and felt he could tell her just about anything.

"Well, it's something for sure." Maggie put her hands on her narrow hips.

Liam leaned against the wall and carefully chose his words. "I think things are strained because we don't agree on some stuff at work."

"That's basically what she said. But I think there's something else going on here."

"Like what?"

"Oh, I don't know. I think you guys are attracted to each other and neither of you want to admit it."

"Mags, I think you got it wrong. She's all business. The only thing we have in common is that we both work at the school. Who knows how long she will even be there." Liam denied having any feelings for Rachel and explained that they were completely different people who had nothing in common.

"Okay, if that's your story and you're sticking to it, I'll let it go—for now." A playful grin crept across Maggie's lips.

"Thank you," Liam said, relieved.

\*\*\*

### Rachel

Rachel sat next to Maggie and her daughter at the large dining room table, and Liam and Daniel sat directly across from them. As the sounds of chatter and utensils clinking against plates echoed off the walls, Rachel quietly took in the affection this family shared and how ordinary moments were somehow special to them.

Liam's gaze would constantly find hers, even when he was busy laughing at something silly the twins had said or as he listened to something Melanie was telling him.

Daniel was spooning more vegetables onto his plate as he said, "Wow, dinner is great."

Patrick nodded as he turned his attention to Rachel. "So, Rachel, how are you liking Birch

Valley?"

"It's a very nice place. Everyone has been really kind, and the students are great," she replied, feeling Liam's gaze burning into her. Avoiding it, she focused her attention on Patrick.

A thought rolled into her mind suddenly. Chelsea would have just loved being here. She wouldn't have enjoyed the whole cooking part, but getting to stare at the handsome O'Brien brothers would have been well worth the trouble.

"Well, I'm glad. I'm sure the students and the *staff* are pleased you're there." Patrick smirked at Liam.

Liam shot him a glare, and Rachel licked her lips in nervousness. She went on to explain how different the school was compared to the one she'd worked at in California. Liam's family then bombarded her with an array of questions, especially about her home state, and she graciously answered each one. Sadness washed over her when she told them about her family, but she perked up when she talked about Chelsea and about the ocean, both of which she missed terribly.

All too soon, dinner was finished, and the men retreated elsewhere while the women cleared the table. As Mary broke out her Tupperware, Rachel playfully reminded Liam's mother to pack her cut of the muffins before trying once again to encourage Mary to let the bakery sell the yummy treats.

Rachel exchanged numbers with Maggie and said good-bye to the children. As she hovered near the front door, fully loaded with goodies, she glanced at Liam, who was on the floor playing with one of the twins. She hoped to leave unnoticed, but he looked up at her and stood quickly.

"Here, let me help you out to your car," Liam offered as he grabbed their coats. Mary threw a look to Maggie, then raised her eyebrows approvingly at Liam.

"Oh, it's fine. I got it," Rachel said, despite struggling to balance the Tupperware and her purse in her hands.

Not allowing her to shoo him away, Liam grabbed several of the containers as he worked the door open. Giving up, Rachel took her coat from him and waved good-bye to the family. Daniel gave him a thumbs-up as Liam closed the door behind them.

"Really, it wasn't necessary for you to come out here," Rachel stammered while she fussed with her keys.

"I wanted to." Liam placed the containers in the trunk of her car as she stood beside him.

They then looked at each other in silence, waiting for the other speak. Snow had started to fall gently, landing on Rachel's hair. Liam carefully swept it away and looked down at her. Then he leaned in and planted his warm lips on hers.

Bolts of shock blasted through her as she accepted his kiss. The connection was hot and electric, but his lips on hers were warm and soft. It was perfect.

Liam lifted his head, searching her eyes as if waiting for a response.

She felt dizzy as she begged the panic that had

suddenly reared up in her to vanish. "I need to go."

Disappointment flickered through his eyes, but he simply nodded and opened the driver's side door for her, then closed it after she got in.

Almost too stunned to drive home, Rachel told herself she had to regroup as she pulled out of the driveway. She wasn't exactly sure what had just happened and wondered if she had just imagined it. She was thankful that the drive to her home would be brief.

\*\*\*

### Liam

Liam walked back to the house, not knowing what had come over him. What the hell was he thinking? Why would he just kiss her like that? It was the way her glacier-blue eyes had looked up at him, all crystal and perfect, and the way the snow had decorated her blonde hair. The moment just felt right. But while he'd love kissing her, he really wished he would have thought things out better.

# Chapter Twelve

## Rachel

Monday morning came too soon, and Rachel was filled with dread. As she entered the foyer of the elementary school, Karen stopped humming while she filed papers into the teachers' mailboxes.

"Good morning, Rachel. How was your weekend?" she asked without looking up.

They had developed a nice routine. Rachel arrived at exactly the same time every morning to find a pot of coffee brewing and Karen busy with her clerical duties. "It was okay." She didn't care to elaborate. She'd spent most of Sunday trying to digest the kiss she had shared with Liam. On one hand, she was completely steamrolled by the incredible way his lips felt against hers. On the other, she felt as though whatever was between them couldn't go anywhere.

Rachel had called Chelsea to see what she thought, and they'd rehashed the kiss over and over again. Chelsea was thrilled Rachel had finally gotten a little lip action and tried to reassure her it wasn't the end of the world. Rachel wasn't convinced, though. She had already been having a difficult time ignoring and avoiding Liam. Now she couldn't forget the way his kiss left a tingling sensation on her mouth.

Karen turned to face her. "You doing okay, sweetie?" she asked, interrupting Rachel's thoughts.

"Oh, sorry, I'm fine. Was thinking about when to draw up that memo about the staff meeting," she replied quickly.

"Okay, well, anytime you want me to write that up, you let me know." Karen smiled and turned back to her work.

Rachel shut herself in her office and plopped her briefcase down on an empty chair before spilling into the chair behind her desk. As she held her head in her hands, someone knocked.

"Come in," she said, straightening up in her seat.

Liam poked his head into the room. "Is it okay if I come in?"

*Oh Lord.* Her stomach started doing flip-flops. "Sure, um, of course."

After shutting the door quietly behind him, she watched Liam's throat as he swallowed.

"Okay, I wanted to say I'm sorry," he said as he moved closer to the desk. "I feel like I put you in a really awkward position, and I don't know what came over me."

She hadn't expected that. "Uh, yeah, it's okay. I appreciate the apology, but you didn't have to."

"Okay, good. I just didn't want you to feel uncomfortable."

"Nope, all good here." *Please leave.* Being in the same room was difficult enough, but hearing him go on and on about making her feel uncomfortable was starting to irritate her. "Also, Liam," she said as he opened the door to leave, "we'll be having a staff meeting tomorrow to go over some of the curriculum. Testing is at the end of the month, as you know."

She meant for her tone to remind him who was in charge, and that it certainly wasn't him.

*** 

The weather grew menacing and dark as the day slowly wore on. The sun was clearly hiding until spring, and Rachel was starting to feel the effects. As she stared out her office window, she wondered how people here coped with the long winters and if she would stick around—or even want to stick around—long enough to see another one.

The only intrusion she'd had to deal with was a couple students who had been sent to her office for acting up in class. Because of the storm brewing, the kids had been forced to stay inside for recess, and they were all restless. By the end of the day, all the teachers looked exhausted.

The following day brought even more bitter-cold and fierce weather. Rachel had layered up the best she could but still felt chilled to her bones all day. By early afternoon, she wandered into the teachers' lounge in search of something, anything, hot to drink. Inside, she found Liam filling his mug with coffee, wearing a cream-colored, cable-knit sweater and dark-wash jeans that made his legs look even longer than usual. The casualness with which he stood there, apparently not knowing Rachel was only feet behind him, let her anchor herself before she moved closer to him.

When she managed to conjure up a little cough to get his attention, he simply moved a foot or so away from the coffee station without taking his attention away from his beverage.

"Good afternoon, Liam," Rachel said coolly, keeping her guard firmly up.

"Afternoon, Rachel," he replied, his tone just as even and cool as he stirred sugar and cream into his coffee.

"I wonder when this weather is going to warm up," Rachel said, trying to make small talk as she followed him to one of the long tables in the lounge.

"Probably by spring, like it always does," he said curtly.

Rachel sighed loudly. "Look, Liam, I think you and I need to talk."

"Is there really anything to discuss?"

"Well, we've got to figure out something, because whatever this is—" Rachel waved her arms around in frustration, "—it's not working."

Liam matched her sigh. "I thought you felt whatever this is too." Sadness crept into his striking green eyes.

Rachel didn't really know how to respond. She was in an impossible position. Of course she felt an attraction to him. Who wouldn't? The man was kind, came from a wonderful family, and was about as gorgeous as they came. The problem for Rachel was that she'd moved here to further her career, not to start dating anyone, let alone someone she supervised.

"Liam, I'm sorry. I feel we need to keep our relationship strictly professional." Rachel bowed her head, not wanting to meet his stare.

"Okay. I need to get back." Liam got up from the table and left the room without another word.

Rachel felt awful as Karen strutted into the room, humming lightly.

"Oh, Rachel, I forgot to tell you, we always have a little bake-sale fundraiser in February. We use the proceeds to hold a Dr. Seuss party in March. It's the neatest event. We buy books and treats, and everyone comes dressed up as their favorite character or in some wacky costume," Karen rambled on without looking at Rachel as she opened the freezer to retrieve a frozen meal. She continued talking as she pressed several buttons on the microwave and went to sit by Rachel. "Oh, and last year, Liam dressed up like that cat character in one of the books. It helps that he's so darn tall. The kids just loved it."

Rachel was able to nod and give Karen a smile. "That sounds so neat. Please let me know what I can do to help."

"You bet." The microwave beeped, and Karen stood to retrieve her food.

Realizing she had mentioned a bake sale, Rachel pushed her thoughts of Liam aside. "You know who would bring in a ton of money? Mary, with those amazing muffins of hers."

"Oh, aren't those simply the best? But yes, she

brings all sorts of treats every year, and they always sell out first," Karen agreed as she brought a steaming cardboard dish to the table.

"Not surprising," Rachel added as the lunch bell rang and children began filing into the halls. "Well, I better go. I need to prepare for the staff meeting."

"Okay, and I'll let you know more about our bake sale a little later," Karen said as she fished a romance novel out of her purse.

Rachel headed back to her office and closed the door. She felt safe in this small room, despite its bare walls and shelves. She wondered if she hadn't bothered to decorate it yet because she was still deciding if she wanted to stay here.

The staff meeting was only a couple hours away, and it would be the first meeting she would oversee by herself as principal. Her nerves were a little rattled, and her conversation with Liam earlier hadn't helped. Rachel reviewed her notes and had even created a slideshow presentation so the teachers could visualize her ideas and see the statistics that backed them. But the difficult part of the entire meeting would not be speaking in front of the group. It would be knowing the teachers didn't agree with her methods. Rachel now realized she should have expected this "if it's not broke, don't fix it" attitude when coming to a small town.

But that wasn't how she operated. She always wanted to see growth and improvement. But then, she also didn't like her life to be messy or complicated, and thanks to her job and to the mess of feelings she had around Liam, it was now both.

When the final bell screamed out, Rachel and

Karen had already set up the cafeteria for the meeting. Rachel was preparing her laptop for the presentation when the flood of students took over the hallways, so Karen left her to corral some of the end-of-school madness. Rachel looked up from her work just as Liam entered the room with Megan trailing close behind him, followed by several other teachers from different grades.

Liam took a seat near the front, and Megan sat next to him and inched her chair closer to his. Liam didn't pay her much attention as she fussed with her blouse and batted mascara-thick lashes at him. Instead, he was scrutinizing one of the agendas Karen had laid out on all of the tables.

Megan leaned in close to him, obviously pretending to be study the material as she whispered in his ear. Whatever she shared caused Liam to laugh a little too loudly. Rachel frowned, feeling a tad irritated as she waited for the remainder of the staff to get seated. Finally, Karen scurried in and took a seat at the table where Rachel's laptop was.

Several minutes later, when she was sure everyone was there, Rachel stood and thanked them for attending and for keeping an open mind. She started by going over how the students had prepared for the statewide tests in the past and explained how their results measured up to other schools in nearby cities and counties and the state at large. Rachel had done her homework and had pulled from every resource she could. She wanted the teachers to understand she wasn't some nitwit who had come in from another state with no idea of what she was talking about when it came to their school and their state. Nope, she had definitely covered all her bases.

Rachel started the visual presentation with a series of graphs that showed the school's decline in test scores over the past few years. She spoke slowly and confidently and only faltered when she noticed Liam staring at her. She couldn't tell if he was truly engaged in her talk or if he was trying to intimidate her, but she suspected the latter.

When she finished her explanation and provided a clear and easy route for the teachers to follow to bring up the test scores, Rachel asked if there were any questions.

Liam's arm immediately shot up.

"Yes, Liam?" she asked, feeling the pit of her belly fill with nervousness.

Liam stood, and the teachers turned their attention to him as though he were a god. "I guess my only question is, do you have any charts or graphs that show how this testing will actually benefit my students in their lives? How do these tests measure their actual abilities as people that we will be releasing into society someday?"

Several teachers whispered in agreement, and a couple actually clapped.

"Well, I understand your question and obvious concern. Testing provides information that can eventually lead to better teaching. It gives us a good gauge on where we are as teachers and about areas we can improve on," Rachel tried to explain just as Megan raised her arm.

"Yes, Megan?"

Liam remained standing as Megan stood, fixing her skirt along the way.

"I have to agree with Liam on this and would also like to add that I feel this testing puts pressure on us as teachers and isn't an accurate gauge on how we are teaching our kids. What about children that don't perform well on these stupid things but are amazing in class? I don't see why we are having to focus more of our valuable teaching time on figuring out how to better prepare them for being tested." Megan's tone grew angrier as she stared Rachel down.

Readying herself for a confrontation, Rachel bit her lip, seething with annoyance just at the sight of Megan.

Another teacher raised her hand and softly commented that while she understood the importance of testing to a point, she felt this over preparation was a bit daunting and conflicted too much with the regular curriculum.

Rachel listened to her, but the gears in her head were already turning. "I understand your concerns, and they are valid. However, this is the game plan we are going to try," Rachel said. "Also, I want to add that we will be sending home weekly progress reports on each student to their parents. I expect these reports to be signed by parents and returned to me."

Surprised faces stared back at her.

Liam squared his broad shoulders, his stance firm. "Wait, what? Why are we going to be doing that?"

"Because we need to get the parents on board as well if we are going to make our goals. It's that simple."

Liam let out a deep breath of irritation. "I think these requests are ridiculous. Mr. Anderson allowed the teachers to actually teach, Rachel. Mr. Anderson–"

"I am not Mr. Anderson. The sooner you realize that, the better, Liam."

Several people shook their heads and offered Liam a sympathetic look.

*Oh good grief.* Of course they were on his side. Everyone always was. But frankly, Rachel had had enough.

Karen stood up before she had a mutiny on her hands. "Okay, everybody, pipe down," she said, sounding like a protective mother. "Honestly, you're acting like Rachel personally created testing, for Pete's sake. I know you all went into teaching because you want to help these little people grow and learn all the amazing things the world has to offer, and that is why you are so valuable and important. But Rachel is important too. She is here to make sure we can continue to have a school for you to teach at. She is here to help us show how talented our students and staff are. That is her only agenda."

The teachers stopped murmuring, and Rachel appreciated how quickly Karen was able to get them to see reason. But Liam was still glaring at her.

"I want you all to know that Karen is right," Rachel went on. "I think you are fantastic educators and that your students are incredible and have so much potential to succeed. I only want our school to show the state we are providing the quality education I know our kids are receiving. I know we can do better."

Some of the teachers nodded, but most picked up their handouts and quietly exited the room as soon as Rachel ended the meeting.

*** 

Rachel felt completely worn out upon returning home that night. She was sprawled out on her couch, snuggling against a throw pillow while reading a book when her cell phone let out a chirp.

"Hello?" she answered.

"Hi, Rachel, how's it going for my favorite bestie?" Chelsea bubbled on the other end.

"Hey. It's going."

"That doesn't sound good. So what's going on? I haven't heard from you all week."

Rachel sighed. "I don't know. I'm dealing with a lot of opposition from the staff regarding some stuff I'm trying to have them do in order for us to score better on the state tests. But we need to make these changes so we can show the state how well we're doing and bring in more money from them. You know how I am; I want to succeed."

"Um, and they're aware you're their boss, right?"

Leave it to Chelsea to always be in Rachel's corner. That was one of the reasons Rachel loved her so much. She wished she lived near her again so they could be hang out over a bottle of wine after the week she'd had.

"I mean, they're allowed to disagree; I'm not a dictator. I think what bothers me the most, to be honest, is Liam. He pretty much spearheaded the whole opposition today."

"Oh, so the problem is actually him. I could give you some suggestions on how to get him to see things your way," Chelsea teased.

"Good one. Yeah, right now, I'm more worried about killing him than jumping his bones."

Chelsea's loud laughter vibrated through Rachel's ear, causing her to pull the phone away.

"Yeah, but it might shut him up at least," Chelsea said when she calmed down.

"Hey, whose side are you on here? I don't want to reward him, Chelsea."

"Always on yours, but I'm just saying there is some serious tension between you guys."

"I know. We actually sat down and discussed it. We both realize it can't go anywhere, especially with me being his boss and just the whole fact that I didn't come up here to get involved with anyone," Rachel explained, partially trying to convince herself.

"Whatever you say."

"I'm serious."

Chelsea sighed. "Oh, if only I were in your position. Lots of role-playing ideas are popping into my head right now."

"I can only imagine." Rachel laughed and tried to toss the idea out of her mind, not wanting to picture Chelsea having anything to do with Liam.

They talked for a little while longer before hanging up. Feeling better after hearing her friend's voice, Rachel repositioned herself on the couch and started reading again. This time she was able to focus.

***

## Liam

Liam spent the evening lounging in his recliner before the fire, sipping on a whiskey and cola as he started the new mystery novel he'd grabbed from the grocery store on the way home from work. The meeting this afternoon really didn't sit well with him. He wasn't trying to turn it into a three-ring circus, but hearing Rachel go on and on about all these new requirements they were going to put the kids and the teachers through rubbed him the wrong way.

His phone shattered the silence. "Hello?" he answered as he looked at his watch, unsure of how much time had passed since he'd eased into his comfortable recliner.

"Hello, sweetheart." Mary's cheery voice sent warmth across the frozen telephone lines.

"Hi, Mom."

"What's the matter, dear? You don't sound too happy," Mary said, sounding concerned.

Liam swallowed another sip of his cocktail. "I'm fine. It was just an extremely long day at work."

"Oh, well, it's the weekend, love. Don't bother your mind with work on your time off."

"Hey, Mom, how about you and me go to Herrick's tomorrow for a little breakfast?" Liam suddenly felt the need to be near his mother. She had an uncanny ability to make anyone feel secure and loved. He also wanted to see if she had any ideas on how to deal with this whole matter at the school.

"Why, son, I would love that. Just you and me, how lovely. Is it okay if I meet you there? I have some shopping to tend to tomorrow."

"Sure," Liam said.

They chatted for a while longer, then confirmed their meetup time and said good night.

Liam swirled his small glass of melted-down ice cubes, which clinked together as they further diluted the now-watered-down drink. As he finished it, Liam decided to turn in for the night. He was looking forward to his visit with his mother tomorrow, but he hoped her newfound friendship with his current enemy wasn't going to sway her to side with Rachel.

Liam shooed away the thought. He was her son, after all, and besides, he'd offered to take her to breakfast, so that had to earn him some extra points.

# *Chapter Thirteen*

### Rachel

Rachel stared out the sliding-glass door that led to her backyard. Outside, several wild turkeys were pecking at the frosty grass. She snapped a couple pictures to send to Chelsea. She still was amazed, and a bit frightened, every time she had a little run-in with some of the Birch Valley wildlife.

Feeling adventurous, she decided to bundle up and go explore the shops on Main Street. She figured she deserved a little retail therapy for surviving over a month at her new job and after all the grief she'd taken on Friday from the teachers.

Rachel planned to have breakfast at Herrick's, then walk up the street to burn off her meal and check out the shops. She had struggled to squeeze into a pair of her favorite jeans the other day and hoped spring would get here soon so she could start jogging around the wooded park across from her home. She could only imagine the lecture she would get from Chelsea about her plumping up.

Walking inside the already-full diner, Rachel scanned the room for an empty booth. She had brought a book and wanted to escape into her coffee and possibly some waffles. She passed several customers, who nodded and smiled politely at her, and a waitress she remembered seeing the last time she came in greeted her warmly.

Then she saw Liam. He was seated at a booth facing the direction she was walking in. He locked eyes with her, then quickly looked down at his breakfast as Rachel tried to sneak past.

"Rachel, dear, good morning!" Mary's lovely voice exclaimed.

Rachel stopped walking, turned, and smiled down at her. "Good morning, Mary. Liam."

"Coming in for a bite of breakfast, are we?" Mary asked as she slid closer to the window. "Please join us, won't you?" she asked before Rachel could respond.

"That's okay. I can see you're enjoying a nice breakfast with your son."

"Oh, heavens, and now you can enjoy one with us too." Mary smiled and eyed Liam, who nodded.

As Mary wasn't exactly giving her the option to decline the invitation, Rachel sat down next to her.

"So what were you thinking of ordering, my dear?" Mary asked as she waved down the waitress who had greeted Rachel. "My treat," she whispered to Rachel.

Liam looked up disapprovingly, but Mary ignored him.

What Rachel really wanted was one of Herrick's amazing coffees, a giant cinnamon roll or waffles, and some quiet time to read. But because that wasn't going to happen, she ordered coffee and a small bowl of fruit.

"Are you sure that's all you want? The waffles are quite wonderful here, aren't they, Liam?" Mary said.

"Pretty wonderful," he replied, grabbing his coffee mug. He clearly wasn't too thrilled with his mother right now.

"I think I'll pass this time, but thank you, Mary."

Rachel was adding cream to her coffee when her cell phone chirped with a message. Being the inquisitive woman she was, Mary didn't hesitate to ask who was contacting her. She and Liam both looked surprised when Rachel told them it was Maggie.

"Yeah, Maggie and I really hit it off when I came over to cook with you, Mary. She's terrific. I'm so glad you introduced us," Rachel said, avoiding Liam's glare.

"That's so nice. I'm glad you two got along so well. Rachel, do you mind letting me out? I need to visit the little girl's room."

Rachel quickly got up to let Mary out, then watched as Mary weaved her way through the maze of tables before she sat back down.

"I'm really sorry," she said softly.

"No, it's fine. She means well," Liam answered.

Rachel's fruit bowl arrived. It was a sad assortment of grapes, cantaloupe, and pineapple in a tiny plastic bowl. She regretted not ordering the waffles.

"You really should have gotten the waffles,"

Liam said with a smirk, echoing her thoughts, before forking a bite of waffle drenched in pure maple syrup into his mouth. Rachel wasn't sure which she was lusting after more, the sexy mouth the waffles were entering or the golden bread covered in pure sugar.

Rachel popped a grape into her mouth out of spite. "The fruit bowl is fine."

Mary had been gone for quite a while, or so it seemed, and the uncomfortable silence was killing both of them.

Liam was the first to speak again. "So about yesterday."

Rachel put her hand up. "Nope, I don't even want to go there with you right now."

"How do you figure that's fair?" Liam said as his brow wrinkled.

Rachel didn't want to get into a fight with him, especially when his mother would be returning to the table at any moment. "I'm not saying it is or isn't. What I'm saying is that I refuse to get into a full-blown argument with you, especially here, and especially in front of your mother." Rachel glanced at her delicate silver watch. Where was Mary?

"Well, for the record, it isn't fair, and you may call the shots at work, but you don't get to here," Liam snapped as he grabbed his mug and turned his gorgeous eyes toward the window.

"You know, maybe I should go and check on her," Rachel offered, looking for any excuse to get away from him. But as she was about to stand, she caught sight of Mary heading toward them, a large smile perched on her soft, round face.

"Sorry I took so long. I went ahead and paid for breakfast because I just realized I better get started on my errands before it gets too late. I need to get lunch going for Grandpa Paddy and your father before too long," Mary announced. She bent down to kiss Liam and whispered, loud enough for Rachel to hear, "Be nice."

Then she leaned over to Rachel and whispered, "You two get along. Also, I went ahead and ordered you a couple waffles." She smiled as she strutted past them, leaving them gaping in surprise.

Rachel was considering getting up to leave when their waitress placed a plate of steaming-hot waffles in front of her.

*Oh darn you, Mary O'Brien*, Rachel's brain screeched as she stared at the perfection before her.

The two were quite a pair as they ate in silence, sharing furtive, uncomfortable glances when they thought the other wasn't looking. Somehow they managed to finish their food. Liam had choked his down first and very well could have left Rachel in peace to finish hers, but he either wanted to her to suffer as he had or he wanted to be a gentleman and not leave her unattended. Rachel wasn't really quite sure. As soon as she thought she had him figured out, he would turn the tables. One moment he seemed to desire her, and the next he was downright annoyed by her very presence.

\*\*\*

## Liam

Liam chewed his last bite of waffle slowly and carefully, unsure of his next move. He knew that if anyone saw him leave, they would quickly form opinions about his departure, whether they were accurate or not. He also was drawn to the complicated creature in front of him. Her eyes were the exact same color as the lake on his property when the evening light danced across the surface: a shiny, silvery blue, deep and mysterious.

He watched as she placed her napkin on the plate, indicating she was done. He withdrew his wallet and left several dollar bills on the table for a tip, then they both got up quietly, and Liam allowed her to lead the way out.

Rachel had parked a couple cars away from his and seemed a bit stunned when he continued walking with her. She quickened her pace, which was no match for his long legs. When she reached her car, she turned, placed her hands firmly on her small hips, and cocked her head to the side as she pressed her tongue against the inside of her cheek in annoyance. Seeing her so agitated only fueled his desire.

"What do you want?" Rachel snapped.

"I was thinking it's still early, so how would you like to make a day of it? I could show you around town," Liam suggested as he inched closer to her, causing her to back up against her BMW.

Rachel inhaled deeply as she moved her hands off her hips and shoved them in her soft gloves. He only moved in more, looking down at her. Sighing,

Rachel pressed a gloved hand slightly against his stomach, and he nearly moaned as her fingers seemed to feel the muscles beneath all his layers of clothing.

"You have no idea what you do to me," he groaned into her ear. Seizing the moment, he leaned in and placed his lips on hers. As he kissed her, electricity seemed to race from his mouth straight to his toes. It drove him to push the kiss further until the rumble of a passing logging truck brought him back to reality.

"Wow," Rachel murmured.

"Now you cannot tell me that you don't feel it," Liam said, his voice husky as he fought to keep from kissing her again.

"God, Liam, we just can't. But yes, I won't deny there is chemistry here."

Liam only stared at her. "Please, let's spend the day together. Let's just see if this tension disappears when we're hanging out."

He was trying to be cautious. He knew if he pushed her too fast or too hard, she would fly away. Having her backed up against the car, he was already leaving her with little room to think.

"Oh Liam. It's so complicated. But what if we did, for the sake of an experiment, 'hang out' together? I'd love to see the town. I have only really visited a couple shops, mainly the grocery store."

She was rambling. To calm her, Liam leaned in and planted a soft kiss on her forehead. "I think we should, then," he said.

"Okay, when?"

Liam smiled. "Now."

"Um, I guess so." Rachel bit down on her lip, looking rather unsure about what she had just agreed to.

"Great. Want to take my truck?" Liam offered.

Rachel hesitated for moment, looking nervous. Feeling her discomfort, he suggested, "How about we walk?" He took her by the elbow lightly and led her in the direction of Main Street.

\*\*\*

### Rachel

They visited practically every shop along Main Street, and Rachel couldn't recall the last time she'd had such a great afternoon, especially with a guy. As they enjoyed all the wonders each store carried and the charm of the business-lined street, she wasn't at all surprised by all the waves and greetings Liam received. He flashed his kind, boyish smile at everyone they passed, then looked at her and give her a sexy grin that she knew was only for her.

Liam was the perfect tour guide, answering her endless questions and trying to point out anything she might find interesting. He knew everything there was to know about each place they visited, and Rachel learned so much about the town as the afternoon wore on. She supposed it helped that he was born and raised in this adorable community.

Soon enough, white flakes drifted down onto them and the sidewalk. They ducked inside a small coffee shop, and Liam suggested they have some hot chocolate to warm her up. While he ordered for them, Rachel found a small table in the corner and took in her surroundings. The room was dark and romantic, and the wooden floors and walls smelled of rich history and age. Closing her eyes, she could almost imagine the people who must have walked these same floors, not just in this building but in all the buildings she had visited today.

Although she could feel the past around her, some of the merchants had definitely breathed new life into these old, presumably haunted buildings. Along with pointing out each sight on their tour, Liam had shared every last bit of folklore, town gossip, and actual history he could recall about each property. Rachel's head spun with all the tales, but she devoured the information and the way his words floated off his tongue. Light sparkled in his eyes as he spoke from his soul about his memories of growing up in Birch Valley.

At one point Rachel felt a tad envious. His life here seemed so storybook as he told her about running barefoot in the summer to get ice cream at one of the shops they had visited earlier, or kissing his first girlfriend in the small movie theater with the antique marquee. Rachel couldn't recall feeling such attachment to any one place in particular in her own life, except for the ocean. She loved the ocean, but she didn't relish the fact that it had been the only constant in her life, whereas Liam had been raised by these people, the shops, and the tree-lined streets of Birch Valley.

\*\*\*

## Liam

Liam watched Rachel as he waited for their order. Her eyes were closed, and she almost looked as though she was praying. He hoped she had enjoyed their day together as much as he had. He'd known he was taking a gamble when he asked to spend time with her. For all he knew, they could have spent the day bickering and fighting, or in their constant tug of war for power.

During their time together, he'd learned she wasn't like the stereotypical Californian. She had many facets, and each one created new feelings inside of him. Liam had never felt a connection like this with anyone before. They were barely getting to actually know each other, yet he felt as though he already knew all the dark corners where her secrets lay hidden. He understood so much more about Rachel just by watching her reactions to the things she saw and listening to the questions she asked. The more she spoke, the more he decided he loved her voice, loved the way the pitch and tone would change depending on what her beautiful eyes saw. She seemed so intrigued by his world, which bewildered him, considering how vastly different her former home had been.

The barista called out their order, and Liam balanced two small hot chocolates and an enormous huckleberry scone as he made his way back to their table. He was greeted by a thankful smile from Rachel as she reached out for the warm drink topped with a floating dollop of whipped cream and chocolate shavings.

"This looks amazing," she said before she took the first sip. When she moved the mug away, a small piece of whipped cream clung to her nose.

"As cliché as this sounds, you have a little something on your nose. Here, let me get it," Liam said as he gingerly used the tip of his finger to wipe it away.

Rachel's cheeks turned a shade of rose. "Thanks."

"Have you eaten huckleberries before?" Liam asked as he split the large, sugar-encrusted scone. "They grow in the Pacific Northwest typically, and everyone here pretty much considers them gold. For example, if you find a great picking spot, you don't ever tell anyone—well, except for me. You can tell me." Liam gave her a playful grin.

"Good to know. I will have to keep that in mind. Maybe we can go picking together."

"I'd love to take you. We tend to go in late spring to try to get them before the grizzly bears do."

"Um, excuse me. So there are bears when you guys go picking?" Rachel's eyes went wide, and Liam could see fear flicker behind them.

"Well, yeah, but they're usually still hibernating. They love morel mushrooms too, and those are awesome. They cost a fortune in the stores, but here, if you know where to go, you can pick them." He motioned all around with the long span of his arms.

"Like where?"

"Well, like in the hills and mountains, certain spots," he whispered.

"So top-secret locations, then?" Rachel leaned in closer.

Liam leaned in to meet her. "Very top secret." He kissed her again, and the current shot through him.

As they both pulled away, Liam knew there would be no more denying their attraction.

They watched the snow as it fell, lost in their own thoughts. When they finished their afternoon snack, Liam suggested they head back to the diner to get their cars. He held the door open for her, and as they walked side by side down the sidewalk, he reached for her gloved hand. Rachel allowed the simple gesture for a moment, then pulled away and tugged her coat tightly around her, like a toddler gripping a security blanket. Liam felt them exiting the dream world they had played in most of the day. The farther they walked from Main Street, the more Rachel seemed to distance herself.

When they reached their cars, Liam waited for her to get inside and pull away. The joy he'd felt all day dampened as he got into his truck and sat for a while to reflect.

# *Chapter Fourteen*

### Rachel

Rachel was busy going through her first month of new bills when her phone rang.

"Hello?" she answered.

"Hey, lady, how's it going? I hope you're doing better than you were on Friday. I know you go back tomorrow to face the mob," Chelsea said.

"God, Chelsea, I wanted to call you so bad yesterday, but I needed to process some stuff." Rachel pushed her stack of bills aside and closed her laptop.

"Okay, so what's up?" Chelsea stretched out each word.

Rachel sighed. "I don't even know where to begin. I feel like I kind of screwed up."

"Well, does any of this have to do with that yummy teacher?"

"You are not helping. But yes, it does," Rachel replied as she started to doodle on an empty, used envelope.

"Details, Rachel! Details!"

"Okay, well, yesterday, I decided to go to breakfast at that little diner I told you about. They have, like, the best coffee, and their waffles are heavenly."

"Wait, you ate carbs?"

"Yes, but you're missing the point here. I am setting the scene for you." Rachel then went into detail about running into Liam and his mother and how Mary had kind of set them both up, and how she ultimately hadn't minded that, especially when she and Liam had shared that remarkable kiss.

"I'm so having a hard time understanding the dilemma here. You got to lock lips with Liam, who sounds like he knows what's up. I like him."

"The problem is that we did share a fantastic day together, and I felt so...I don't know."

"You felt like a normal, happy woman who is possibly meeting a really nice but also hot guy, who sounds like he can light your fire just by looking at you. Pretty plain and simple, really," Chelsea said matter-of-factly.

"Ugh, it's so frustrating because, yes, he could totally be great boyfriend material. Hell, maybe, even husband material. But the problem is, again, I'm his boss, and I didn't want anything like this."

"I know you've been fighting wanting to date or do anything that remotely involves a potential relationship. But I don't understand what you are so scared of," Chelsea said firmly.

"The whole work ethic issue is a problem, an enormous problem. This could cost me my job, Chelsea. And you know very well why I shy away from dating." Rachel pressed her pen firmly against the envelope, and her frustrated doodles left hard indentations on the paper.

"Well, if you don't plan on doing anything about this relationship, then you need to stop the lip-locking, because you're sending this poor guy mixed signals. End of story. As for why you don't want to date, come on. It's been almost two years, Rachel."

Rachel agreed. That was why she had tried creating an action plan with Liam, keeping distance between them, but then she'd let her guard down and seen how great of guy he was. And she enjoyed the lip-locking. No one had ever kissed her like that. She could only imagine what it would be like if they went further than kissing. Images of nude bodies, twisted sheets, and cuddling seared her mind. She really shouldn't go there.

Chelsea and Rachel soon got off the topic of Liam as they discussed Chelsea coming to visit Birch Valley at the end of March or during spring break. Chelsea was anxious to see this little hole-in-the-wall town and get a good look at this Liam. After saying good-bye, Rachel tried to convince herself to go back to paying her bills, but she couldn't concentrate on them. All she could think about was the pressure of Liam's lips on hers and how much she wanted to feel it again. Oh dear Lord, she was in trouble.

\*\*\*

## Liam

After dinner on Sunday, Daniel and Patrick retreated quickly from the table, leaving Liam to assist with the cleanup.

"Liam, how did breakfast go yesterday?" Mary asked with a mischievous grin as Liam carried a stack of dirty dishes to the sink where she stood rinsing silverware before placing it into the dishwasher. She wouldn't meet Liam's eyes.

"Yeah, thanks a lot for that, Mom," Liam said as he leaned against the counter. "Breakfast itself was awkward, but I did end up showing her around Main Street."

Mary's eyebrows lifted in surprise. "Really? Well, that was awfully sweet of you, son. How did that go?"

"It was okay. She really seems to like our town."

"So just okay, huh?"

"Yes, Mom," he said, knowing she was probing for more details. "We had a nice time, and then it started snowing, and she was ready to call it a day." He didn't feel the need to go into it any further. He didn't want to have to explain the kiss, the light touches they'd given each other throughout their walk, or the fact she'd grown distant and cold toward the end. He was still trying to sort it out himself.

"I was thinking of inviting Rachel over the next time Maggie visits. I'm so glad the two of them hit it off. Rachel sure seems like she could use a friend, and, well, to be honest, so does your sister." Mary's voice grew quiet as she mentioned her daughter.

"How is Maggie doing? I talked to her last week, and she seemed okay."

"She's fine, I suppose. But something seemed a tad off when we spoke the other day. She was telling me how much Michael has been working, and then she said he's been begging for them to have another child."

"She doesn't want more kids? I'm surprised they don't have more. Melanie is already six," Liam said thoughtfully.

"Well, I think it's a little more complicated than that, Liam. Of course she would love to have more children, but I think she would also like Michael to be in their lives. He's hardly around now as it is for Melanie. So Maggie isn't so sure bringing another baby into the mix is what they need right now."

"I guess you're right. I bet Melanie would love a playmate, though. She would make such a great big sister." Liam adored Melanie and hoped if he were to ever have a daughter that she would be as sweet, bright, and loving as that little girl.

"I know she would. But being a mom is a hard job. When I had you kids, I had your father around to help. Granted, he worked, but it was just up the road, and he always found time to be here, especially for important things, like when you guys played little league or when Maggie took ballet. Michael, unfortunately, isn't able to quite pull himself away as easily. He misses a lot, apparently," Mary explained as she continued rinsing the dishes with warm, soapy water and placing them neatly into the dishwasher.

"Well, someday, when I become a father, I hope

to be a lot like Dad, and you're right, he was there for everything. Still is," Liam commented, remembering all the events in his life that his father had been a part of. Pat and Grandpa Paddy had helped shape him into the man he was today.

"I hope you start considering the idea of settling down soon. I could use a grandchild from you," Mary teased.

"You're more likely to get one from Maggie and Michael. I need to meet someone first, Mom. Isn't that usually how it works?"

Mary splashed a little of the soapy water onto Liam. "Well, I could think of a possible prospect. Or, son, there is always the mail-order bride option."

"Good grief. But going back to Maggie, I think it would be cool if they had another kid. I know Michael would love it, and maybe he'd try harder to be there for his family if they did."

"I know Michael wants to be there. I see how much he adores both Maggie and Melanie, and maybe, in a little while, after he makes partner, they can have another baby," Mary said.

Seeing that the cleanup was mostly finished, Liam bent down and gave his mother a peck on the cheek. "Thanks for dinner, Mom. I better be heading home."

Liam said good-bye to the rest of his family and saw Patrick getting ready to load his sons into his car. "You want some help with those kiddos?" he asked.

"Sure, thanks," Patrick said, handing Liam one of the sleeping twins. Each man then headed outside, cradling a heavy toddler.

After they buckled each child into their car seat, Patrick turned to Liam and thanked him.

"So Mom says you had breakfast with Rachel. How did that go?" he then asked, leaning against his car.

"God, you too?" Liam laughed. "Mom just hit me up for details when I got stuck helping with dishes. It went okay, but yeah, Mom completely ditched me yesterday after she invited Rachel to join us."

"Well, I'm sure she meant no harm. Plus, Rachel's not bad-looking. I could think of a lot worse people to share breakfast with."

"Yeah, but we had this meeting on Friday, and suffice to say, we don't see eye to eye," Liam explained.

Patrick nodded. "Yeah, but you have to admit there's some chemistry between you and Rachel for sure."

"I feel like there might be some. Yesterday, we went around to all the shops on Main Street and had a great time. I'm starting to really like her, and she seems like she's into me too. But then, it's so weird, she starts pulling away and getting all distant."

"So what I'm hearing is that nothing official is going on between you," Patrick said.

"Why, are you interested?" Liam teased.

Patrick rolled his eyes and shook his head, "No. I mean, she's pretty enough and seems very sweet, but when you two are in the room, it's filled with tension. It's like you both are doing this little dance, and honestly, we're all a little surprised you guys haven't gotten together yet."

"Well, don't go blabbing this to the rest of the family, but we have kissed a couple of times. I kind of started it, though, but she didn't pull away or slap me. But it was so strange how different kissing her felt compared to other girls, you know?"

Patrick's expression grew thoughtful. "You know, it was like that with Beth. Something about her just turned me inside out." His voice had a tremor in it. Patrick didn't discuss Beth too often. Even after three years, the pain was still too close to the surface.

"So what do I do?"

"Honestly, I'd say how you feel. I mean, have you told her?" Patrick looked through the rear window of the car to see if the boys were stirring.

"We both have talked about it in a roundabout way. It's just that with her being my boss and everything, she's all freaked out by the idea of seeing where it goes. She also said she didn't move up here to get involved, so I sort of took that as her not being interested."

"I can see her concern there. Well, I'm sure you guys will figure it out. I better get these boys home now. Good seeing you, and if you ever need to talk, I'm here," Patrick offered as he opened the driver's-side door and got in.

"Same goes for you, man, if you ever want to talk."

Patrick smiled and looked down. "Have a good night, Liam." He closed the door and started the car.

Liam got into his truck and headed home. The roads were a little slick, and he could see a sheen of ice on them beneath his headlights. Although Liam didn't care for these cold temperatures, he was also grateful it hadn't snowed all day.

\*\*\*

### Rachel

When Rachel woke up Monday morning, everything was frozen solid. The snow that fell over the weekend was now hardened and ugly. But the sun had started to peer out from behind the clouds, tempting everyone with its elusive warmth.

Inside, though, chilly air dominated the house. Reluctantly departing from the warmth of her bed, Rachel grabbed a sweater and went to make coffee. As she turned on the faucet to fill her coffeepot, Rachel frowned in confusion when no water came out. She turned the knob again and again. Nothing. She grabbed both the hot and cold knobs and twisted them frantically. Again nothing. Not a single drop.

Rachel sprinted to the bathroom and worked the knobs on the sink and the shower, and again no water appeared. Panic started to set in as she paced for a moment. She had to be at work in an hour and didn't know what to do or whom to call. Maybe she could catch Karen if she hadn't left for work yet. Or what about Mary? Maybe if there was an issue with her plumbing, she could send Patrick or Daniel over. Eyeing the clock on her microwave, she decided Mary was probably her best bet.

"Hello?" Mary answered in a cheery voice after

picking up on the second ring.

"Good morning, Mary. It's me, Rachel."

"Oh, hello, dear. Everything all right? You sound a bit upset."

"Actually, I don't know what's going on. I went to fill my coffeepot this morning, and literally nothing came out. I tried the bathroom sink and the shower, and I just don't understand why it isn't working." Rachel looked at the clock again as her anxiety started to spiral out of control.

"Oh no. I bet your pipes froze last night. It was downright frigid, so I bet that is what happened. I actually cracked mine before I went to bed," Mary said in her usual kind tone.

"Cracked?"

"Yes, that's when you turn the handle and leave just a trickle of water running. Keeps the pipes from getting frozen," Mary explained.

"I see. Well, I had no clue. So now what do I do?" Rachel asked, her patience running thin. The phone beeped, indicating another call was coming through. "Hey, Mary, I have another call on the other line. Can I call you back?"

"Sure, dear."

Switching to the other line and hanging up with Mary, Rachel let out a huge breath. "Hello?" she answered roughly.

"Hi, Rachel, it's Liam."

"Oh, I was just on the phone with your mom. I think my pipes might have frozen," Rachel groaned.

"That's why I'm calling. Apparently, you aren't the only one. The school's partially froze too, and one of the boilers went out. Karen called and said we're going to have to cancel class today. I offered to call you."

"Wow, really? Okay, okay, um, so what do we do?" Rachel tried to contain her racing thoughts. She wasn't prepared for this. She hadn't encountered a problem like this back at her old school.

"It's really going to be fine, Rachel. So here's the plan. Karen has already put the message out to the parents and staff. This has happened before, so it's not our first time at the rodeo," Liam soothed.

"Well, it's my first time. How do we fix this?" she snapped.

"All right, try and calm down. I'll call my brothers, and we can come over and take a look at your pipes, okay?" Liam's voice was cool and relaxed, which only annoyed Rachel more.

"I don't understand why you aren't a little more worried."

"Because this kind of stuff happens here. It isn't a big deal. Yeah, it might be a pain, but it sure isn't the end of the world." She could hear the smile in his voice. "How about you go over to my mom's place? My brothers and I can see what's going on at your house. We got a crew coming out to the school to work on the problems there."

Rachel inhaled deeply as she calmed herself. "I don't want to be a bother to your mom, Liam."

"She would probably enjoy the company, especially yours."

"I don't know," she said hesitantly.

"I'll give her a call. I know she'd want you to come over. She might make you learn some more cooking, though. Not sure if you're up for that," Liam teased.

Rachel smiled at the thought of getting another lesson in the culinary arts. She'd had such a great time being in Mary's kitchen. "Okay, I guess that's fine. But only if I'm not interrupting any plans that she might have."

"You won't be, I promise. Well, how about I give you a call back in a little bit. Sound good?"

"That works. Liam, thank you," she said softly.

"No problem, Rachel," Liam answered before hanging up.

Rachel couldn't get over how calm Liam and Mary were acting about this whole thing. She recalled during their outing that Liam had told her that people often referred to this area as God's country and you had to be made of some pretty tough stuff to survive here. She was starting to wonder if she was up to the challenge.

*** 

Every pound of Mary O'Brien radiated joy when she opened the door for Rachel to come in.

"I'm so glad Liam had you come over. So sorry about your pipes, but my boys will get you all fixed up, so please don't worry, dear," Mary said as she ushered Rachel inside.

"I hate to bother you on such short notice," Rachel apologized as she hung up her coat.

"Bother me? Honestly, I'm thankful for the company." Mary swatted gently at her.

"Well, I do love spending time with you, so it's

equally a treat for me."

Mary smiled. "Why don't we start with a cup of tea."

As the women migrated to the kitchen, Mary explained what they would be making today. She said she was going to take advantage of having Rachel there so they could do some practice runs for the bake sale.

Rachel pushed up her sleeves and got about wrist deep in dough. As she worked the mixture, letting the cool combination of ingredients squish between her fingers, she felt the stress melt away. *This must be why Mary was so calm and collected all the time*, she thought.

***

After Liam called Mary to say he and his brothers had fixed Rachel's pipes, Rachel hugged Mary good-bye and thanked her for a positively lovely day. She left cradling a warm Dutch apple pie she'd helped create and drove home feeling warm and happy. As she turned onto her street, she found Liam's pickup parked in front of her house.

As she grabbed her purse and stepped out of her car, Rachel noticed her neighbor was outside. "Hello, Sue-Ellen," she said as she waved at the older woman with her free hand.

"Why hello there, Rachel. I saw the O'Brien boys here earlier. Heard your pipes froze. Sure was colder than heck last night."

"Yes, I really appreciate the guys helping me out. Looks like Liam is still here." Rachel nodded toward the truck.

"Yeah, he stopped by here to see if we were all right. Such a nice boy. Always has been such a sweetheart. His brothers left a few minutes before you pulled in," Sue-Ellen explained. "Well, it isn't getting any warmer, so I think I will be heading back inside. So nice to run into you, dear."

Rachel watched Sue-Ellen waddled back to her home before heading to her door. Liam must have heard her coming, because he stepped out before she could grab her key.

"Good, you're home," he said with one of his sexy grins.

Heat started to simmer in her belly. It didn't matter what the man said or did. Everything about Liam stirred her up.

"Sue-Ellen said your brothers just left." Rachel frowned with disappointment.

"Well, don't look so happy to see me," Liam teased as he moved out of the doorframe he was filling to let her in.

"Thank you so much for everything," Rachel said, dropping her purse on an empty chair before going to put the pie on the kitchen counter. As soon as she did, she lightly smacked herself on the forehead. "How rude of me! Liam, did your brothers say how much it cost to repair the pipes?"

"They said no charge. Take care, and it looks like it might be cold again tonight, so keep the handle turned a bit to let some water run," Liam said as he let himself out of her home. As Rachel stood facing her front door, she instantly felt his absence.

When she got ready for bed, she made sure to do what he suggested. She was now paranoid about her pipes freezing.

# *Chapter Fifteen*

The cold snap that had taken hold of Birch Valley finally loosened its grasp on the sleepy town. The weeks that followed Rachel's frozen-pipes nightmare went by quietly, except for the fact that every teacher but two were turning in the progress reports she'd requested. Rachel groaned at the thought of having to confront Liam and Megan. Liam's reasons for refusing to participate were obvious, and it was crystal clear why Megan decided to followed suit.

As if that wasn't enough, Valentine's Day was rearing its ugly head again, and the school seemed to go all-out for the holiday, so there was no escaping all the red and pink. Everything seemed to be plastered with tiny hearts and mini cupids. Love was not only in the air, it was leaving its chocolate and rose stink everywhere. *Nothing like being reminded just how single you are*, Rachel thought.

Rachel entered the teachers' lounge one afternoon to find Megan flipping through a magazine intended for teenage girls. Rolling her eyes, Rachel cleared her throat. "Hi, Megan."

As Megan looked up from a glossy page filled with photos of new lipsticks and eyeliners, her face twitched with irritation. "Hello, Principal Rachel."

*Seriously, that's what we're calling me now?* Rachel thought in annoyance. She honestly couldn't stand the woman seated before her.

"Well, Teacher Megan," Rachel continued. *Two can play this game, sweetheart.*

Megan's eyes glimmered with an unspoken challenge.

Rachel smiled as she sat down next to Megan, who moments ago had looked ready to for a standoff. Now she just looked uncomfortable. *Good.* "I've been collecting progress reports for almost two weeks from the other staff, and I haven't received any from you," Rachel continued. "I was curious as to why."

Megan shifted uneasily in her chair, closing the magazine. "Because I haven't had a chance to turn them in, sorry," she said curtly.

"I see. Well, if you could please have those on my desk by the end of today, I would greatly appreciate it. I'll be meeting with the superintendent to discuss them, and I would hate to have to explain why yours are missing." Rachel's tone was thick and sweet as honey, and she was thrilled to be able to unnerve the woman beside her, whose dress was several sizes too small and exposing far too much of her ample cleavage.

"Also, I wanted to let you know about several dress code revisions. I'll be having Karen put the memo in your box. Thank you so much, Megan, and

I look forward to seeing those reports on my desk." Rachel smoothed the invisible wrinkles from her black dress slacks as she rose from the table.

The shocked look in Megan's eyes was priceless as she started to adjust the top portion of her dress, and it gave Rachel a little buzz. Rachel didn't like abusing her authority, but this woman had been taunting her since she arrived, and she'd had about as much as she could take.

As Rachel passed Karen's desk, she motioned for the secretary to follow her into her office. Once they were inside, Rachel closed the door.

"Oh my goodness, Karen. I have just about had it with that woman," Rachel said as she slid behind her large desk and flopped into her oversized chair.

Karen took a seat in front of Rachel and grinned. "What did you say to her?"

Rachel appreciated the fact she and Karen were so in sync that she didn't have to tell the secretary whom she was talking about. They both shared the same opinions about Megan and almost everything else.

"Well, apparently, you'll be drawing up a memo about the new dress code we will be enforcing here at the school." Rachel burst into laughter.

Karen's laugh followed. "Just so we are clear, does that mean no more skintight sweaters or dresses that cause me to fear what would happen if she bent over? I have been worried about one of those puppies falling out for so long. What if the kids saw it, could you imagine?"

"Pretty much. You should have seen her trying to pull her dress over her chest to cover up. Oh good grief. Also, she hasn't turned in any of those reports, so I told her I want them on my desk by the end of the day. She says she has them but has forgotten to give them to me. Baloney!"

"You know who else hasn't turned in any?" Karen's face grew serious.

"I know. But I know why he's doing it. She's just playing Simon Says—well, I guess Liam Says."

Karen shook her head. "Liam feels pretty strongly about the negative impact the reports will have on the kids."

"I know he does. I plan on having it out with him later. For now, I had to let off a little steam, and she just happened to be in the teachers' lounge. I promise I was only going in there for coffee." Rachel put on an innocent face.

"Sure. So Rachel, I have to ask, what's your beef with Valentine's Day?" Karen asked as she smoothed her satin floral skirt.

"I don't know. I could use the excuse that it's the whole commercialization of love and that greeting card companies, florists, and chocolate manufacturers are just raking it in due to the pressure society puts on people," Rachel ranted and waited to see how Karen would react. When the secretary's expression remained unchanged, she continued, "Or I could say I experienced a very— well, possibly the worst breakup of my whole dating career, and it happened on the so-called day of love."

"I figured it was something more like that, because come on, who doesn't love chocolate or flowers?" Karen teased.

Rachel couldn't help but laugh. "Quite true."

"Now this leads me to my next question. What's going on with you and Liam?"

*Boy, no pulling any punches here*, Rachel thought. Then she wondered if Mary had mentioned anything to Karen. "Nothing. I mean, I don't know."

Rachel almost felt like opening up about her feelings for Liam. The tornado of unexplained desire, pent-up frustration, and attraction to a man whom she wouldn't have even considered back in California was wreaking havoc inside her.

"Rachel, I see the way you both light up almost to the point of spontaneous combustion around each other," Karen said playfully, then became serious. "I know you're trying so hard to gain the respect of everyone here, and you're doing a great job as principal. I only wonder if exploring a relationship with someone, who in my humble opinion is one the finest men we have here in Birch Valley, would be something you are interested in doing."

Rachel shook her head and felt the air leaving her. "Nope, I think he's a great guy and comes from an amazing family, Karen, but I didn't come all this way to get involved with someone, let alone one of my teachers."

Karen stared at her, searching her eyes. "You'll come to your senses."

Rachel rolled her eyes and smiled. "I think I already have, and that's why I haven't started dating Mr. Liam O'Brien."

Karen smirked right back. "Well, I better get to that memo. You think about what I said. Someday,

Valentine's Day will be special to you again."

"Easy for you to say, you have a fantastic husband. But I won't say never," Rachel joked, thinking about how Karen's husband brought her flowers almost every other day to keep the vase on her desk full with fresh and bright bouquets that were the envy of almost every woman who passed by.

Karen left then, promising to bring the memo by in a little while to get Rachel's approval. Rachel then spun her chair around to look out her window. The sky was a faded blue with white and gray clouds smeared across it. She almost thought she heard the distant chirp of a bird, but with the terrible cold weather, she hadn't seen many signs of wildlife. When she'd gone to the grocery store a few days ago, Rachel had heard several clerks saying spring would come early this year. She hoped they were right. She was getting real tired of winter.

\*\*\*

## Liam

Liam stood in front of his class, showing them slides of presidents. In the middle of explaining the life of President Lincoln, the phone in his classroom rang, interrupting his lecture. He excused himself to answer it.

"Hello? Mr. O'Brien's room."

"Howdy, Liam," Karen said.

"Yes, Karen, how can I help you?" he asked

pleasantly, winking at one of his students.

"Well, I wanted to remind all the teachers that the progress reports are due this afternoon."

Liam swallowed. "About those, you and I both know why I'm not participating. I have no intentions of ever doing so."

"I know, but I'm making my calls to all the teachers. I don't know why you have to be so stubborn, Liam O'Brien," Karen teased.

"You know why. Anyhow, Karen, I need to get back to these kiddos before I lose them completely. Catch up with you later," Liam said before hanging up.

Clapping his hands together, he turned back to his students. "Where were we?"

\*\*\*

## Rachel

The bell chimed loudly, signaling the end of the day. Because it was Friday, the roar of the students was even louder as they moved through the halls. Rachel waved good-bye to the students and wished each one she passed a great weekend. At one point a small girl, who was probably in kindergarten, wrapped her arms around Rachel's waist and told her to have "the bestest weekend ever." The sentiment melted her heart. Kids were kind, selfless, and continued to surprise her.

Rachel watched the last bus pull away before she headed back to her office to finish up for the day. As she passed Karen's desk, she stopped to ask,

"Did any more reports get dropped off?"

"Yes, actually. Megan turned in an enormous stack, probably a couple weeks' worth."

"Wow, really? Well, that's good. Maybe our little chat scared some sense into her," Rachel said, grabbing the hefty stack of papers from Karen. "Any others?"

"Nope, and I called him too."

"I figured you would." Rachel's irritation soared as she took the reports to her office. She couldn't wrap her head around why Liam was being so stubborn about this new policy. She was even more annoyed that he thought he could get away with not turning any reports in. Well, she planned on changing that.

Feeling determined, she locked the front door to the empty school. Her school. She was going to have to hash this matter out with Liam. As she walked to her car, Rachel rehearsed what she planned on telling him. She needed to finally make him understand that he would follow protocol or face the consequences. Rachel felt strong and confident when she got into her car and dialed Liam's number, hushing any butterflies with a gulp of diet cola as she waited for him to pick up.

"Hello?"

"Liam, it's Rachel. I need to meet with you," she announced, trying to make her voice stable. *Cool and calm* was the mantra she kept reciting in her head.

"Okay, what about?" His annoyance was obvious.

"I think we both know what about."

"Good grief, about those reports?" he said with irritation.

"Liam, I want to discuss this matter and come up with some kind of solution. We can't keep sweeping this issue under the rug. Those reports are very important," Rachel said, trying to maintain her professionalism.

He sighed. "Well, we can discuss them on Monday."

Rachel didn't want to wait. She wanted this matter figured out now, because she knew he would only keep putting her off.

"I'm afraid that's not going to work, Liam. I'm headed over now." She didn't allow him to respond before hanging up.

Rachel punched Liam's address into her car's GPS system, which indicated he wasn't even five miles away. She knew he wouldn't expect her to arrive on his turf, but she needed to corner him and get him to understand that she'd had enough. As far as their feelings for each other were concerned, that issue was settled and buried. She had kept things professional and distant since their outing and assured herself that was the right call, especially when he defied her like this, making her look like a fool.

Sitting in her running car as the heater kicked in and began warming her up, Rachel decided to call Chelsea. *Getting her input might not be such a bad idea*, she reasoned as she dialed her friend's number.

"Hello?" Chelsea answered quickly, her voice perky.

"Hey, Chelsea, what are you up to right now?"

Chelsea grunted lightly. "Not really doing anything at the moment. I have a yoga class I'm going to in a little bit. Why, what's going on?"

"I wanted to get your opinion on something," Rachel said slowly, wondering now if calling her for advice had been wise. Now they were talking, she wasn't so sure Chelsea could relate to her situation or that she would know how to handle someone like Liam.

"I love to give my opinion, as you know," Chelsea said, her tone curious. "Where are you right now? Your phone sounds weird."

Rachel let out a huff. "I'm in my car, that's sort of what I need your help with," she answered as her mind started to race.

"Uh, like, if you have a car question, unless you need help deciding what color you look good in, I have no mechanical skills. Maybe go to the nearest Beamer dealership."

"No, it isn't anything like that. I'm in my car and going to drive over to Liam's. We need to have a serious talk."

"Oh, so you are headed over there. Finally going to get with him?" She could almost hear Chelsea smiling.

"God, no! He's still refusing to turn in those progress reports or do any of the testing curriculum I'm having the teachers do. Besides, nothing has changed," Rachel said sourly. "I don't want to get involved with him."

A nagging feeling tugged at her as she waited for her friend's response.

"Wait, so you are headed to his house right now?"

"Yeah, I figured we need to settle this."

"Oh Rachel, do you really think it's fair to be going to his home to have a fight about something work-related? I don't think that's a good idea."

Rachel considered her words for a moment. "What else should I do? I can't keep having him not comply. Besides, whose side are you on here?"

"Well, of course I'm always on your side. It's just that going to his house to reprimand him doesn't seem right. Imagine if your boss just showed up at your door and started giving you hell. Not cool, Rachel."

"Oh good grief, I'm not going over there to yell at him or anything."

Granted, anything was possible when the two of them were together.

"Well, you asked for my opinion, and there it is. I don't think you should go to his house unless you are finally coming to your senses about dating him. If that's the case, then I say get your ass over there!"

Rolling her eyes, Rachel muttered that she'd call Chelsea later before she hung up. She then steered her car out of the empty parking lot and weaved her way through the quiet neighborhoods of Birch Valley until she got onto the highway that led her out of the heart of town.

*\*\*\**

Doubt crept into the car with her and was her

only companion as she drove along the dark highway. The moon sat bright and high in the early evening sky, and the trees cast thin shadows on the desolate road. Rachel kept her eyes focused tightly on the asphalt ahead. The faded yellow lines that divided the single lanes were her only guide in the dark wilderness that surrounded her. The highway had no streetlamps or any other source of illumination besides her headlights. Even switching to her high beams didn't seem to pierce the darkness.

*Sure feels like a lot more than five miles.*

Her GPS beeped loudly and informed her to take a sharp turn ahead, and Rachel slowed her car to ease onto to the street. She drove slowly until she came to a marker with bronze numbers that confirmed the address. Rachel drove up a gravel driveway, listening as her tires crunched over the pebbles and hardened snow until she arrived at a cabin with several windows that emitted a soft glow in the murky blackness.

As she parked next to Liam's truck, she considered what she wanted to tell him. After completing some deep breathing exercises and trying to calm the wild adrenaline coursing through her veins, she unbuckled her seat belt. She needed to be concise and keep her cool. She didn't want to appear rattled or give Liam the upper hand. It was best to have a game plan when going into battle, and Rachel was sure this was only the beginning of a much larger war.

# *Chapter Sixteen*

Wood smoke blended with the crispness of the harsh air in a dance of scents Rachel still was not quite used to. Inhaling deeply, she trudged through the compacted snow on the walkway, trying to reassure herself that this was the best way to handle the problem with Liam. Reaching deep inside and searching for some kind of inner strength, she knocked, almost too hard, on the heavy wooden door. She heard movement, and then Liam's tall figure filled the doorway.

His hair was wet from showering, and he wore comfortable jeans, a sweatshirt with a sports logo on it, and thick socks. The lingering scents of soap and shampoo wafted from him, exciting her. He smelled amazing.

*Focus, Rachel.*

"To what do I owe this unexpected visit?" Liam smirked.

Rachel rolled her eyes. He knew full well why she was here. "Do you mind inviting me in? It's freezing out here," she snapped as her teeth chattered. She wrapped her arms tighter around her thin frame, desperately attempting to keep any more body heat from escaping.

Without speaking, he moved aside to let her in. As she entered, Rachel scanned the inside of Liam's home. A remarkable fireplace framed by river rocks proudly stood front and center in the living room with a crackling fire that was burning slowly inside it. Exposed wooden beams supported the vaulted ceilings. His leather recliners and large, plaid couch were masculine but cozy and inviting. The lighting from several side-table lamps was soft, almost romantic. This home oozed Liam, and Rachel was worried she'd made a huge error in judgment coming here.

"You want some coffee or something to drink?" Liam asked as he brushed past her, heading away from the living room.

"Sure, coffee would be great," she replied, taking her coat off and draping it carefully over the oversized plaid couch in front of the fireplace.

Rachel followed the sounds Liam made as he roughly opened and shut cupboards. The kitchen she entered was large and bright. A breakfast nook was tucked in the corner, and the walls had several windows. She could imagine how lovely it must be to enjoy a cup of coffee as the early-morning sunlight filled the room.

Liam's back was to her, and he ignored Rachel as he prepared the coffee. The coffee grinder loudly churned the raw gourmet beans, creating a delightfully pungent aroma. *If anything, at least the man had great taste in coffee*, she thought.

Rachel swallowed. "Liam."

As he turned to face her, she felt drawn to him, which only upset her more. Being here, in his home, perhaps wasn't the smartest idea, and regret for having intruded on him gnawed harder at her.

"I guess I just want us to resolve this issue," she continued.

Liam slouched casually against the counter, which only made Rachel even more frustrated. She wanted to catch him off guard and make him feel nervous in the same way he constantly had her in knots.

"Okay, and which issue is that?" His eyes scanned her body, causing Rachel to shift her weight nervously.

"Liam, I'm talking about the reports. There aren't any other issues to discuss," Rachel answered firmly. "I propose you start turning them in."

Liam rolled his eyes. "There are no reports to turn in."

The bitter smell of the coffee filled the room, and Liam turned away, grabbed two generous-sized mugs, and started to fill them. "You take anything in your coffee?" he asked as though an argument wasn't brewing.

"Wait, what do you mean there are no reports to turn in? You haven't even given them to the parents?" Rachel's voice turned pitchy with anger.

"So nothing in your coffee? Just black, then?"

"Screw the coffee. I want to know why you haven't even sent the progress reports out. I figured you just were refusing to turn them in to me."

Liam turned back to face her, clenching his jaw

and biting his lip in an attempt to stifle a laugh from escaping his sexy mouth. This only aggravated her even more.

"I guess I don't see what's so funny," Rachel said.

Liam only nodded, covering his smile with a hand.

"You have nothing to say?" Rachel raised her voice as she planted her hands on her hips. "So basically, you think what I'm telling the staff to do is some kind of joke? That the rules don't apply to you?"

"I'm not saying that."

"Well, you seem to find all of this pretty damn comical, Mr. Liam O'Brien. But I don't see this as a joke. I take what I do very seriously, and I won't tolerate this kind of insubordination." Rachel moved in closer, eliminating the space between them. She moved her finger to his chest and began to poke him.

"Ouch," Liam said as he grabbed her hands. His own were so much wider and larger than hers.

Thick tension hung in the air between them. She tilted her face toward his, and Liam looked down at her. For a moment, she thought he was struggling not to kiss her, then he released her hands slowly.

Rachel pulled his face down to hers and kissed him hard. She didn't understand what had possessed her but decided not to fight it. Instead, she allowed her free-flowing emotions and desire to burn through her as she continued to kiss him deeper.

The radiant current that surged through her whenever they touched returned stronger than ever and seemed to be capturing them both. Liam circled his long arms around her body and brought her closer. The softness of his lips now smashed hard against hers, demanding more of her. As their tongues probed wildly, Rachel nipped at his lower lip.

She wasn't sure quite what was happening, but her feet were no longer planted on the ground. Her mind was swirling, and heat blazed through her body. Rachel felt herself being lowered and placed on a plush surface, and she tightened her arms around Liam and pulled him to her. She wasn't certain if the room was dark, and she was too frightened to open her eyes in case this was a dream. She tangled her legs with his as he roamed his hands over her body, discovering her soft flesh. Her anger had dissolved into a raging passion, a fire fueled from weeks of smoldering desire and frustration.

Her moaning only seemed to encourage him further to seek her hidden treasures. Sparks burst behind her eyes as lust pulsated hard and quick between their bodies. Pent-up want and need drove them as they each searched for release together.

Rachel welcomed Liam's weight on her body. They were equally desperate for closeness as they rid themselves of any space between them. She had never felt anything like this before. Her mind raced as it struggled to keep up with her body, and she ignored its attempts to make her see reason. Passion vibrated through her, leaving her entire body humming.

Likewise, Liam also seemed to be reacting

instead of thinking. Each of his movements was in sync with hers, perfecting a rhythm that caused her mind to blur. Their lips fused again as each demanded more until their need was spinning out of control. They gripped each other tight, consuming each other with an animalistic hunger.

He found her burning fire and buried himself deep, carrying them to a higher plane of physical awareness. Exhaustion enveloped them as they crashed over the peak, leaving them in the wake of rippling waves of pleasure.

As they lay together in the dark room, Rachel's eyelids grew heavy and her body drifted far away into a heavy slumber. Other than their soft breathing, the room was quiet.

Liam wrapped an arm gingerly over her and whispered in her ear, "This feels so right, Rachel. It's too perfect to be wrong."

\*\*\*

As gray morning light filtered through the room, the smell of coffee and bacon startled Rachel awake. Her brain was foggy, and as she tried coming to her senses, she looked around the room and realized she wasn't in her own bed or even at home. A pleasant ache filled her body, and she recalled the incredible sensations of last evening right before panic flooded her.

Rachel mentally slapped herself. What had she been thinking? She threw back the heavy comforter and hopped out of bed. She found her clothes and shoved her limbs through them rapidly. She was so furious with herself and her lack of control the night before. She definitely wasn't prepared to face Liam this morning.

After walking down the dark hallway that led to the kitchen, she eyed Liam. Dressed only in dark green plaid pajama bottoms with his naked chest facing the stove, he was busy frying bacon and didn't seem to notice her. Feeling pangs of regret, Rachel took the chance to sneak through the front door.

A few minutes later, she was speeding down the highway on autopilot while her mind replayed their encounter. Tears stung her cheeks, and the confusing mix of emotions shook her to her core.

As soon as she parked in her driveway, Rachel rushed inside the safety of her home and headed straight for the shower. As she welcomed the hot water cascading over her, her thoughts floated back to Liam. Guilt plagued her for leaving him as she had. It wasn't fair to him, and she felt like a coward, but she didn't have it in her to deal with the consequences of her out-of-control behavior.

Rachel lathered a loofa with lavender-scented body wash and scrubbed at the shame that crawled on her skin. Still in awe at what she had allowed herself to do, Rachel stood under the water and cried some more.

\*\*\*

## Liam

Liam sat in his kitchen with a plate of cold food

before him as the cold morning sun spewed rays of light across the wood floor. He had lost his appetite after Rachel had left without as much as a word. He knew they had gotten carried away last night, but that passion and desire had been lying right below the surface for a while now, so he wasn't surprised it had finally broken through. Still, he regretted and blamed himself for not slowing things down and making certain Rachel really wanted what had transpired. Liam knew now more than ever that he wanted her, and being able to touch her last night made him want to feel her even more now. His house was too quiet without her, his loneliness more potent. His heart was missing, and he knew Rachel now held it.

Maybe he could reason with her, show her what they had done was only the beginning of something wonderful. He grabbed his cell phone, dialed her number, and waited for her to pick up.

Last night had been amazing. Surely she could see how perfectly they fit together.

\*\*\*

### Rachel

Rachel had just wrapped her head in a towel and was drying off when she heard the familiar chirp of her cell phone. It was probably Chelsea bugging her.

As she picked up the phone, she noticed the number was not her friend's, so she hit the Ignore button and sent the call straight to voice mail. She knew who was calling, and right now she couldn't muster up the courage to speak with him.

Rachel then curled up on her couch, attempting to distract herself with a new romance novel she had picked up at the grocery store. When her phone rang again, she looked at it to see who was calling and was happy to see Chelsea's number this time. While she had been reading, Liam had tried several more times to call her, but she wasn't ready to face him. Instead, she was already trying to come up with possible ways to avoid him at work.

"Hello?" she answered.

"Rachel, I never heard back from you last night. Wanted to see if you had tried calling. My phone was having some issues. Plus, I went on a little impromptu date with my yoga instructor," Chelsea rambled.

"Yeah, I'm sorry." Rachel paused. She didn't even know where to begin this conversation. Did she really want to rehash the whole event and relieve all the details? "So what's up with this instructor?" Rachel tried to sound interested, but she felt as if she were miles away.

"Nothing." Chelsea sounded bored. "He might be in super-great shape, but honestly, he's just a yoga instructor, so, like, how far can it really go, you know?"

"Too bad," Rachel said.

"Well, how'd it go with Liam? You tell him off?"

"God, Chelsea, I don't even know where to start." Her voice grew shaky as uneven waves rocked her stomach.

Chelsea sighed. "Oooh, so it went pretty bad?"

"Let's just say it didn't go as planned. Like at all."

"Start from the beginning. After we hung up, you were pretty determined to read him the riot act and let him have it. So did you?" Chelsea's tone was direct and calm.

Rachel swallowed. "Yes, I drove over there. I thought about what I wanted to say. I had a game plan, Chelsea."

"I take it things didn't quite pan out the way you had hoped."

"You know, the thing with Liam is he gets me all tied up in knots, and I get so frustrated with him. I thought he would have had a different reaction to me coming over. But he didn't. Instead, he stood there, all sexy and gorgeous like usual, making me feel like a puddle of jelly. Ugh!"

Chelsea laughed her sweet laugh. "Well, at least now you admit he's hot."

"It's just that I don't want to get involved. But, well, I kind of got a little too involved." Rachel grimaced.

"Holy cow! Are you serious? No way, Rachel."

"I really screwed up, Chelsea."

"It's okay," Chelsea said, her voice low and soothing. "You finally listened to your heart and, well, other regions, but you finally ignored that annoying brain of yours. I'm actually sort of proud of you."

"Well, don't be. I'm totally mortified by what I did. I think I got overwhelmed because Valentine's Day is coming up and, well, it isn't exactly my favorite holiday, as we both know." Tears burned at her eyelids. "This is not like me, you know?"

"I know. It's not like you to hop into bed with some guy, but Liam isn't just some guy," Chelsea said softly. "I think there might be something very special between you two, but you're way too stubborn to see it. I know Valentine's is hard for you, but maybe this will change that for you."

"I can't have any kind of relationship with him. Don't get me wrong. If things were a little different, then maybe, but it can't work."

Chelsea sighed, then added sympathetically, "It will be okay. Trust your heart for once."

Rachel shook her head. "I can't."

"Oh Rachel, I wish I was there. This sounds like a 'large bottle of wine and chick flick' kind of situation. Maybe moving up there wasn't such a great idea. I almost thought I was wrong about that too. You always sound happy, even when you are frustrated with work."

"I'm starting to think I may have really messed up by coming here." Rachel's heart squeezed a little, and she suddenly felt homesick. She hadn't felt this ache for a while and had thought she was settling nicely in Birch Valley. She had begun to feel like an important part of the school and truly loved her job. She had made wonderful friends in Mary O'Brien and her daughter Maggie, and she adored Karen. She'd made great strides, and thinking she had actually failed now did not sit well with her. But Rachel missed the comfort of having Chelsea, who knew her better than anyone.

More tears escaped her eyes, and she wiped them

away before saying good-bye to her best friend and promising to call if she needed to talk some more.

# *Chapter Seventeen*

### Liam

Sunday dinner was in full swing at the O'Briens'. Liam sat next to Daniel, who immediately started digging in after they all said grace. When Liam just sat there, plowing an imaginary field in his potatoes, Daniel looked over at him.

"What in the heck are you doing, Liam?"

"Huh?" Liam looked up.

Daniel forked some potatoes into his mouth and motioned toward Liam's plate. "You seem kind of spaced out," he said quietly. "Everything okay?"

"Yeah, everything's fine." Liam turned back to his plate, trying to focus on his food. He hadn't regained his appetite since Rachel had run away yesterday morning. Instead of eating, he watched Grandpa Paddy tease one of the twins by pretending to steal his roll.

"Oh dear, must you torment the child?" Mary scolded as she entered the dining room and placed a gravy boat on the table, then gave the boy a small peck on his head.

"Only having a bit of fun with my little lad here." Grandpa Paddy winked and replaced the roll.

"So Valentine's will be here next week," Daniel said. "Anyone got any plans?"

Patrick and Liam looked at each other, and Patrick shot Daniel a cool glare.

Clearly noticing the look that passed between them, Mary took the opportunity to redirect the question. "Anyone need any more rolls?" She smiled as she held up the large basket.

"I could always do with another, my love," Pat answered.

The meal continued without incident. As the other men scurried away after eating, Mary asked Liam to stay behind and help her clear the table. He picked up the large casserole dish from the center of the table and followed her into her kitchen.

"Thanks, hun. So did you enjoy dinner?" she asked.

"Yeah, it was good, Mom. Always is."

"I'm glad. I noticed you didn't seem to have much of an appetite, so I wanted to ask."

Liam sighed. "Sorry, I wasn't very hungry today."

Mary watched him, and Liam could tell she was trying to figure out what was going with him.

"How's work going? I know we have that bake sale coming up soon, and I was thinking about trying something different this year—lemon bars."

"Yeah, that sounds good." Liam's turned away and went to grab more dishes from the dining room table.

"So how are things going with Rachel? I haven't heard from her since the poor dear's pipes froze. We had such a lovely time baking, and I know she appreciated you and your brothers helping her."

Liam avoided his mother's stare as he returned to the kitchen. He knew what she was doing. She was probing for information so she could fix whatever was wrong, but he doubted she could help him with this problem.

"Well, I better get home. I have some papers I need to grade. Thanks again for dinner, Mom." Liam kissed her on the cheek and practically ran out of her kitchen.

\*\*\*

### Rachel

Monday morning showed up with rain; not a quiet drizzle but pounding sheets of wild precipitation. Rachel hurried out of her car to take shelter inside the warm elementary school, and Karen smiled as she entered.

"Good morning. A little wet, isn't it?" Karen teased. "Coffee's ready."

"Morning. My goodness, I can't believe how it's coming down out there. My windshield wipers didn't even help. I wasn't sure if I was going to be able to drive. Might have been better to take a boat." Rachel laughed.

"What this means is that spring is near," Karen added confidently as she grabbed a stack of paper to put in the teachers' mailboxes.

Rachel weaved her way into the teachers' lounge and added some more coffee to the mug she had already been working on. She had slept terribly and was already on her third cup of coffee.

Rachel's body tensed as she heard Liam greeting Karen. Quickly planning an exit strategy, she zoomed into her office.

\*\*\*

## Liam

Karen watched as Rachel sped past. "Boy, she must be in a hurry," she commented to Liam.

He watched as Rachel shut the door to her office, knowing full well why she had fled. So the avoiding game now was in full swing.

For the remainder of the day, Liam didn't see a trace of Rachel, but he didn't press the issue or try to confront her. He wanted to give her a little space as he tried to figure out how to mend things between them.

After work, Liam decided to drive by the O'Brien Construction shop to see if Patrick was in. He wanted to get his brother's advice on what to do about Rachel because he had failed to come up with any ideas on his own.

Walking inside the large metal building, he saw Patrick leaning against the counter sorting some papers.

"Hey, Patrick, how's it going?" Liam called out.

Patrick looked up, and his mouth turned into a

slanted smile. "It's going. Just got done with a small job; we barely just got back in. Glad you stopped by, though. I wanted to see how things were. You seemed a little down at dinner."

"Yeah, that's kind of why I came by. I wanted to get your advice on some stuff."

"Sure. I'm assuming this has to do with Rachel?" Patrick gave him a knowing look.

Liam nodded. "Yeah, I'm sort of stuck right now. Basically, she came over on Friday to discuss that issue we've been having at work."

Thinking about their encounter left him wanting more, needing more. God, he wanted her again so badly, it made his body hurt. The thought it may never happen killed him.

"So how did that go?" Patrick asked. "She probably gave you an earful, I imagine."

"She did, and then, I don't know, things happened so fast."

Patrick focused his eyes on Liam with intense curiosity. "What do you mean 'things happened so fast'? What the hell happened, Liam?"

"Let's just say it went from fighting to making up real quick," Liam said. "Then the next morning she took off without saying good-bye or anything, and today at work, she completely avoided me."

"Wow." Patrick rubbed his dark evening stubble. "You really like her, don't you?"

"I do. I can't explain it, either. That's why I wanted to come to you. I feel like we finally got to a point where we both see that we are attracted to each other, and I think this could turn into something serious."

"So now how do we fix this? Basically, your biggest problem is work, right? Maybe we should start there. What about those reports she has been hounding you about?" Patrick was deep in thought, and Liam was glad problem-solving was his gift.

Liam rolled his eyes and grunted. "Yes, work is our main problem and her not wanting to get involved because of work. I think she came up here to really prove something to herself or maybe her family. Patrick, I don't agree with what she is asking us to do with all this focusing on testing and dragging the parents into that big mess."

"I know you don't, but if you play ball, she might be a little more willing to talk to you at least. Maybe she won't be so quick to put up that wall," Patrick offered helpfully.

"Man, I don't know. That's asking me to go along with something I firmly don't believe in," Liam countered.

"Do you think you might love her?" Patrick looked hard at him.

This was why Liam had come to Patrick. He was only a little bit older but had lived so much more. He knew what love was, and he would be straight and honest with Liam. There would be no sugar-coating from Patrick.

Liam swallowed and inhaled, then let out a lungful of air. "I think I do, Patrick."

***

## Rachel

Rachel was in her kitchen heating up some water for tea when her cell phone buzzed.

"Hello?" she answered as she dunked a teabag into a large mug, mesmerized by the steam.

"Hey, lady, how's it going?" Chelsea chirped.

Rachel smiled. She could always count on her best friend to be happy and cheery. Maybe it was all that California sun. Rachel sure missed that, especially now, when the gray clouds controlled the skies of Birch Valley and matched her own gloomy disposition.

"Raining like crazy here," Rachel responded as she grabbed her mug, then took a sip, careful not to burn her mouth.

"Well, I better not tell you how gorgeous it is here," Chelsea teased. "So the big question is, how was work today, and did you see him?"

Rachel sighed loudly. "I'm such a coward, Chelsea. I avoided him like the plague. I just feel awful. Any time I heard his voice today or even caught a glimpse of him, I booked it in the opposite direction."

"Oh, Rachel."

"Next week we have this bake sale to raise funds for our Dr. Seuss day in March. I have to sort of lead the event, and all the teachers participate. I'm completely dreading it now."

"Do you have to bake too? Remember that time we tried making brownies? What a disaster!"

Rachel chuckled. "Yeah, I have to bake too."

"There is a grocery store or bakery nearby,

right?" Chelsea suggested sweetly.

"No, I'll actually be baking. I already know how to bake something pretty awesome." Rachel smiled at the thought.

"Really?" Chelsea seemed surprised but then continued, "So let's talk more about Liam. What are you going to do?"

"I have no idea. I do know we can't go on like this, with me running to my office every time he's near."

"Maybe it's time to talk to him, Rachel. What if you explained how you feel? Honestly, where do you stand with this guy? Where do you want to stand with him?"

It was a good question, and Rachel really wasn't sure of the answer. A large part of her was terrified, but another part wanted something with Liam, and that part seemed to keep growing. Although Rachel continued to try to fight any feelings she was developing for Liam and that was getting harder and harder to do.

"It's so incredibly difficult. There's a part of me that, to be completely honest, is attracted to Liam. He's unlike any guy I have ever met. He's sexy, funny, and smart, but he's also a teacher and I'm his boss. My God, I can't even begin to explain the effect he has on my body."

Thinking about Liam caused her to feel warm all over and desire to simmer right below the surface. She was shocked how quickly her body reacted.

"Damn, that sounds like enough of a reason right there to be with him," Chelsea responded with eagerness.

"He comes from this amazing family. I love his sister, Maggie. You would too." Rachel went on to explain how her relationship with Maggie had developed over the last several weeks.

"She sounds really sweet." Rachel thought she detected a hint of jealousy in Chelsea's voice.

"Seriously, you'd like her. I bet she would adore you too," Rachel said gently.

"I guess the only problem is, you need to figure out if you can get past the work stuff. Then, if you can, maybe you can try and give it a shot. He sounds wonderful, and I want to meet him and his brothers," Chelsea said in her fake sultry voice.

Imagining how Chelsea would react to Liam made Rachel squirm with a bit of jealousy this time. "When you come up for spring break, you're going to have to meet everyone here. There are so many nice people. As for his brothers, they are both single. Patrick is, like, wow, I mean, just wow. 'Tall, dark, and handsome' barely describes that man. And Daniel is so adorable and sweet."

"Ooh, Patrick. I like tall, dark, and handsome very much. Now I can't wait to come and visit you."

Rachel laughed. "I bet."

"Hey, have you heard from your parents at all? My dad says he had drinks with your dad last week. Said he didn't even discuss you being up here," Chelsea said quietly.

"No surprise. I got an email from him a couple days ago, asking if I had come to my senses yet. My mother sent me a lovely text too, asking me if I had met anyone and also when will I come to my senses and come back," Rachel said. "Ethan and you are honestly the only ones who seem to have supported me doing this. Ethan says he hopes to come up for a visit too, but he has been so swamped."

"Maybe Ethan and I should come up together," Chelsea offered seductively.

"Good grief. I can't wait to show you this place. It's so different, but I think you will like it, and everyone says it's so pretty in spring. Right now, there are dirty chunks of snow everywhere."

The two friends chatted for a while longer, and when they hung up, Rachel felt more at ease about her problems and eager for Chelsea's visit in the spring. She considered herself lucky to have such a great friend and realized how much she truly missed her.

\*\*\*

The following days only brought more rain and worsened Rachel's mood. Continuing to avoid Liam was proving to be more difficult each day. It also didn't help that Karen was watching her like a hawk, knowing full well what she was up to. To top that off, Valentine's Day was tomorrow, and Rachel could feel herself becoming more irritated as it neared, not only because it reminded her of that awful breakup a couple years back, but because it made her realize how lonely she was. Then there was the bake sale. Even though it wasn't until Friday, the day after Valentine's Day, Karen had already started decorating the cafeteria, going for a full-blown Valentine's theme that made Rachel nauseous. She couldn't wait to be done with this holiday.

\*\*\*

## Liam

Liam sat behind his desk in the quiet classroom as his students took a practice test in preparation for the major state test. He stared out the window, watching the rain pelt the glass. He then turned his attention to the large stack of neatly signed papers in front of him. He was setting a plan in motion. A plan he hoped would set him and Rachel on the right track. He may not fully agree with her decisions, but knowing that conceding to them might bring them closer eased his conscience.

\*\*\*

## Rachel

Rachel strolled into work the next day feeling even more down in the dumps. She was wet and cold and had slept horribly the night before. Today was the dreaded Valentine's Day. A large vase filled with flowers sat proudly on Karen's desk, and Rachel groaned as Karen peeked out from behind the mailboxes, her arms filled with memos printed on pink paper.

"Happy Valentine's, Rachel," Karen sang happily.

Rachel nodded and shuffled to her office without

replying. *Must Karen be so perky today?* she thought as she closed the door behind her. When she looked at her desk, she saw several goodies waiting for her there. Her frown softened as she sat down to get a good look at them. Karen had given her a small vase containing a festive floral arrangement, and a few parents had given her boxes of chocolates. She couldn't help but feel touched by the sweet gesture.

She then noticed a small crystal and silver paperweight sitting atop a stack of papers. Confusion washed over her as she read the inscription:

### *You have my heart.*

She turned her gaze to the papers beneath and couldn't believe her eyes. They were the progress reports from Liam's fourth grade students.

A smile appeared on her face. Maybe this Valentine's Day wouldn't be so terrible after all.

***

### Liam

Liam was organizing the treats he'd brought for his students when he heard a soft knock at his door. Butterflies swirled in his stomach, and he smiled broadly and turned as Megan slithered in. A brilliant red sweater and pink skirt hugged her body, and she wore her long brown hair in loose waves. Tiny heart-shaped diamonds twinkled at her ears.

"Good morning, Liam. Happy Valentine's," she cooed.

His broad smile vanished as disappointment overtook him. "Morning."

"Why so cranky? You were just smiling a second ago," Megan said, sounding slightly offended as she inched closer to him.

"Sorry, thought you were one of the kids," he replied coldly and turned back to his task.

"Need any help?" she offered as she touched his arm.

He shifted his body away from her grasp. "No, I got it, but thanks."

"Okay," Megan whined, "well, I guess I will head back to my room. Just wanted to wish you a Happy Valentine's."

"Same to you. Hope your students have fun today."

"Oh, I almost forgot, what are you bringing for the bake sale tomorrow?" Megan asked, clearly scrambling to find any reason to continue their conversation.

"My mom's bringing in lemon bars, I think," Liam replied, finally looking back at her.

"Yummy." Megan licked her lips slowly.

Liam had had about as much as he could stand. "Well, I really need to get some stuff done. They will be here any minute now."

Looking disappointed, Megan sashayed out of his classroom. That woman put it all out there, and Liam wanted nothing to do with any of it. Granted, she was sexy, he supposed, but she wasn't anything like the woman down the hall, with the sun-kissed pixie haircut, overgrown bangs, and the beautiful, deep cobalt eyes.

***

By the end of the day, Liam had had his fill of overly hyper students bouncing everywhere in a love-infused sugar high. He was grateful when the last bell sounded.

"Don't forget, you guys, bake sale tomorrow night. Give those fliers to your family, and tell anyone you know," Liam shouted over the sounds of backpacks being gathered.

After the last of the students fled, he began tidying up his classroom, pushing in a couple forgotten chairs and picking up candy wrappers and scraps of paper. He was savoring the quiet when he heard a soft knock at the door. Mentally preparing for the return of Megan, he was surprised and relieved to see Rachel. Her soft, pink sweater highlighting rosebud lips that were turned upward in a nervous smile. He watched as gray pants that fit snugly around her hips and legs made their way toward him.

"Liam, are you busy? Did I interrupt you?" she asked cautiously.

He could sense her fear. *Why*, he thought, *why would she be scared of him*? She was the one who held his heart now; she had all the power. Didn't she know this? He was frightened by how deeply she made him feel.

"No, not at all. Please come in." He led her toward his desk after he closed the door. As she wrung her hands, he noticed how supple they were. He wanted to touch her and feel them on his body again.

"I wanted to thank you." She didn't meet his eyes.

"Rachel, there's so much I want to say—"

"Liam, I appreciate what you did. But I can't really discuss the other night, if that's okay." Rachel looked down, picking imaginary lint from her pants, still avoiding his gaze.

"Oh Rachel, I want us to talk about it. I need you to know how you make me feel." Liam leaned in closer. Her light perfume smelled like summer, floral and warm.

"I'm so sorry, I just can't." Rachel pushed past him with a speed he wasn't prepared for and fled the room.

He could practically feel the light leaving him and a cold, sinking weight of loneliness replacing it. The only silver lining he could see in this internal storm was that she'd finally come to him. They were making progress, slowly but hopefully surely.

***

### Rachel

Rachel went to the grocery store right after work without saying good-bye to anyone. As she navigated the aisles, her phone buzzed loudly in her purse.

"Hello?" she answered after fishing it out quickly.

"Happy Singles' Awareness Day," Chelsea shouted on the other end.

Pulling her phone away from her ear, Rachel shook her head. "Thanks. How has your day been?" she asked as she gathered more items from her list for the muffins she'd be baking.

"Eh, you know, it's lovers' day, and I don't have one, so I guess not an entirely great day. Where are you? You sound distracted."

"Getting stuff for the bake sale." Rachel scanned for the aisle that had the last ingredients on her list.

"How was work today?" Chelsea asked carefully.

"Okay, get this. I get to work and find a bunch of neat stuff on my desk, flowers, chocolates, all that good stuff, but the thing that really wowed me was what Liam left for me," Rachel said as she considered two different bags of sugar. "Hey, Chelsea, what's the difference between a name brand and store brand, like, say, for sugar or flour? Does it really matter when you are baking?"

"You know you're asking the wrong person, right? I'm telling you, just wander over to their little bakery section and grab some cupcakes or something," Chelsea said. "So wait, what did Liam get you?"

"Maybe I should call Mary," Rachel thought out loud.

"Earth to Rachel, what did he get you? You're killin' me here."

"A beautiful paperweight."

"A what? Why?" Chelsea demanded, sounding irritated. Clearly, that was not the answer she wanted to hear.

"A paperweight. It was heart-shaped and said, 'You have my heart,' but it's what it was on top of that really surprised me: those progress reports I've been after him about." Rachel smiled at the thought of Liam.

"Oh, well, that's nice, I guess. I really would've thought he would've done the whole dozen-roses bit or something super romantic. Hmm, I'm a little disappointed, actually."

Rachel could almost hear her friend frowning. She shrugged. Chelsea didn't understand how much Liam finally turning those in meant to her. Now she didn't have to worry about reporting to the district without all of them, which also meant she didn't need to fear losing her job just yet. The district still wanted to make sure the school did better on the tests, so she knew she would be on pins and needles waiting for the overall results and standings. "It's a very big deal, Chelsea. I mean, he fought so hard against those. I was worried I was going to lose my job if I showed up empty-handed."

"Okay, so this is big, then? Like, 'it's the end of the war, and now you can go and see if you can recapture the magic from last week' type of big?"

"Yes. Wait, no. I mean, yes, it's a big deal, and no, I don't want to recapture the magic. I just think this is a step in the right direction for us to be able to coexist at work now."

"Rachel, you do understand why he turned those in and did the paperweight thing, right? It's not really my idea of a great gift from a lover, but he obviously has lost his heart to you."

"First off, we are not lovers," Rachel defended.

"Nope, you are. I'm afraid that what went on a week ago between you is what would define a lover, and it sounds like he's an amazing one at that," Chelsea rebutted, sounding quite pleased with herself.

"You are impossible, you realize that?" Rachel fought back a laugh. She felt warm every time she had to defend herself against the word *lovers*. Her body agreed with Chelsea but her stubborn brain refused to.

"But you love me."

"I do, but for the record, Liam and I are not lovers. And I know he may have ulterior motives for turning those reports in, but I'm thankful he did."

"Well, I will drop this for now, but it's totally a 'to be continued' conversation, just so you know. I have yoga and need to head out."

"You going to go out with the instructor again?" Rachel said playfully.

"First off, he's an instructor, and secondly, he has a man-bun thing going on, Rachel. Not too sure I'm into this whole man-bun hairstyle. I don't think I like a guy having better-looking hair than me. He actually suggested I needed to switch my hair products, can you believe that?" Chelsea laughed.

Rachel couldn't imagine anyone having nicer hair than Chelsea, and considering how much she spent to make it look fabulous, she could picture how insulted her friend must have been. Then she thought about Liam's slightly shaggy hair. She had a difficult time seeing him wearing it long and in a bun. He wasn't that type of guy. Running her fingers through her own pixie cut, she realized she was way overdue for a trim. It was also getting a little shaggy.

After saying good-bye, she hung up with Chelsea and double-checked her list before paying, feeling lighter and happier after her chat. She was now ready to go home and bake.

\*\*\*

On Friday night, Rachel entered the cafeteria with an armload of muffins, and Liam instantly jogged up to her.

"Here, let me help you," he said as he grabbed several trays from her hands. "These smell great—and very familiar." A boyish grin replaced the sexy one he had given her as he walked over.

"Thanks. I'm sure you are pretty familiar with that recipe. I hope I did hers justice," Rachel said, following Liam to a partially filled tabletop to set the remainder of her trays down.

"I'm sure they're great."

Megan sauntered up to Liam, carrying a colorful tray of cupcakes frosted with a baker's precision and decorated with the touch of an artist.

"Excuse me, Rachel," Megan's voice oozed sugary-sweet desire as she pushed past her. "Liam, could you help me carry these?"

Rachel watched as Liam assisted Megan, unable to help feeling more than a bit annoyed that he was helping her. After talking to Chelsea the evening before and then working so hard on Liam's mother's recipe, Rachel felt almost territorial toward him.

She was lost in thought when Karen came up to her with a large smile on her face.

"So is it true?"

Rachel's brow furrowed with confusion. "Is what true?"

Still smiling from ear to ear, Karen said, "I think it's so sweet."

Now Rachel got it. "Oh, with Liam and the reports."

"Oh goodness, no, not that. Even though that was also very good of him, and sweet I suppose. I'm referring to what you baked." Karen's soft-lined face seem to be glowing.

"The muffins."

"Not just any muffins, my dear, but Mary's. I spoke with Liam a couple of minutes ago. It really touched him that you made those. Everyone is raving about them too. Several have already sold."

"Wow, I didn't even think I could replicate her amazing muffins. It's the first thing I actually learned how to bake, thanks to Mary."

"Well, good job, Rachel. They turned out fantastic." Karen patted her shoulder, then went to help a parent who was flagging her down.

Rachel decided to go by each table and check in with the staff to see how things were shaping up. Along the way, she noticed the stacks of various cakes, pies, cookies, and treats on many of the tables had dwindling down to near nothing The cafeteria was filled with so many people that Rachel was sure they'd raise a decent amount of money to buy new books for the library and have one heck of Dr. Seuss party this year.

\*\*\*

## Liam

Liam stood guard at a long table as he watched Rachel working the room, chatting to teachers, parents, and students alike. She gave each person her undivided attention as well as her warm, kind smile. He felt proud to have her representing the school.

"She really seems to be in her element," Mary commented.

Liam turned to her. "Yeah, I think so too."

"All of my lemon bars are gone. I should really have brought extra. I didn't think they would go this quick."

"I'm not surprised in the least." Liam embraced his mother. "Did you see what Rachel brought in for the sale?"

"No, I didn't." Her eyes grew wide.

"Well, let's go see if they are still at that table over there," Liam suggested as he guided her through the small sea of people.

As they arrived at the table near the entrance, Liam searched for one of Rachel's trays, then pointed it out to his mother. Only a few muffins, which Rachel had made in several different flavors, were left now. A small place card with the words *Mary's Muffins* written in an elegant font stood beside the remaining ones.

Mary clutched her chest, beaming with pride. "Oh my, she made them."

Joy spread through Liam at the sight of Mary's smile, which was quickly killed as Megan approached.

"Mrs. O'Brien! How lovely to see you. I have to say, your lemon bars looked amazing," Megan rambled as she devoured Liam with her eyes.

Mary seemed to have been caught off guard as well. "Why, thank you, dear. What did you bring? Something lovely, I'm sure." She patted Megan lightly on her arm.

Liam pressed lightly on his mother's elbow to steer her away, and Megan began engaging in a little game of tug of war with him.

"I'd love to show you what I brought, if there are any left, of course," Megan said sweetly.

"Well, then, let's go have a look," Mary agreed politely.

Liam was always amazed at his mother's patience and kindness. He spotted Rachel and noticed her gaze dart away quickly. He would much rather be with her instead of having to play nice with Megan.

Mary excused herself after being shown the cupcakes Megan had made, complimenting her more times than necessary in order to escape. As soon as she had, she looked up at her son. "Where do you suppose Rachel might be? I would love to talk with her."

Liam smiled. His thoughts exactly.

# Chapter Eighteen

### Rachel

The bake sale had been an enormous success. Rachel was surprised by the amount of townspeople who had come out to support the school. She still couldn't get over the overwhelming sense of community and caring in these people. In the beginning, she had felt like an outsider, but now she had been wrapped tightly in the fold. So many people wanted to talk to her, and their words were encouraging and full of praise and hopes for the future. Rachel wasn't experiencing much doubt about belonging there now, aside from the uncomfortable awkwardness with Liam, and even that was starting to dissipate slowly—very slowly. Now, instead of wanting to run and hide when she heard the sound of his voice or caught a whiff of his spicy cologne, she longed to be near him, to maybe even touch him again. Seeing him interact with Megan only made her want him more. The sight of him acting tenderly toward another woman and the mere thought of him being with someone else brought out a sense of jealousy she hadn't experienced before. She had left the bake sale more confused than ever.

Rachel sat at her kitchen table, looking out into her backyard as thoughts swirled in her mind. Could she be in a relationship with Liam? How would that translate to their working relationship? What if things got serious, or if they didn't work out? As she breathed in the rich aroma of her coffee and sipped it, feeling the warmth travel down her throat, someone knocked at her door.

She set her cup down and got up instantly, curious about who was there. She wasn't used to getting visitors. *Maybe Sue-Ellen needed help*, she thought. But as she glanced through the window, she saw Mary O'Brien on her doorstep, swaddled in a thick, green wool coat. A heavy, gray, knitted cap covered her curly, auburn hair.

Rachel smiled as she opened the door. "Mary, what a nice surprise."

"Good morning, Rachel. I am so sorry to drop by unannounced."

Rachel waved her hand to stop her from apologizing. "Mary, no need. I'm happy to see you. You're welcome anytime." Rachel smiled as she reached out to her. "Please come on in. I just made coffee. Join me for a cup."

"That sounds wonderful," Mary said softly as she crossed the threshold and followed Rachel to the kitchen, where she took her coat off and planted herself at the table. "Wow, this place is so pretty, Rachel. You have really turned it into something quite lovely, dear. I remember when Bob lived here. He was the nicest man, but it never looked like this."

"Oh, thank you. Do you take anything in your coffee?" Rachel asked as she busied herself refreshing her own mug and taking out another one for Mary. "And would you care for a muffin?"

"A wee bit of sugar and cream, if you have it, dear," Mary answered as her eyes lit up. "And would that be one of the muffins you made for the bake sale, by chance?"

"Why, yes, it is." Rachel laughed. "Now don't be too critical. They are hardly as amazing as yours, but they aren't half-bad, considering it's my first shot at baking them. I cannot thank you enough for teaching me."

"I was happy to, just like when we made that pie when your pipes froze. I love having you in my kitchen. I enjoy our time together."

Rachel gave Mary her coffee and placed a plate with a couple of muffins in the center of the table before sitting down.

"Why, thank you, these look delicious. Coffee is splendid too. Just the pick-me-up I was needing." Mary closed her eyes and seemed to savor the strong caffeine as she sipped.

"I didn't see you last night, Mary. I heard you brought in some lemon bars, but I never got a chance to see them, and they were already gone before I could purchase one. No surprise there."

"I'd be more than happy to bring you some. I didn't stay too long. I tried looking for you as well, but it was such a full house. I'm happy so many people turned out for it. You guys probably made a decent amount for the Dr. Seuss party," Mary added before sipping slowly at her mug again.

"Why, yes. Karen was thrilled with what we brought in. She says it has to be a record. She teased that I was the draw." Rachel rolled her eyes and swatted her overgrown bangs away. She was in need of trim and needed to see who did hair in town. Maybe Mary could suggest someone.

"Well, you have to realize Mr. Anderson was the principal for years, so now that we've got some new blood in that school, of course you're going to be quite an attraction. Everyone really seems to like you, though, Rachel. I hope you see that." Mary patted her hand.

Rachel smiled and blushed slightly. "Thank you. I like everyone so much. They were all so kind and genuine."

"Do you find you're making many friends?" Mary inquired as she broke off a piece of her muffin. "Oh my, this is wonderful. You nailed the recipe. I think it might be better than mine."

"You are too kind, Mary, but trust me, yours are better." Rachel smiled. "Maggie's great. I feel like her and I have so many things in common. She mentioned she might be heading out here in a week or so."

"She thinks the world of you too. I'm so glad the two of you are friends now."

"Me too. I really can't wait to see her again."

"Yes, and that's actually why I stopped by," Mary said. "I was going to talk to you last night, but like I said, I couldn't find you anywhere. Our family goes on this little outing every year where we go moose watching. I wanted to see if you would like to join us. It's just a simple camping trip, only a couple nights. We have a few motor homes, so we don't have to rough it too bad."

Rachel paused for a moment. She had never seen a moose before and had no idea there were any in this area. At first thought, the prospect of joining the O'Brien family for a trip sounded like fun, but then she considered seeing Liam. Could she handle an overnight trip with him? She wasn't so sure.

"How neat! So where do you go to see these moose?"

Mary told Rachel about the various mountain locations and some of the campgrounds that were home to many different kinds of wildlife. She added that their trip was sort of the O'Briens' kickoff for spring, now that the snow was turning into rain and the weather was warming up slightly. She also described how her family spent their time together by playing games, keeping warm with hot chocolate, and making wonderful memories. She wanted to include Rachel so she could see more of Birch Valley and experience the outdoors.

It sounded like a lot of fun, and Rachel decided she couldn't disappoint Mary. She also wanted to try something different, and going to see moose was way different than anything she had ever done. Besides, this would give her the opportunity to see Maggie and meet her husband. A large part of her also jumped for joy at the idea of being alone with Liam inside a motor home, cuddling with a cup of hot chocolate. Another part of her was completely terrified. She couldn't trust herself around that man.

After finishing her coffee, Mary excused herself and said she would call Rachel later to set up the details of the trip. When they hugged, Rachel squeezed Mary tightly. She really appreciated how thoughtful and sweet Liam's mother was and wished this was the kind of mother she had. A thought struck her then. Mary would be the type of mother-in-law she could have if she and Liam married. The thought of marrying Liam should have scared her, but it actually brought a smile to her lips.

***

## Liam

Liam was washing the last dish when his phone rang. After drying his hands on the back of his jeans, he answered. "Hello?"

"Good morning, son."

"Hi, Mom," Liam said as he leaned against his counter.

"I was calling to check in with my handsome son. I stopped by Rachel's this morning and shared a lovely muffin and cup of coffee with her," Mary said. "I have to say, she really has that home looking quite nice."

"Yeah, I saw it when her pipes froze. So you had coffee with her?"

"Yes, and a muffin. Those were delicious, by the way."

"So why did you go over there, Mom?"

"Because we never got a chance to visit with her last night."

"I see. What did you guys talk about?" Liam inquired, his curiosity running wild.

Mary sighed. "It wasn't about you, dear, if that's what has you worried. I had a nice chat with her, just catching up, really, and we got to talking about Maggie and their friendship. I thought how great it'd be if she joined us for our little moose-watching adventure."

Liam swallowed, almost choking. "You invited her to go with us?"

"Well, yes. I thought it's probably something she's never done."

"What was her reaction? Did she want to go?"

"Sweetheart, she seemed really excited about the idea. I think at first she might have seemed a tad unsure, but I suppose that may have had something to do with you two," Mary said lightly.

"It might." Liam couldn't help but feel a little anxious about the trip. He was thrilled Rachel was going, but he was more than a little surprised she'd agreed.

"I think it'll be good for you guys," Mary added. "Besides, Maggie'll be there. Rachel and her get along so well, and it will be wonderful to have everyone all together. Your father and Grandpa Paddy thought it was very nice that I invited her."

"I appreciate you inviting her, Mom. That was kind of you. I guess I just didn't expect her to want to go."

"Well, she is, and I want you to try and work out whatever mess you got yourself into with her. I really like her, Liam. And if my mother's intuition tells me anything, I think you do too."

"I do, Mom. A lot," Liam admitted.

"I know you do, son."

\*\*\*

### Rachel

Rachel was reading when her phone rang, though she had been having a hard time concentrating on the words of her romance novel. Her mind kept wandering to the upcoming trip with the O'Briens.

"Hello?" she answered.

"Hey, I was out getting lunch by the pier and thought of you." Chelsea sounded sad.

"Ah, I would've loved to have had lunch with you there today," Rachel said. "But I did have an unexpected visit today."

"Really? Who stopped by, Liam?"

"No, his mother, actually. She came over, and we had coffee and chatted for a bit. Then she invited me on this family camping trip they take to go see *moose*."

"Moose? You guys have those up there?" Chelsea asked in horror.

"Apparently. I've never seen one or anything, just deer and stuff. But it's an overnight camping trip in RVs."

"Wait, overnight? Oooh, so will you be sharing an RV with Liam or with his mother?"

"I'm not too sure about the sleeping arrangements, but I can say I'm actually excited about this."

"What? Okay, what changed in, like, the day and a half since we spoke?" Chelsea's voice rose in excitement.

"I don't know. I mean, not a whole lot has changed. I only spoke with Liam for, like, a minute last night." Rachel wasn't quite sure how it had happened, but something definitely was different, and it scared her.

"Well, at least you are talking to him. How did the bake sale go?"

"Really well. In fact, we sold just about everything and made some serious money too. The people were so nice to me, Chelsea."

"They better be nice to you!" Chelsea laughed. "That's great the sale went good."

"So what are you up to today?" Rachel assumed her friend had tons of plans on what she could imagine was a gorgeous and sunny Saturday in Newport Beach.

"Like I said, I had lunch and did a little shopping. I don't know, I'm sort of bored today," Chelsea muttered.

Rachel was surprised to hear her friend sound so melancholy. Usually, Chelsea was like a bursting ray of light, bright and cheery. "Really?"

"Yeah, I don't know, I just feel sort of out of it today."

"I'm sorry." Rachel considered how lately she hadn't really been involved in Chelsea's life. She'd been making everything about her, not even thinking about what might be going on with her friend. It was so easy to get lost in her own problems, especially when Chelsea was so helpful, happy, funny, and carefree.

Guilt overcame Rachel as she listened to Chelsea explain how she had been feeling down for a while. She felt lonely mainly because she was missing her friend and not finding anyone to date who truly interested her. Rachel came to understand that in some ways Chelsea was feeling a bit left out of Rachel's life and a little jealous that she had found a great guy. She was also mad at Rachel for fighting something that could potentially be wonderful.

"I really hadn't thought about it that way, Chelsea. I am so sorry."

"That's okay, Rachel. Now enough about me." Rachel swore she could hear her friend wiping tears from her eyes.

"Hey, look at it like this. You'll be here in a little over a month!"

"I can't wait. I almost want to just sneak away now and hide out at your place for a while."

"Well, you could come up after we finish testing, which is, like, in less than two weeks," Rachel offered as she looked at her calendar, examining the dates when she wouldn't be quite as busy.

"That might work. I feel like I need to get away for a while. I haven't done anything fun in such a long time. Plus, I miss you like crazy and am dying to see where you live."

"I think it'd be great. You are welcome to stay as long as you want. I have an extra room here, and this might give me a little motivation to get it set up finally," Rachel said with a huge smile. "I can't wait for you to come up here and see this place. It really is great."

"Well, it's settled. You tell me when that testing junk is over, and by then, you will be so fried you'll be needing some fun too. That's where I come in."

"Sounds perfect to me."

They continued to plan out Chelsea's stay, discussing the things they could do while she visited. Chelsea said she didn't mind that Rachel would be working part of the time and even commented that it'd give her an opportunity to explore Birch Valley.

As she ended the call, Rachel was glad they had finally cemented plans for Chelsea's arrival, and now she was eager to get that extra room looking amazing. With her newfound energy, she decided to drive to Spokane tomorrow and spend the day shopping.

# Chapter Nineteen

The following week brought something Rachel was not used to seeing in Birch Valley—a tremendous amount of sunshine. Granted, it wasn't especially warm sunshine, but it did melt down the snow, leaving puddles everywhere. Having the sunlight every day made the world feel bright and happy. People seemed friendlier than usual, and Rachel noticed she was smiling more, but the joy blooming in her had been brought on by more than just some sunny weather. Liam had left another stack of signed reports on her desk, along with a token of his affection. Twice this week, he had left a flower on top of the pile, and the small action had left Rachel wandering around like a giddy schoolgirl.

One morning as Rachel exited her office, Karen noticed her grin. "Wow, someone sure looks to be in a good mood again today. The sunshine really agrees with you."

Rachel blushed. "Maybe."

"Or maybe it's something special in that coffee

you are drinking." Karen motioned at the mug Rachel was refilling.

"Oh, Karen," Rachel said before taking a sip.

"So you think our kids are ready for next week?" Karen asked as she helped herself to more coffee as well.

"I think so, especially now with the staff working so hard with them. Every teacher has been committed to getting these students ready. I feel pretty confident that our school is really going to shine."

The halls were quiet this morning, and all the classroom doors were closed as the students worked hard studying for the state test. Rachel knew they were going to do well next week. She had even been thinking of a fun reward she could to do for the entire school, maybe a root beer float party. On the week following tests, the students would also have an extended weekend because of the President's Day holiday, and the Dr. Seuss party would be held soon after.

"Wow, so every teacher is committed, you say?" Karen asked, tearing Rachel away from her thoughts.

"Yes, every last one of them, Karen." Rachel smiled knowingly.

"That's a turn of events for sure. Glad he finally came around."

"Me too. I will be so happy to get next week over with," Rachel said. "I'm looking forward to our Dr. Seuss party too. Have you started ordering any of the new books yet?"

"With all that money we got from the bake sale, I

was able to get quite a bit. The kids are going to have such a great time, and I bet they will be just as happy to be done with testing too."

\*\*\*

## Liam

Quiet had quickly fallen as students filed into the cafeteria for lunch and then swarmed the playground to enjoy the sunny weather. Liam had entered the teachers' lounge to grab his lunch when he noticed Rachel munching on a small sandwich and lost in her book.

"Hey, how's it going?" he said carefully as he sat across from her after pulling his sandwich from the fridge.

"Oh, hi, sorry," she replied, closing the paperback in front of her.

"I can let you get back to reading. I didn't mean to bother you."

"No, it's okay. You can join me. So how is the pretesting going for your class?" Rachel asked, before taking a nibble off her sandwich and motioning for him to sit.

Liam stared at her and swallowed. He'd been having a difficult time dealing with the whole testing thing. He thought he could get past it, but after turning in those pesky reports the parents had been forced to sign, he was honestly starting to hate it even more. In the past, the kids just took the test without all the pressure like there was this year, and he didn't like having to base his whole curriculum on how to fill in the right bubbles with a number two pencil. He really wanted to say something to her about how he felt.

"I want you to know, Liam, I really appreciate you turning in those reports." She blushed.

Seeing her get a little flustered lightened his mood considerably. That was why he had been dealing with those reports, he reminded himself. For her, his Rachel. "Rachel, I want it to be known that I still don't agree with all this focus on testing," Liam said cautiously, waiting for her reaction.

Rachel took in a deep breath. "I know you don't. I didn't think that would change overnight. But the fact remains that we have to test, and the more effort we put into practicing, the better the students will do when they actually take it. Besides, it'll be over before you know it, and then you can go back to being the fabulous teacher you are."

Her reaction surprised him. Based on their past confrontations, he figured she would've let him have it. Instead, she was patient and even gentle with him. He could get used to this. Liam sighed, deciding to switch gears. "So my mother told me she invited you on our little family moose watching trip next weekend."

"Yes, I got a message from Maggie this morning about it. Michael will be coming along, and she seems very happy about that."

"It's pretty hard to tear Michael away from work. I didn't realize he was going to make it. That's pretty cool." Liam felt a little dejected, though. He had just spoken with Maggie the other night, and she had failed to tell him about Michael.

"Yeah, I'm looking forward to meeting him. I'm very excited about the trip."

He eyed her suspiciously to see if he'd heard her right. "We usually have a lot of fun. The hardest part is getting up early to see if we can even find a moose."

"I'm happy your mom invited me." Rachel smiled, her mouth pink and soft.

Those lips were all Liam could focus on. He wanted to feel them on his. When the bell interrupted them, he tried to regain some composure before he rose from the table. "I'm glad she did too," he said, giving her a mischievous grin.

*** 

### Rachel

The weekend brought with it a wicked rainstorm, and Rachel's lights flickered as the wind toyed with the power lines. Rachel didn't leave her home once. Instead, she threw herself into preparing for Chelsea's visit. She was busy organizing some of the new items for her guest room when the phone rang.

"Hello?" she asked as she discarded the plastic wrapping from a new picture she had purchased for her guest room.

"Rachel, I wanted to see how you were holding up in this storm." Liam's voice was filled with concern, and it flooded her with instant warmth and need.

"I'm good. Just keeping busy with a little

project," she managed to say.

"It's a pretty bad storm. I was worried about your power. I lost mine a couple of times," Liam explained.

"Yeah, it's pretty crazy outside, but luckily I haven't lost mine yet. But I'm prepared. I have candles and stuff laid out."

"Candles, huh? Sounds like the makings of romantic night. Want me to come over and bring dinner?"

Liam's offer made her body flood with warmth. "Nope, but thanks for checking on me." Not letting him come over was almost painful.

"Well, if you need anything, please don't hesitate to call me." Liam sounded a little disappointed, but his voice was still smooth and sexy.

"Thanks, I will. Have a good night, Liam," Rachel said before hanging up.

She had to push herself to go work on the guest room, but she was thankful for the distraction. The O'Brien boy was giving her tingles everywhere.

***

## Liam

By Sunday evening, the storm had moved on, and the O'Briens were gathering at the table for their ritual dinner. Patrick helped his sons into their seats, trying to tame their young energy. Daniel wasn't helping much by constantly making silly faces at each boy, thereby causing them to break out into unstoppable giggling.

"Thanks, Daniel," Patrick said sarcastically. In response, Daniel crossed his eyes at the twins and made them laugh even more.

Liam chuckled as he carried a large pot of soup to the table. Mary's famous chicken noodle soup was filled with wide, homemade egg noodles and large pieces of chicken and vegetables and topped off with freshly baked homemade croutons. When the family was all seated, Grandpa Paddy led them in prayer before Mary ladled servings into bowls.

"This is delicious, Mom," Daniel stated as he sprinkling more croutons on his serving.

Liam nodded in agreement as the twins slurped the noodles loudly, causing Patrick to give them a stern look.

"So who's excited about next weekend?" Daniel asked the group.

Mary smiled at Liam as he said, "I'm looking forward to it. I'm happy to have a long weekend, and I'll finally be done with that testing."

"That's all?" Patrick smirked.

"No, that's not all."

Grandpa Paddy cleared his throat and pointed his spoon in Mary's direction as he said, "Mary says that pretty lass, the principal one you fancy, is coming along with us."

Mary tossed him a glare before giving Liam a sympathetic look. "Never mind him, but yes, Rachel will be joining us. Though heaven only knows why she would want to subject herself to this rowdy lot."

Daniel turned to Liam. "So, what, are you guys like a couple now?"

"No, not yet." Liam couldn't help the smile that

found its way to his face.

"You better step on it, son, before some other guy snatches her up," Liam's father pleaded.

"I know, Dad," Liam said before he spooned some soup into his mouth.

"He's right, lad. Another man gets wind of a pretty little thing like her, you will be straight out of luck," Grandpa Paddy added.

"Patience is a virtue. Some things aren't meant to be rushed; they take a little finesse," Mary quipped. "Besides, they only just met less than two months ago."

"They're right, though, Mom. It isn't like we always get a shipment of new women in the area," Daniel commented.

Liam rolled his eyes. For his part, Patrick kept his lips tightly together, and Liam appreciated it. He had only told his older brother about what had happened the night Rachel paid him a visit, and he was sort of shocked Patrick hadn't slipped up and told Daniel or even their mother.

"Thanks for the advice, guys. All I can say is that I'm working on it," Liam said, hoping that would be enough to get them to move on to another topic.

Thankfully, dinner continued without any other comments or unwanted advice. Afterward, Liam helped his mother clean up, and she made sure he was well stocked with plenty of leftover soup.

"Are you concerned at all about Rachel joining us, especially after tonight? I hope those men don't give her a hard time," Mary said with a mock frown.

"Don't worry, Mom, she has you to protect her,"

Liam assured her.

"I would hope it'd be you, son, who would be doing the protecting." Mary winked as she placed the full Tupperware bowl in his hands.

After kissing her good-bye, Liam started for the front door. On the way there, he passed by the den to let his father and grandfather know he was leaving. Patrick was seated with the men and got up to walk him out.

The air was slightly chilly and damp as the brothers made their way to Liam's truck.

"What's up?" Liam asked after putting the bowl of soup in the cab.

"I was curious how things were going with Rachel. I got to admit, I was kind of shocked when Mom told us the other day that she had invited her."

"I know, it threw me for a loop too. I'm glad Mom did, though. It was nice of her. She really likes Rachel, and I guess Maggie has taken a shine to her as well. They apparently have some kind of friendship going on," Liam said. "I took your advice about meeting her halfway about those reports, and things are getting better. A lot better."

"I'm glad. I know it's hard to have to compromise. Hopefully, this trip can bring you guys together."

"I think that's why Mom wants her to come with us."

"Oh, I'm sure it is. We need to figure out who is going in which RV. Before Rachel was invited, I figured you, I, and the kids could share one, but now I'm thinking we will have to bring all three RVs now." Patrick looked at Liam thoughtfully.

"Well, as long as I'm in the same one Rachel is in," Liam said.

Patrick rolled his eyes and grinned sheepishly.

"You wanting to chaperone us now?" Liam joked as he climbed into his truck.

"All things considered, probably not a bad idea," Patrick answered playfully before saying good night to Liam.

\*\*\*

## Liam

Liam stood in front of his students on Wednesday afternoon, beaming and clapping his hands. "That was the last test! You did it! You guys are awesome!"

Cheers erupted from the class as Liam thanked them for putting their best work out there. He was proud of them, and no test could ever change that. He had never seen his students disappear quicker when the last bell rang. They were just as eager for their long break as he was and had no problem showing it.

\*\*\*

## Rachel

Rachel yawned as she sat at her desk. Even though the week was short because of the holiday, she felt exhausted. There had been so much stress in just three days. She wasn't sure if she was happier that the testing was done or that she was about to embark on a family vacation with the O'Briens.

A soft knock interrupted her thoughts, and Karen peeked through the open door. "I wanted to let you know I have all the test booklets from all the classes."

"Even from Liam's?" Rachel questioned with a hopeful grin.

"His were the first to be turned in." Karen smiled as she let herself into the office and closed the door behind her. "I hear you're going on a little family trip," she said as she sat down in the chair in front of the desk.

"You heard right, and from Mary, I assume?" Rachel returned the smile as a nervous blush crept along her neck.

"Yes. Mary is thrilled to have you join them. She also said Maggie was headed in tonight."

Rachel had received a text from her earlier. She seemed excited to get to finally visit with Rachel again, and the feeling was mutual. "I know. I can't wait for us to leave tomorrow."

"Well, I'm so glad you and Maggie are becoming friends. She is truly a lovely girl." Karen gave Rachel a hard look. "But I'm more curious about you and Liam. You two seem to be getting along a tad better these days."

Rachel let out a little huff. "We are."

"Come on, Rachel, you don't have to hide it from me. It's plain as day, just so you know," Karen gently chided.

"What is?" Rachel said, surprised.

"Honestly, I know I'm old, but I'm not blind or stupid," Karen said as she leaned forward and patted Rachel's hand. "I see the looks you two exchange, and I've seen how you light up when he's near and the joy that radiates from him too. There's something special between you two."

There was no point in arguing. Rachel knew Karen was right.

"I hope this weekend that maybe you guys can finally figure out what you're going to do about it," Karen added. "Liam's a good guy, Rachel."

"I know he is." She looked down at her hands, knowing she had struggled long enough with her emotions.

"Why are you not interested, then?"

"Oh Karen, I don't know." Rachel paused. Admitting defeat was hard, and admitting she might, in fact, love Liam was even more difficult. "I am interested, but I just don't see how it can work."

"Well, I'll be praying for you when you are out there this weekend." Karen got up from her seat and waved good-bye. "Have a lovely time, Rachel."

***

Rachel had started the process of packing, an activity she didn't enjoy. She had several pieces of clothing strewn across her bed when she decided to take a break and plopped alongside them to call her friend.

"Hey Chelsea," Rachel said as she snuggled further onto the bed

"Haven't heard from you for a couple days. How

did that testing stuff go?"

"It's over, so that's good. Now I pray for good results and the district signing me on for another year."

"So you think you want to stay another year?" Chelsea questioned.

"Well, I don't want to get fired, and I hope I did make a difference with the school."

"I'm sure you did. I know you made an impression on more than just the students. Speaking of which, aren't you headed out for your little adventure tomorrow?"

"Yup, I'm trying to pack now."

"That's why you called. You need help from the wardrobe goddess. It will be my pleasure to assist you," Chelsea teased.

Rachel laughed. "You are the best. Besides, you are just so good at it."

"I know, it's a gift."

"Hey, I almost forgot to tell you, the guest room is officially amazing. I had ordered some bedding online, and it's so pretty."

"Ah, you didn't have to go to all that trouble for me. I know how busy you are. I could've helped you," Chelsea whined sweetly.

"No, honestly, it was a great distraction."

"I can't wait to see it."

"So when do we want to get your plane tickets?" Rachel asked as she leaned over to look at her calendar.

"I actually already purchased them."

"Oh, okay. I wanted to get them for you, my treat, since you are my guest."

"I know, but I haven't taken a trip in forever, and when I went online, I saw a couple great deals and figured I better snatch them up," Chelsea explained happily.

"Well, I'm glad you got them. I'm so excited to have you come up."

"Okay, so enough about my trip. We need to figure out what you need to pack for yours."

Rachel sighed. "True. It's still kind of cold here, so jeans and sweaters are sort of a must."

"Do you have leggings or skinny jeans?" Chelsea asked. "Something cute to showcase those great legs of yours."

"I don't want to wear anything too tight or revealing. His family will be there."

"Oh, you mean that hot brother of his is going. Dang, I should have come up for this trip," Chelsea complained playfully. "So how do you think it will be with you and Liam?"

"I'm not sure. We've been getting along okay, no fighting or anything. Then again, we've been too busy at work to argue. I want to have a nice time with him and his family. I hope we see a moose. I will try to get a picture for you if we do."

"What are the sleeping arrangements?" Chelsea said with interest.

"I have no idea, actually. I know we're taking RVs, so I assume we'll have to bunk together. Come on, his parents and siblings are going to be there. This isn't like a romantic weekend getaway or anything."

"Maybe you need to turn it into one," Chelsea suggested.

Rachel had barely gotten over her shame and guilt from sleeping with Liam, and she had no intention of doing that again unless they were going to try to have a relationship. She hoped being out in the woods would help clear her mind and give her some much-needed answers.

A beeping sound interrupted their conversation.

"Hey, Chelsea, I have another call. It's my mom, and I better take it. I'll call you a little later."

Switching calls, Rachel inhaled before answering, "Hello?"

"Hello, darling, it's your mother," Evelyn Montgomery's voice chimed at the other end of the line.

"Hi, Mom. Everything all right?" It was unusual for her mother to call her.

"Oh yes, nothing wrong at all. I had lunch with Chelsea's mother, and she informed me her daughter was going to be coming up for a visit soon."

"I was actually on the phone with her when you called. I'm excited about her coming."

"I'm sure you are. Chelsea really is quite a lovely girl."

Rachel could tell Evelyn was holding something back. "Mom, I hate to sound ungrateful for your call, but we haven't talked on the phone in a very long time, so it seems a little out the blue."

"I must say, I have some concerns I wanted to address."

"Concerns? Everything all right?" Rachel repeated as she sat upright in her bed, on edge now.

"Yes, everything is fine. My concerns are with

you, darling. Chelsea's mother mentioned there might be a young man you may possibly be interested in dating."

Rachel felt the sudden urge to kill Chelsea. Why would she tell her mother anything about Liam? Mentally gearing up for an all-out war with Evelyn, she tried not to blame Chelsea, who, after all, had a much better relationship with her mother. They were able to actually open up a bit to each other about what was going on in their lives, unlike Rachel and her family.

"My concern, dear, is not that you're finally interested in dating again. I'm actually quite thrilled to hear you are. I am concerned, however, about the type of man you seem to be eyeing."

Rachel groaned. "Mom, first of all, while I think I may be interested in dating again, I'm not seeing anyone right now." She decided acting nonchalant was the best option for now. She didn't want her mother to know anything about Liam, whom she was falling hopelessly in love with despite herself.

"Oh Rachel, it's been over two years since you and Trevor broke up. But I can imagine why you had such heartbreak. That man was perfect, and somehow you let him slip through your hands. I think you made a huge mistake when you refused to quit working and marry him."

No, that wasn't the only reason they had broken up. Of course, her mother didn't want to recognize that he had decided Rachel wasn't enough and had slept with almost every nurse on the hospital floor where he worked. The sad part was that Rachel was almost willing to forgive the infidelities, but she refused to stay home with no career, letting everything she'd worked for turn into dust, while her potential husband screwed anything with a set of boobs. Trevor had only wanted Rachel so he could join her father's celebrity-filled practice. She had been naive, and his good looks and charm had let him deceive her easily. It was her first serious relationship, and instead of having a fairy-tale ending as she'd hoped, it became twisted and ugly.

"Mom, you know it was more than that. I don't even want to get into this with you right now." Rachel was steaming mad. Why couldn't her mother take her side and actually defend her like a mother should—like how she knew Mary O'Brien would?

"Stop being dramatic, Rachel. I don't want to see you be a fool and get involved with someone who isn't up to par with your station in life."

Rachel almost laughed. "You don't care who I marry as long as he is rich and successful and runs in the same stupid circles you do."

"That isn't what I'm saying. I think you need to have someone who is equal, or even better than you."

Was she hearing her mother correctly? Did she seriously think her daughter needed to find a man who was better than she was?

"You know, Mom, I think it's best we agree to disagree. Thanks for the advice," Rachel said before hanging up. As she lay back down on her pillow, hot tears immediately flowed in small rivers down her cheeks.

\*\*\*

## Liam

The sun was peeking out from behind stark white clouds as Liam pulled up to his parents' home, fully packed and ready for the adventure they were about to embark on. He noticed the family's three large RVs parked alongside the home and across the street.

Melanie burst out the front door and made a beeline for him. "Uncle Liam!" she cried and wrapped her arms around him the second he got out of the truck.

He couldn't believe how much she had grown in only a month or so since he had last seen her.

"How's my favorite niece in the entire world?" He scooped her up into an embrace and swung her around in a full circle before setting her back down.

"I'm so excited, Uncle Liam. When are we leaving?"

"I'm not sure, kiddo. We have to see what Grams says, okay? I know we are waiting for someone to arrive." He hadn't see Rachel's car when he'd pulled up, and worry started to gnaw at him.

Melanie loudly announced his arrival as they walked inside, and Mary gave him a kiss.

"Morning, sweetheart. The guys are loading up the last of everything. Rachel called and is on her way." She smiled knowingly.

"Yeah, I didn't see her car." Liam tried to play it cool, but he knew he wasn't fooling anyone, especially his mother. He gave her a quick hug and set off to see if he could help the guys.

A few minutes later, Rachel's silver BMW crawled slowly up the street, making Liam worry. Maybe she had doubts about going on this trip. But then Rachel parked and emerged from her car, dressed in a pale pink sweater and jeans, and Liam couldn't help but think how touchable, soft, and purely feminine she looked.

"Good morning," he stammered.

"Oh, hi. Sorry, I was running a little late. But I brought a peace offering." She seemed distracted as she retrieved two large boxes from her car. "Donuts."

Daniel must have smelled the fresh-baked goodies, because he rounded an RV instantly. "Morning, Rachel."

"Hi, Daniel. Do you mind taking these for me?" She handed off the boxes.

"I'll run these in to Mom." Daniel turned quickly toward the house.

"Can I help you with any of your bags?" Liam offered, a little upset that his brother had come to Rachel's aid.

"Sure, thanks." She unlocked her trunk, where a medium-sized suitcase sat along with a backpack.

Liam hefted the suitcase out. It wasn't very heavy, so he swung the backpack onto his shoulder.

"Oh, I didn't mean for you to get everything," Rachel said, following him.

Liam stopped at one of the RVs and stepped inside. The interior was clean, cozy, and comfortable. Each RV had a bathroom and a bedroom, as well as a decent-sized kitchen and large sitting areas. He hoped she liked it.

"Maggie insisted we bunk with them," Liam said as he placed her suitcase near the sitting area.

"Oh, that's great." Rachel seemed to be relieved.

A couple minutes passed in awkward silence before Maggie joined them.

"Hey, roomie!" she cried as she embraced Rachel. "I hope you don't mind," Maggie said as she quickly exchanged looks with Liam.

"No, this is amazing." Rachel squeezed Maggie back before adding, "Do you or your mom need any help before we leave?"

"I'm sure she does," she answered.

Rachel followed Maggie out of the RV. When she turned back and gave Liam a broad smile, his heart lurched inside his chest. He couldn't explain the hold this woman had on him. But judging by her expression, he was pretty sure Rachel knew.

# *Chapter Twenty*

### Rachel

"Mary, can I take anything out for you?" Rachel asked as she stood in the living room with Liam's mother.

"No, I think we have it, dear," Mary replied as a man Rachel hadn't met walked through the front door.

"Got anything else for us to load, Mary?" he asked.

Maggie grabbed him by the arm and led him toward Rachel. "I would like you to meet my husband Michael." She turned her green eyes to him. "Michael, this is Rachel."

He extended his hand to her, and Rachel noticed it was soft and well manicured. His smile was filled with perfectly white teeth.

"Pleased to meet you, Rachel. Maggie talks nonstop about you. All good things, I promise." He laughed as Maggie softly punched his arm.

"Nice meeting you as well," Rachel said. He was

handsome, too sharply dressed for a camping trip, and his demeanor screamed professional. She recalled Maggie saying he was a lawyer or something along those lines.

"We better get on the road, guys. Everyone out," Mary ordered playfully as she shooed everyone out the door.

Rachel followed Maggie to the RV they would be using, noticing Liam was already behind the wheel of the massive vehicle. Their gazes connected immediately.

"Michael, why don't you ride up there with Liam?" Maggie suggested. "Rachel and I will hang out back here with Mel."

Michael climbed into the passenger seat, and Maggie led Rachel to the large sitting area. Melanie was curled up in the corner on one of the couches, her gaze glued to the screen of her handheld game system.

Rachel took a seat across from Maggie as the RV started to pull away from the house.

"So how far away is this campground?" she asked, feeling a little queasy as they rolled down the street. She wasn't use to this jarring motion and tried to calm her nerves by looking out the window.

"About an hour or so. It's really beautiful there. We go every year, and it's a lot of fun, huh, Mel?"

Melanie looked up and smiled but quickly returned to her game.

"I'm glad your mom invited me. I've been looking forward to this since she told me."

"I know, I'm so happy she asked you too. So how are things going at work?" Maggie said, looking toward the driver's seat as if trying to tell if Liam was eavesdropping.

Rachel had been keeping Maggie in the loop for the most part through email and text messages. However, she had avoided discussing anything too deep about her and Liam. She knew she was walking a fine line here. After all, Maggie was still his sister, and Rachel knew the two were close. So divulging any information about her feelings for Liam could complicate their new friendship.

"Honestly, things are much better." Rachel wasn't lying; things were better.

Liam stole a glance at Rachel, and she gave him a small smile in return as she spoke with Maggie. She was completely at ease with his family, and she hoped she would get that way with him too.

Aside from the constant jostling of the RV as it worked its way over the wet, muddy ground along the curvy mountain roads, the drive to the campsite was incredible. Snow lingered on the walls of the mountains and hills, and they were surrounded by majestic tamarack and cedar trees.

"Mom, are we almost there?" Melanie whined, tossing her game to the side. "I'm hungry. Can I have a snack, please?"

"We're almost there, Pumpkin," Maggie answered as she fished around inside a large bag for a box of graham crackers for her daughter.

Michael leaned over and whispered something in Melanie's ear. It must have been quite funny, because she erupted into wild giggles.

Liam tossed a look at Rachel. "You doing okay back there?"

"Yep. Eyes on the road, mister," Rachel commanded nervously. Her stomach still hadn't gotten used to the constant jiggle of the RV. Liam smiled as he turned his focus back to the road.

A little while later, Liam followed the caravan of RVs to a partially secluded campground that offered a splendid view of a decent-sized lake. The RVs created a wall as they parked with their doors facing the lake.

Rachel sighed in relief. Now that they had stopped, hopefully her insides could go back where they belonged.

Everyone fled the RVs and sprung into action making camp. Mary led the women, including Melanie, in setting up portable chairs and tables. The men secured the RVs and discussed going out for firewood, even though they had brought a decent amount of dry, seasoned logs.

Rachel soaked in the damp, fresh scent that can only be found in the deep forest as she absorbed the rugged crevices of the mountains that surrounded them. She had never been camping before and couldn't help but feel a bit uneasy about the animals or monsters that might be lurking in the thick trees. An image of Bigfoot crossed her mind. If that thing existed, it would be living out here for sure. Still, being outside among the greenery and stone made her mind feel free and clear. She felt as though she could finally think and breathe.

The campers settled in around lunchtime, and Mary had already started an assembly line for the women to organize the meal. One table acted as a buffet filled with homemade barbecued baked beans, potato salad, condiments, plastic cups, and cutlery. Paper plates were neatly stacked next to several packages of hotdog buns. Mary had already ordered for a campfire to be started, and it was billowing large plumes of smoke as the flames licked the iron grill where they would cook the hot dogs.

The older O'Brien men had planted themselves in front the calm, mirror-like lake. As they sipped beers and enjoyed the view from their canvas chairs, Liam and Daniel tried to help the young twins burn off some energy with a game of catch. Meanwhile, Patrick stoked the fire and chatted with his father and grandfather.

Rachel wished she'd brought her cell phone so she could capture the family enjoying the tranquility of nature and one another's company. Her gaze then shifted to Maggie's husband. Michael had his laptop out and was desperately trying to find a signal with his cell phone. She couldn't help but think how out of place he looked. Dressed in khakis and a cream sweater, he didn't fit into this picture of rugged O'Brien men who were dressed in jeans, thick hiking boots, and thermal or flannel shirts that hugged their broad chests.

Liam wore a deep olive-green thermal shirt under a warm brown flannel, and both colors brought out the emerald and gold tones of his eyes. His worn, soft, and comfortable-looking jeans fit well against his long legs. He oozed sexy mountain-man appeal with his unshaven jaw and slightly shaggy hair.

Shaking away those thoughts, Rachel asked

Mary what else needed to be done.

"I think I'll have Pat and Grandpa Paddy roast the hot dogs now. I'm sure everyone is getting a little hungry," Mary replied as she hugged Melanie.

Sitting around the fire and balancing their paper plates in their laps, the family devoured their lunch. Conversation flowed as they shared old memories and made new ones. Rachel and Liam sat next to each other, and their arms occasionally brushed as they ate or talked.

"Liam, you should show Rachel that trail that leads to the other side of the lake," Mary suggested as she started to gather up the plates after they had finished eating.

Liam turned to Rachel. "What do you think?"

"Mary, are you sure I can't help you first?" Rachel asked, not wanting her to get stuck with all the cleanup.

"Oh no, it's fine, dear," Mary answered, giving Liam a slight nod.

"Well, okay then. Let me grab my gloves real quick, Liam," Rachel said as she set off toward the RV where her luggage was stowed.

\*\*\*

The ground crunched under their boots as they walked together at a steady pace to keep warm.

"This place is gorgeous. I can see why you guys all come out here," Rachel said as they worked their way onto a small trail of flattened, worn ground. She guessed that animals heading to the lake had made it over the years.

"Yeah, it's one of my favorite places." When Liam took Rachel's hand, she didn't flinch or pull back. "I'm glad you came with us."

She smiled, enjoying the quiet as they continued to walk hand in hand alongside the lake. Up close, she could spot layers of ice she hadn't noticed before on the water. Along the way, Liam wrapped his hands around her waist to lift her over several old, decaying logs that had fallen in their path.

"God, you're beautiful, Rachel," Liam sighed, his voice heavy as he leaned in closer.

Rachel stood rigid but didn't pull back. She told herself not to worry and not to think but just to let go and be in the moment.

The kiss was gentle, not rushed or demanding. The same current that had surged between them each time they had kissed returned, but this time it spread through her slowly, as if this kiss were seeking new meaning, new promises.

Liam pulled back slowly, took her hand again, and continued to guide her on the trail. As they reached the end near a small tributary that fed into the lake, Liam took a seat on a large fallen tree. Rachel watched him gaze at the landscape as he breathed slow and easy, clearly contented. She envied his calm. She had been rattled by their kiss. Though it wasn't as passionate and wild as their previous kisses had been, it was still wonderful, but in a way Rachel couldn't quite understand. She tried to seem as interested as Liam was in the beauty of the scene around them while her brain struggled to work out her feelings.

"Well, we probably should get back before they

send a search party," Liam said after they shared about twenty minutes of quiet reflection.

He extended his hand to help Rachel up, and they traveled back, exchanging comfortable conversation. Finally, Rachel realized what had been different about the kiss. This walk felt just like the time they had explored Birch Valley together. She had loved spending that time with him, and now she was finally able to accept that she needed to be with Liam. The only major roadblock now was how they would handle being a couple while working together. But if she wanted a relationship with him, she knew she needed to figure out a way around that obstacle.

\*\*\*

As they approached the camp, Rachel heard lively music. Grandpa Paddy was singing an Irish folksong, his rich brogue bringing it to life. Rachel released Liam's hand and instantly felt the loss of their connection.

"There they be. Mary almost had us call in the troops for you," Grandpa Paddy declared before resuming his singing.

"Never mind him." Mary shooed the old man away. "Rachel, did you enjoy the trail?"

"I did. It's really breathtaking. This whole place is beautiful. Thank you for bringing me here." She couldn't help but look up at Liam.

Liam smiled at his mother as he gently placed his hand on the small of Rachel's back. "You want anything to warm you up?" he asked her.

"I started a pot of coffee if you would care for some," Mary said.

"That would be wonderful," Rachel answered. Even though she was warm to her toes from kissing Liam, coffee was always welcome.

With Styrofoam cups in hand, the group sat around the fire again and listened to Grandpa Paddy sing. Rachel was in awe of his spectacular voice as it took her to a different place with green, rolling hills, a cold ocean crashing violently against cliffs, and an old world that was magical and alive with heritage.

Shortly thereafter, the kids all went back to the RVs for a nap, and Rachel studied Liam's family in fond silence. Mary was huddled close to her husband's side with her eyes closed and a contented smile on her face. Grandpa Paddy was lost in his music, his eyes teary as he sang. Daniel was oddly quiet and almost appeared lonely, and Patrick looked deep in thought as he stared off into the distance. Maggie clutched her cup and was staring at her husband, who seemed a million miles away as he kept raising his cell phone in frustration to try to locate a signal. Liam was humming along with Grandpa Paddy with his long legs extended toward the fire. He had that familiar look on his face of overall happiness and being content.

Even without speaking, the O'Briens shared a closeness, and Rachel could feel the love and security hovering over them. She had never had any moments like this with her family, had never felt that sensation of love and effortless togetherness. She realized then that being with Liam would also mean having a place among his family. Her heart squeezed with an odd longing when he put his hand on her knee and rubbed it lightly. The connection was instant.

The afternoon quickly transformed into night, and the air was cold without the cloud cover. The family had finished a dinner of stew and homemade biscuits, Rachel was washing dishes in one of the RVs, and the children were watching a movie in the sitting area nearby. Looking at their small faces mesmerized by the dancing characters on the screen, she couldn't help but feel domestic and maternal in this homey setting. When she imagined herself being a mother, a thought she didn't have often, she was surprised that it didn't frighten her but filled her with longing instead.

Maggie entered the RV with a few more used bowls, stirring Rachel from her fantasy.

"Are they being good for you?" she asked, nodding in the direction of the children as she set the dirty dishes in the sink.

"They haven't even moved," Rachel joked. "Apparently, that movie is riveting."

Maggie laughed and braced herself against the counter near Rachel. "So are you enjoying yourself?" she inquired, her gaze still on the children.

"I don't know if I have ever had such a nice time," Rachel said as she rinsed soap from the bowls. "It's so relaxing out here. I've never been camping and had no idea what I was missing out on."

"Yeah, I always like coming out here with the

family. Now that we have Mel, I wish we were here more."

"She's such a sweet little girl, Maggie. She seems to be having a blast."

"I know. That's what makes being over on the coast so hard." Maggie's eyes turned sad as she looked at Rachel.

Instantly, Rachel wondered what was going on with her new friend, but she didn't know if it was her place to ask.

"I want her to grow up with her cousins and with my parents and brothers," Maggie said as she looked at the children again.

"You guys all seem very close, despite the fact you don't live here. I can't get over how neat your family is," Rachel said. "My family is nothing like yours. In fact, I got into this argument with my mother last night. Keep in mind, Maggie, her and I, like, never speak. She only sends me a text message here and there, okay?" Rachel swallowed before she began to relive the conversation with Evelyn. "So I get this call from her, and she isn't calling to check in on her daughter who moved fifteen hundred miles away, so I assume something must be wrong."

Maggie looked concerned. "How sad. So you two aren't very close, then, I take it?"

"Nope. She has always been kind of hands-off with me and my brother. My father isn't much better, to be honest," Rachel explained. "Anyway, she calls, and I finally get her to tell me the reason behind her call. She had lunch with my best friend's mom, and I guess she mentioned to my mother that I was dating someone up here."

Maggie's eyes grew wide. "Liam?"

"See, I had told my friend about him, and obviously, as you know, we have some sort of thing we are trying to really figure out, but that's a whole other ball of wax," Rachel rambled, drying her hands on a dish towel. "So I used to be in a relationship my mother thought was absolutely perfect, only it was far from it. Well, she accuses me of ruining that relationship, and well, she just got so nasty," Rachel said, feeling the hurt from last night return.

"Oh, I'm sorry, Rachel." Maggie rubbed Rachel's arm soothingly. "Why doesn't your mom support your reason for not being with that guy?"

"I could give you a hundred reasons why that woman never supports me, but you see, he's a doctor, like my dad, and also a pretty big scumbag, as it turned out. She just wants me to marry and have kids and play in the same ridiculous social circle she's in," Rachel confessed.

Maggie frowned. "Yeah, I can't say my mom is like that. I mean, she always tries to see the good in everyone, but I know she has my back no matter what," she said as she led Rachel to the couch. "See, I get so lonely in Seattle. Michael is constantly working. He says it's for our future, but it's frustrating."

"Yeah, I've noticed his phone is kind of glued to him," Rachel said carefully.

"I know. I wish he would be more present and realize that him being here with us is far more important than work. I want the memories we're making here to be good ones," Maggie explained.

"So Michael has been talking about wanting more children, which would be great, I guess, but I feel like a single mom half the time as it is. I can't see the sense in bringing another baby into the mix right now."

"Have you guys thought about moving back here? Maybe a slower pace would be good for Michael," Rachel said, smoothing a wrinkle on her jeans.

"We have tossed the idea around, but he's so damned focused on making partner at the firm he's at," she whispered, glancing over at the children. She clearly didn't want them to hear her frustration.

"You know, it's funny, because here I am, from a pretty large city myself, and I came to this teeny tiny town not knowing what to expect. I was worried I couldn't adapt. But let me tell you, it has slowed me down in ways that were so unexpected, and I find I'm actually pretty happy here."

Maggie smiled. "I'm glad you moved here, and if we ever do move back, it's comforting to know I have a great new friend in Birch Valley."

"Don't get me wrong. I miss certain things about living in the city, but it is different here. If I ever get married and have kids, I'd want to raise them in a place like this," Rachel said.

"That's how I feel, and now that Melanie is getting older, I want her to grow up here. I think what's hard is that Michael doesn't quite see this place like I do. He was born and raised in Seattle, so the small-town thing is only something he sees when he visits, you know?"

"You can't blame him for wanting more kids.

Look how beautiful your daughter is." Rachel looked at the young girl falling asleep next to her cousins.

Maggie sighed. "I know, and Michael is a good dad. He loves her like crazy. But I just feel so stuck."

"What do you do when Melanie is in school?" Rachel asked, leaning her tired head on her hand as she propped herself up on the couch.

"Well, I used to work, but once I got pregnant, I stayed home. I keep busy for the most part, and I help out at her school a lot."

"Do you have any friends there?"

"Sort of. I know that sounds silly, but mainly, they're the wives of Michael's colleagues or some moms from the school. I left pretty much everyone I knew when I moved over there." Maggie sighed.

Rachel didn't know what to add. She had left Chelsea, her only true friend at the time, and that had been difficult. She had then found that making friends in Birch Valley didn't go quite how she thought it would. She could relate to Maggie's loneliness somewhat, but now instead of wanting to form friendships, the gears inside her had shifted, and something she'd had no intention of wanting now stood in her sights front and center. She now wanted a relationship, possibly marriage and maybe even children.

"I understand being lonely. I miss my friend Chelsea. She is so unlike anyone I have ever met, and we grew up together, so she knows me pretty damn well," Rachel said. "She is actually coming up next week to visit. I haven't seen her since I moved."

"That's so neat."

"Yeah, she's thinking of staying through spring break. Maybe you can come back over and meet her."

"That would be nice. I'm pretty sure me and Mel will be back here for spring break."

The two women talked for a little longer until a soft knock interrupted them.

Liam's tall figure stood in the doorway. "Hey, ladies," he said. "Everyone is heading to bed."

Maggie glanced at her watch. They'd been chatting for a couple hours. Funny how time could disappear when you were locked in a great conversation with a new friend.

"I better tuck these kids in. Is Patrick coming for the twins, or does he want them just to stay in here?" Maggie asked.

"Let me check." Liam vanished.

"Here, let me help you," Rachel offered as she turned off the TV and pulled out some blankets for the children.

Michael appeared a moment later. "Getting the kids tucked in? Patrick said to leave the boys in here tonight."

"Yeah, that works. Sorry, Rachel and I lost track of time," Maggie explained as she hefted up one of the twins onto the double bed.

Michael lifted the second child. "No, it's fine. Everyone just sat around and decided to turn in. Your mom said we need to get up early to try and see those moose," he whispered.

Maggie turned to Rachel. "Oh, I hope we see

some tomorrow. Have you ever seen one?"

"No, and to be completely honest, I'm a little scared," Rachel admitted.

"Well, I'm sure my brother won't leave your side, so you'll be fine," Maggie teased.

Rachel smiled at the thought and said good night as she exited the RV.

\*\*\*

She found Liam waiting for her.

"You want to sit outside for a little bit before we turn in?" he asked as he ushered her to an empty chair.

"Sure."

The clear sky was dazzling with its studded blanket of stars. The temperature was dropping, causing Rachel to shiver and bundle her jacket tighter around her.

"It's really something out here. You never see the stars like this in California," she commented, staring up at the sky.

"Light pollution. Just think, if you didn't have all those streetlamps and lights everywhere, you could see these stars there."

"Yeah, but I've got to admit, I kind of like all the lights. It can be so dark when I'm driving at night around here," Rachel said. "This makes it more special, having to find a secluded spot like this to see the stars," she added in a quieter voice.

Liam's mouth contorted into the sexy grin she'd come to love. "Yeah, I suppose so."

Rachel began to feel a little nervous. They were

alone, the lights were turned off inside the RVs, and only the moon and campfire cast shadows around them.

"Rachel, can we talk?" Liam said cautiously.

"About what?" She was suddenly alert.

"About what's happening between us."

Rachel wasn't entirely sure she was ready to discuss this topic. The guilt and shame of sleeping with him had since washed away, but she hadn't quite managed to fully own the feelings that had replaced them yet.

"Rachel, when I'm with you—"

"I know," Rachel said. "I get it. I'm just having some difficulty figuring out how I can make this work with my position and yours."

"What is there to figure out?" he asked, turning his eyes to her.

"Like what if this doesn't work out? What about our jobs?"

"I think it will work out. I have never felt anything like this before. Have you?" Liam asked as he took her hand.

"No. That's what scares me so much. I've been so mad at myself."

"For what?" Liam begged as he rubbed his thumb against the top of her hand soothingly.

"For so many things. For starters, running away the morning after we were together. That was awful and unfair to you. I didn't consider how that would make you feel, and I'm so sorry, Liam." Rachel's voice was almost a whisper, and she could feel herself beginning to dissolve. Pieces of the hardened wall she had worked so hard to build around her heart were crumbling. Tears started to trickle down her chilled cheeks.

"Oh Rachel, it's okay, baby." Liam smoothed them softly from her face.

"Being here with you and your family feels so nice and perfect. I'm not used to anything like this. I wasn't looking for this when I came up here," Rachel said, allowing herself to feel the range of emotions as they flooded her.

She had left her whole life behind when she moved here because she felt something was missing. She just didn't expect to find it so soon.

"We need to get up early if we want any chance of seeing a moose." Liam led her to the RV, where he guided her to her bedroom in the rear and planted another feathery kiss on her forehead. His arms sought her and brought her closer to him. Rachel's face found refuge on his broad chest, where she breathed in the scent of his aftershave mixed with wood smoke from the campfire. She fought hard against the urge to grab him and pull him into her bed. She could tell Liam was restraining himself too as he released his hold on her and said good night, leaving her alone in the tiny bedroom.

***

**Liam**

Closing the pocket door and leaving Rachel in the RV was one of the hardest things he'd ever done.

The sitting room in the RV was softly

illuminated by moonlight as Liam stared at the ceiling above the couch. He hadn't realized how fragile Rachel was. He didn't like seeing her cry and instantly wanted to protect her and shield her from any pain, emotional or physical. He wanted her in so many more ways too. He loved how she fit right in with his family, like a perfect piece to their puzzle. Her ability to engage so effortlessly with his mother and sister amazed him, and she was sweet to his father and grandfather, particularly tonight when she'd brought them the hot dogs to cook. She also got along well with his brothers, joking and laughing with them as if they were old friends. He had a fleeting sensation that this was what their lives could be like if he and Rachel were married. Marriage wasn't usually something he enjoyed thinking about, not because he didn't want to get married eventually but because he had never met someone he might want to marry. Until now.

Dizzying visions of what was happening between him and Rachel circled his brain until sleep finally invaded him.

\*\*\*

## Rachel

It was still dark out when the O'Brien family gathered the next morning to search for moose. The air was brisk, and a dense fog hovered over the lake and clung to the trees, giving the land an eerie look.

Armed with hot coffee and binoculars, they went off in different directions. Dressed in camouflage clothing, Patrick and Daniel embarked on a trail together. Maggie dragged Michael along with her, securing her arm tightly around his as they followed a more open path closer to the water. Grandpa Paddy and Pat moved slowly, taking easy paces toward higher ground so they could have a view of a wider area. Mary, meanwhile, decided to stay back with the kids and work on breakfast.

Liam and Rachel stalked quietly through the wooded area, eyes peeled for any sign of the elusive moose. Rachel wasn't quite sure where these creatures hid, but they were good at it. They had been walking for a while without any luck, and just when Rachel had lost hope of seeing one, Liam paused, grabbing her arm gently. He put his finger to his lips, silently guiding her with his eyes to a mother and her calf. They were strolling slowly through the thick brush, nibbling and grazing without a care in the world on their way to the lake.

Rachel was in complete awe at the sight of them. The mother was far larger than she had imagined, significantly bigger than the deer that were always in her yard. The baby was a goofy little thing with awkward legs, and it kept close to its mother. The cinnamon-colored animal sniffed the air and nudged her calf, indicating they better get a move on. She suddenly seemed a bit nervous.

"We might want to back off. I think she's getting a whiff of us. They can be pretty protective with their young," Liam whispered.

"Wow, I could watch them all day," Rachel commented as the moose walked toward a series of trees that separated them from the water. She then turned her gaze to Liam's handsome face. The beginnings of a beard lined his jaw, and his green eyes were bold against the gray of the early morning.

Turning back to watch the mother and her baby, Rachel asked, "Wait, where did they go?"

"Probably down to the lake. Quick, aren't they?" Liam said as he pointed in the direction they'd most likely gone. "We should head back."

Rachel was in no hurry to return to camp. Being alone in the woods with Liam felt primal, as if they were the only two people in an undiscovered world.

"Liam," she murmured.

He stood there towering over her, his green eyes piercing as they searched her own.

"I think I might love you," Rachel said.

Liam brought his head lower and pressed their foreheads lightly together before pulling her into his arms.

"I know I love you," he answered before kissing her full on the mouth. The dewy air clung to them as they stood in their embrace.

Rachel had known that moving to Birch Valley would help her find what had been missing in her life, and now, as Liam held her tight, she realized she was holding his heart and their future.

# *Epilogue*

Her nerves were zinging in all directions as she reread the label on the box. Breathing in slowly to steady the uneven waves crashing wickedly in her stomach, she braced herself as she watched one line form in one of the two plastic-covered windows on the test strip, followed by a faint second line.

Maybe she should try again. After all, there were two tests in the box. Perhaps this one was faulty, a dud or something. If it was right, this was definitely not something she had planned for.

After taking out the other test, she straddled the toilet again and let the warm stream leave her body while praying silently that this would yield a different result. The bathroom light shone harshly down on her as she placed the test on the granite countertop and watched and waited. The first line was visible in seconds, and soon the other plastic-covered window proudly displayed a bold line. It was positive.

Looking in the mirror, she saw her eyes were red from crying. What was she going to do?

# *About the Author*

I was born and raised in southern California and relocated to beautiful eastern Washington state. The rural small towns that speckle this vast area have inspired my ideal setting for most of the stories I write. The pine and tamarack trees covering the towering mountains, the shimmering lakes and rivers, the abundant wildlife and a feeling of a time forgotten, stirs so many of my creative juices. I can't thank my parents enough for dragging this city kid on long roadtrips up to this rugged foreign area, because now it is my home and I truly love my life here.

Reading was something that spurred me to begin writing at a young age. I enjoyed creating characters, different settings, and describing anything and everything. Storytelling, I have found is something I have inherited from both of my parents. I love attention to detail, using words to fully bring the picture alive, that is something I got from my dad. Creating characters and figuring out their story and how to achieve their happy ending comes from my mom. Then there is the smell of a book, new or old, the weight of it in your hands as you balance it open, seeing all those beautifully typed words spun and woven into sentences, this was created by a writer. I knew that was what I wanted to be when I grew up.

Over the years I fiddled with a story here and there, but it wasn't until 2015 that I realized it was time. Time to get those dreams down on paper (or my laptop) and so The Cloverleaf Series was born.

Coming from a family that is focused on being involved in each other's lives as much as possible created a great deal of inspiration and ideas for The Cloverleaf Series. My family is one that has weathered several terrible storms and still somehow keeps propelling forward. During those sunny times we can be seen gathered around, eating good food, sharing memories, and laughing until we can't catch our breath. We fight hard and love hard.

Romance, I simply love it, that's why I write it. I remember my mom giving me my very first paperback romance novel. It was a pretty exciting one filled with suspense and an overall excellent storyline, she had just read it and she felt it was suitable for my teenage eyes. That was it, I was hooked. I began to devour these romance stories that varied over the years from sweet to sultry, I consumed thousands of books and stories over the years. Each time I finished reading a novel, the desire to write my own grew stronger. As ideas for books swirled in my mind, it always had a romantic element to it, and I suppose it always will. What is there not to love about falling in love and finding that special person to share your life with? Who doesn't wish for passion, butterflies in your stomach, and that happily ever after?

As a reader, I can't even begin to thank all of the writers that have created so many emotions for me, falling in love with characters, mourning their loss, sighing as I close the final chapter or smiling when everyone lives happily ever after. As a writer, I just want to do the same.

**Facebook:**
http://facebook.com/authorgloriaherrmann

**Twitter:**
http://www.twitter.com/@gloriaiswriting

**Website:**
http://www.gloriaherrmann.com/

**Goodreads:**
https://www.goodreads.com/authorgloriaherrma
nn